MW01701647

Vengeance

by

Jim Hair

DORRANCE
PUBLISHING CO
EST. 1920
PITTSBURGH, PENNSYLVANIA 15238

The contents of this work, including, but not limited to, the accuracy of events, people, and places depicted; opinions expressed; permission to use previously published materials included; and any advice given or actions advocated are solely the responsibility of the author, who assumes all liability for said work and indemnifies the publisher against any claims stemming from publication of the work.

Dorrance Publishing Co
585 Alpha Drive
Suite 103
Pittsburgh, PA 15238
Visit our website at *www.dorrancebookstore.com*

ISBN: 979-8-8868-3084-2
eISBN: 979-8-8868-3944-9

vengeance / **ven**-*juhns* / noun - infliction of injury, harm or humiliation on a person by another who has been harmed by that person; violent revenge

Prologue

1973

Their relationship could best be described as Teacher and Student. To call them father and child really didn't fit by any stretch of the imagination. They simply didn't fit into that mold at all. Not that anyone would have expected them to; they had never had the chance to bond, until now— but not in the traditional sense. With the father serving in the U.S. Navy and the child's mother out of the picture, the two barely knew each other. Now, having been forced into parenthood, the father just didn't know any other way to relate to his child than to fall back into what he knew well—instruction.

The Teacher, affectionately referred to as "The Colonel" by everyone that knew him, was freshly home from Vietnam. As a decorated Navy SEAL, the Colonel was well trained in everything a SEAL needed for survival in a combat situation. He'd spent countless months perfecting Naval Special Warfare tactics, skin-diving skills (as it was called back then), search-and-rescue operational tactics, search-and-destroy tactics, demolitions skills and the art of stealth. During the past 6 years in Vietnam he had employed all of these skills with his men—his true children, just to stay alive. He had been ordered to carry out missions that could never really be discussed now that he was stateside. "Back on the block" is what his men used to call it. Home was not the place to try to explain what went on in Southeast Asia. Sure, everyone was curious and they would ask, but they weren't really looking for answers. The civilian population could never understand the things the Colonel had been asked to do for his country and in reality, they didn't want to know. But that was all in the past now; that part of the Colonel's life was over. He was home and that was all there was to it.

The Colonel now saw his mission as passing on his legacy. It was really all he knew. They would rise early every Saturday and begin the 2-hour drive into the desert. Just the two of them. Every weekend. At 10 years old, the Student had no choice in the matter. There was no debate, there were no questions, there was no discussion. The Colonel was in charge now and around the house orders were orders, and they were to be followed. Period.

Every weekend was about training. It didn't matter that the skills to be passed down were so outrageous that no one would ever have use for them, they would be taught and they would be learned. And so the Colonel taught, and he taught well.

The hunting cabin had been in the Colonel's family for longer than he could remember. It was in such a remote location in the desert that even if it were left unlocked, it would be safe. With the exception of a wandering coyote or lizard that happened to get curious no one would ever find the cabin—it was too remote and too well hidden. Even so, the Colonel made sure to secure the cabin and set booby-traps that would ruin the day for anyone trying to get too close a look at the place.

The training schedule was as meticulous as the Colonel himself. Polishing his boots and shining his Navy SEAL Special Warfare Triton Pin were simple everyday tasks that were never overlooked. In his mind, one's life depended on attention to detail—all detail. It didn't matter that here in the United States there was no threat of attack nor any reason to expect one. The Student would be prepared for any situation regardless of whether there was a threat or not. The Colonel understood how to train; he knew that hands-on training along with classroom training forged the best learning and retention combination. He'd seen it proven time after time. He also knew that skills, when not used for long periods, could be forgotten so he provided the Student with a leatherbound notebook and pen and regularly inspected the notes being taken. The notebooks would become the link to everything being taught and would serve as future tools and references, if needed. The Colonel required the Student to make diagrams along with the notes to solidify the learning process. The Student excelled.

If there were a mistake or if something of importance was missing from the notebook, there would be a price to pay, usually some Physical Training in the sand. The Student began to accept the PT as a part of life. It was the one thing that kept focus on the task at hand. After a few months, it was secretly welcomed as an added bonus to the skills being developed. Physical conditioning became part of the Student's life at an early age and would continue. So much so that the Student would sometimes intentionally slack off to get some exercise in.

Lessons were very detailed; they started with the mundane task of keeping the cabin in order and learning how to secure the building in such a way as to easily know if an intruder had been poking around. Everything had its place and everything was expected to be in its place. These lessons were learned quickly by the Student. The lessons were delivered firmly and matter-of-factly by the Colonel. He offered such devotion to the Student's progress and development and shared in the joy of each new skill attained that there may have been some fatherly pride developing, though it would never show on the surface.

As time went on the Student became more and more eager to learn and proved to be a very good pupil. Reconnaissance was first and came naturally to the Student. The innate ability to see what most would miss was very pleasing to the Colonel; the Student was a natural. The development of camouflage, stealth and patience skills were also picked up very quickly over the next several months. Understanding how to use night vision goggles was a key element of the recon training. They would spend hours each night learning how to maneuver in the dark.

"Own the night and you own the game." The Colonel would drill this into the head of the Student.

"Yes, sir" was the only response from the Student.

Once the Student had mastered the art of movement and observation the Colonel constructed a series of tests for the Student to see just how well the skills could be applied in the field. The Student passed with flying colors. The Colonel was confident that the Student could move undetected in any situation. The training was successful and both of them knew it. It wasn't too long before the Colonel was sure that the Student was ready to step up to the next phase of training.

Just after the Student's twelfth birthday the Colonel began the most important, and fun, part of the regimen—the weapons/demolitions phase of training. Some old military contacts were able to procure a load of "missing" C4 and weapons for the Colonel—part of a debt that had been repaid by grateful Vietnam comrades. The Colonel and the Student spent months preparing the cabin to store the weapons and explosives. They created false walls, hidden compartments in the floor and ceiling, and bolstered the security system. They would bring ammunition to the cabin each weekend and store it in the homemade armory. The outside of the cabin would appear to be an old abandoned shack, but inside was a complete arsenal of weapons and explosives; housing everything needed to create almost any type of reconnaissance mission or assault strike element. The Student was taught everything about weapons and demolitions. Firing any kind of weapon became a natural extension of the Student's instincts. Accuracy and speed were developed over months on their improvised firing ranges. The Colonel was certain that the Student could qualify as expert on any range, in any organization, under any conditions—at 13 years of age.

Demolitions were where the Student found a home. Focus was on how to gauge the right amount of C4 needed for the job, how to place the plastic explosive in such a way as to maximize the damage, how to conceal the C4 from "civilian" eyes and how to construct all types of detonators.

"The detonator is one of the most important aspects of a successful demolition mission," said the Colonel.

"Yes, sir," replied the Student.

"There are timers, trip switches, electronic switches, just about anything your mind can imagine."

"I want to learn them all, sir."

"Well, it takes time. We'll take them one by one."

"Yes, sir."

This was the most conversation the two had had in a long time at the cabin. Mostly, it was the Colonel doing the talking and the Student making notes and diagrams in the notebook. By now, there was an entire bookshelf filled with the leatherbound notebooks. Every once in a while, a question was raised by the Student and, if asked properly, the Colonel would explain with patience. If the question was not asked properly, the Student knew it was PT time.

Field tests were a regular part of the demolitions training. At first, harmless blasting caps were the only ordnance used, to protect both student and teacher. As the skill level progressed, the Colonel slowly added small amounts of C4 to the detonating devices. The excitement was uncontrollable. The Student loved the art of demolitions and became very creative with it, even to the point where suggestions were carefully made to the Colonel as to how explosives could be set up to be almost impossible to find, either before or after detonation. There was no doubt now that the Colonel was a proud father yet still there was no hint of it on the surface. The Colonel showed no emotion and the Student was learning this from him as well.

The Colonel and the Student kept this training regimen steady for over 8 years. The skills taught and learned kept them both as close as one might expect, and kept them both sharp with their skills as they began to compete with one another while in the desert. The relationship was everything the Colonel had hoped for—the Student was ready for any threatening situation that might come along. In actuality, they had become peers, for the Colonel had successfully passed on everything he knew to the Student. In fact, if truth be told, the Student might have passed the Colonel in some areas.

It was a warm spring day during the Student's senior year of high school when things changed forever. The Colonel was making final preparations for their weekend trip to the desert. Actually, the Student had everything ready to go even before the Colonel had slapped the alarm at 05:30. It brought a small smile to the Colonel's face to think of the progress that the Student had made over the years. He felt a strong sense of pride.

He was loading the final case of .45 ammo into the truck when it happened. At first, there was confusion about what was happening, this strange pain. He dropped to his knees and the sudden heart attack ended his life. The Student found the Colonel in the garage with a load of ammunition spilled around him. The Student immediately went into survival mode. There was no emotion—emotions can get you killed. The garage was cleaned, removing any trace of ammo and other supplies that would hint of what their trips to the desert were about. For the first time, the Student visited the cabin alone. The ammunition and supplies were stowed in their place and the cabin was secured.

Training was over. Forever.

PART ONE

Chapter One

November 1989

Alex Coswell sat silently in his 9-year-old Jaguar with his head in his hands. His car was running but the heater fan was on the blink again. His breath was fogging the windows and the interior of the car was cold. He shivered.

It was the day before Thanksgiving and the snow was piling up fast. It was 11:30 in the morning and the forecast was calling for another 6-8 inches of snow before the evening rush hour. This amount of snow this early in the year was a bit unusual but not unheard of. Rochester got a lot of lake effect snow. The drive from the city out to Scottsville was going to be a real challenge, even at this hour. Alex had no desire to drive there. Cold car or not, he feared a colder reception from his wife. There was no doubt that Janey loved him. She'd proven it time and again over the past few years, moving from job to job with him. Each move causing her to uproot her career and start over again. But there was only so much she could take.

He wondered how it had come to this. His entire world was crashing down around him—again. This time, though, it was complete destruction. Everything was in jeopardy. He had reached the end of his rope. Janey wouldn't understand this time. She never really did, but she went along. This time he feared it was going to be different.

As Alex sat in his car he allowed his mind to travel back to happier times.

They met 4 years ago, it was 1985. She was a senior in college and studying to become a computer programmer with degrees in both Computer Science and Business. They met at a job fair on campus. Alex had graduated a year earlier with degrees in Finance and Computer Science and had been heavily recruited by all the big New York brokerage houses. He accepted a terrific job with Sohlmann & Stein—a boutique brokerage firm with an office on Wall Street. He had already moved to Manhattan and started his career but came back to the university to work the job fair for the weekend.

He was looking for bright students that might want to consider an internship with S&S when Janey walked by. She was an athletic blonde and moved with all the confidence in the world, like she owned it. She was striking. They caught each other's eye and Alex struck up a quick conversation.

"Don't I know you?" asked Alex. "You look familiar."

"Sure, if you call being in the same computer lab two years ago knowing me," replied Jane. "I'm Jane Franklin," said Jane, extending her hand with a warm smile and bright eyes.

"I'm Alex Coswell," he said with a sheepish grin. "It's nice to formally meet you."

She had a very strong grip for a woman and from that moment on Alex was toast. He was shy by nature, not having many friends in his formative years, but confident. Jane somehow brought him out of his shell and they both felt comfortable standing there, staring into each other's eyes.

The attraction was immediate for both of them. Jane saw something in Alex that she liked, something that drew her in. She had heard about magnetic personalities, but that was only conjecture—not something that was real. She couldn't really put her finger on what it was, but something was there; Alex was unique. They started dating and spending as much time together as possible. Since neither of them had any family to speak of, they were free to devote weekends to each other. One weekend was spent in Manhattan, the next on campus, and so it went. Alex would help Janey study and prepare for her final exams. She would listen to his stories about the work he was doing on Wall Street at Sohlmann & Stein.

The next thing either of them knew they were engaged to be married. The wedding was a simple formality before the local Justice of the Peace in New York City. After a week in Bermuda on their honeymoon, Alex and Janey settled into a comfortable routine in Manhattan. Alex worked crazy hours at Sohlmann & Stein and Janey landed a computer programming job with a large corporation not far from Alex's office. In her free time she studied for the CPA exam. They were the perfect couple, he was handsome with dark hair and all-American good looks and she with her stunning beauty made everyone who knew them envious.

They had a nice apartment in Manhattan just around the corner from the Broadway Theater district. It wasn't furnished with much, but it was much better than either of them had while growing up. They would spend what little free time they had enjoying the city life and making plans for the future—something neither of them had ever done in the past.

Jane's job was mundane at best. It was easy to get lost in the computer department of a large company and her skills were severely underutilized. She found that she had a lot of free time on her hands at the office and began to develop friendships with other highly skilled programmers that were trying to fill their time at the office. She passed the CPA exam on the first attempt and found that her career very easily allowed her to explore the connection between computer technology and business. She focused all her efforts on new computer technology developments that were expanding at a very rapid pace. She would be successful—whatever it took. It was the way she lived her life.

Chapter Two

Alex was the Golden Child at Sohlmann & Stein. He was the rising star that could do no wrong. His insights and ability to understand the nuances of the world of finance, coupled with his computer skills vaulted him to a position in the company that every new employee could only dream of. He met regularly with Mark Stein, the Managing Partner. Together they would discuss strategy, market direction and speculation, when to walk from a client and how to steal big fish from the competition. They also explored new areas of finance that might yield big results.

Other new associates should have been jealous, but they saw something in Alex that they could never measure up to, so instead there was respect. This gave Alex the freedom to formulate friendships among his peers that were quite rare in the cutthroat arena of high finance. Alex was able to talk to all the employees and get insight into what was needed at the firm to improve morale and build greater success for S&S. Whether it was a better coffee maker, a better band for the Christmas Party (David Sohlmann and Mark Stein didn't push their religious beliefs on their employees) or a revised bonus structure that reflected the efforts of everyone's part in the success of the company, Alex could bring these requests to Mark and things got done. Everyone loved him.

Alex had never met David Sohlmann, but he didn't care. No one had ever seen the old man at the office, scuttlebutt was that David Sohlmann was about 68 years old, but who really knew? Even HR didn't know anything about him. Some wondered if he even actually existed. He kept an office there, but Alex, along with every other S&S employee believed that it was only for show when clients visited. There were no family photos, personal mementos, or other typical things one would expect to find in an occupied office. There was nothing that would indicate anyone had ever stepped foot in the 1,100 s.f. corner office with a 71st-floor view of Midtown Manhattan—or ever would.

Mark Stein was in his early 50s and outwardly wealthy. His suits were imported from London along with his custom-made shoes. His Rolex was about as gaudy as Switzerland had ever produced—diamonds on the bezel and face. It had to cost at least $30,000.00. His shirts and ties were custom made by a local Italian tailor over on 35th Street. He never drove in the city, or anywhere for that matter. His driver, William, was on call 24/7. William had been a personal servant for Mark Stein for over 20 years. Of course, he was on the S&S payroll, but worked only for Mr. Stein. Knicks games, Jets games, Rangers games, trips to his house in the Hamptons; William knew the fastest way to navigate to any of these locations. He was a trusted insider in Mark's world and quite valuable. His "hood" connections came in handy when he was running late or needed to find some recreation for the "Boss" as he referred to Mr. Stein.

Mark Stein was never married, so he spent as much time in the office as any of his employees—except for Alex. He would arrive most days before 6:00 A.M. and find Alex in his cubicle. He'd stay until 7:30 P.M. most nights and Alex was still there, grinding it out, finding ways to generate money and more money. This work ethic was not lost on Mark. Alex Coswell was special. He knew it. Everybody knew it. He could do things for the firm that would make Mark Stein a much richer man than he already was. He only needed to be groomed and conditioned for the things that David Sohlmann and Mark Stein had in store for him. Big things.

As months churned by, Alex grew more and more comfortable with his unique position in the firm. His ability to relate with both sides of management and regular employees was invaluable. He was loved by everyone at the firm including Mark Stein and purportedly by David Sohlmann. He was quick with a joke, a birthday card, and the occasional flowers at just the right time for just the right person.

The strategy meetings were taking place more and more regularly, Alex was given more responsibilities and his ability to offer suggestions were received with respect and anticipation by Stein. His peers and the staff also held him in very high professional regard. He had developed a continually flowing pipeline of information throughout the firm, from the mailroom to the managers of every department that gave him a unique ability to direct actions and generate positive results. He knew everything that was going on. He was just easy to be around and people felt comfortable sharing seemingly meaningless bits of information with him. Alex was making money for the firm and the future was bright.

One night as Alex was finishing up his day, Mark called him into his office.

Mark Stein was standing at the window looking out at the lights of the city. He was swirling the ice in his crystal tumbler and making sure he got every drop of alcohol out of the glass. With his back to Alex, he asked, "How do you feel things are going, Alex?"

This was a loaded question. Mark knew the answer, but wanted to see how Alex would respond. He wanted to see where Alex was mentally with his experience over the past 2 years at S&S. Alex had been instrumental in taking the firm's revenue to heights that no one had expected.

Alex was sitting on Mark's new Italian leather sofa that had recently been imported directly from Milan. He studied the floor before answering.

"I'm having a ball," replied Alex. "We have some exciting new clients, markets are up across the board and the computer system should be ready for implementation across the entire platform in the next month or so."

Mark smiled. He knew that Alex had spearheaded the computer idea for the firm. Overall efficiencies would propel the profits even further if this internet thing really took off. Alex was confident that it would, but believed that they had to act now to get in early. He called it being an early adopter. Mark agreed. It would allow them to be the industry leader and offer consulting services as an additional revenue stream.

"Would you like something to drink?" offered Mark.

"No thanks, I'm not much of a hard liquor guy, you know that."

Mark said, "I want to talk to you about heading up a new project for the firm. It's pretty loose right now and very confidential, so I can't go into much detail, but David and I feel you're the man for the job."

"Sounds like an interesting challenge. Anything you can share at this point?" asked Alex.

Mark started to walk out of the office while Alex sat there. "Just that we want you to run with it, details will come later. Oh, and your salary will be bumped another $100,000.00 if you accept." Mark said this over his shoulder as he was walking away and turning off the lights. He didn't want a response right now. The plan was to just let it sink in.

Alex was speechless. Not in his wildest imagination did he think he'd ever make that kind of money. He stood in the darkness of Mark's office and let his mind wander while he took in the lights of Manhattan.

Alex arrived home at 8:15 with a bouquet of flowers for Janey and found the kitchen table in their apartment set with china and candles. The candles were even burning. Soft music was playing in the background. The aroma from the oven was mouthwatering. This was highly unusual; he either got something out of the microwave or they ordered takeout.

He turned to see Janey standing in the hallway looking as beautiful as he had ever seen her. Her blonde hair was in a tight bun, the little black dress fit tight in all the right places and the black heels were simply icing on the cake. His head started to spin. He had so much to tell her, but all this... it was causing him to reel a bit.

"It's not our anniversary, what gives, babe?" asked Alex. "Did I miss something?"

"Why do you have flowers?" asked Janey with a cocked head and a confused look on her face.

"I... I have some news," stammered Alex.

"I just thought that we'd celebrate tonight," replied Jane at the same time.

They were both confused, it was an awkward moment. They both stood there wondering what each other was up to.

Alex was really at a loss. What could she possibly want to celebrate? There was no way she could know about the conversation he just had with Mark Stein. And whatever was in the oven must have required some forethought and the aroma was something that a master chef would need to work on for at least 2 hours. He was completely stumped.

"Did you talk to Mark?"

"Who? What? No!" exclaimed Jane. "Why would I talk to Mark?"

"Well, I just had an interesting conversation with him that could be worth celebrating, is all."

"It's going to have to wait, Alex. Right now, you and I are going to sit at our table and enjoy a real homecooked dinner, together. Then we have to have a serious talk." She said this firmly. There would be no questions.

"You're starting to scare me a little." He stood there staring into those steel-blue eyes that didn't give a hint of anything going on behind them.

Alex thought back to their first date after the job fair. Her confidence was contagious and he liked it. She caused him to feel like he never felt before, like he was finally at home in his own skin. Right now, her confidence was again giving him a feeling that was hard to explain. He wasn't sure what to expect.

They ate dinner together in their apartment and made small talk, neither of them wanting to share their news just yet. The food was great, but the anticipation was wreaking havoc on Alex's stomach. He was uncomfortable not being in control.

As they both cleared the table and cleaned the kitchen, Alex said, "You're dressed up pretty nice for dinner at home. Are you going to tell me what we are celebrating?"

Janey just stared at him. With her heels on, she was eye to eye with Alex. She wrapped her strong arms around his neck and pulled him in close. She was clearly in control of the moment. Alex hesitated for just a split second, then he closed his arms around her waist and stared back at her. They enjoyed the embrace for what seemed like an eternity. Janey never took her eyes from his. They were lost in a moment that would be remembered for as long as they both lived.

He felt something on the back of his head; it was something he did not recognize. Alex never saw it coming or from where she had pulled it. Slowly she brought it to the side of his head and let it rest there. As he slowly turned his head toward the unknown object, his mind tried to understand the meaning of what he was seeing.

It finally sunk in. At first, terror filled his entire being. He couldn't move and found it hard to breathe. Slowly, he began to understand.

"Read it to me. Out loud," she said. "I want to hear the words."

Alex looked at the object Janey was holding in her hand."I love my Daddy!" he said as tears filled his eyes. The little yellow bib was no bigger than a cocktail napkin but it hit him with the power of a freight train. Suddenly, his earlier conversation with Mark was lost. Completely gone.

"Can you believe it?" said Janey in a level voice."We're going to have a family!"

Tears were streaming down her face. Alex was a mess. He couldn't think straight. Everything was spinning. He tried to regain control but found it impossible. It was too much.

"How? Who? When did this happen?" It was all he could utter. "Really?" He was completely happy for the first time in as long as he could remember.

Chapter Three

David Sohlmann was indeed a very real person. He was actually only 55 years old but looked much younger than his years. His short-cropped hair was always in place and his chiseled facial features were almost menacing. He was a health nut by anyone's definition of the phrase, spending at least two hours every day pushing his body to its limit. He was a gifted athlete, able to compete in any type of physical activity. He was a fierce competitor in every aspect of his life. He was driven to win his share of both friendly and not-so-friendly competitions. He would often seek opponents that were 15 to 20 years younger than him just to revel in their loss. He was addicted to the thrill of victory.

He was even stronger and more driven when it came to business. He was truly a mogul, but preferred the silent behind-the-scenes role when it came to his dealings. Controlling events and outcomes from an invisible position might sound like cowardice, but it was more his powerful need to develop a strategy, watch it unfold, and then control the events to achieve their final result. *His* desired result.

The level of wealth that he had built for himself was massive. He was involved in many business ventures; from his brokerage firm in Manhattan to manufacturing to banking to real estate. His holdings were enormous. They were surpassed only by his ever-consuming obsession to control every situation in which he found himself. So much so that he could easily blur the line of moral ethics, if he had one, to ensure the end result.

He had been married and divorced four times, or was it five? He honestly couldn't remember anymore. The women he found attractive were drawn to his power and wealth, some even loved him, but not one of them could handle his controlling personality. Obviously, there were prenuptial agreements in place with every wife—but they were more than willing to walk away with only what they entered the relationship with. They just wanted to get David Sohlmann out of their lives.

He was sitting on the afterdeck of his 165-foot luxury motor yacht in Key West with what promised to be his next wife. They had just finished a wonderful dinner of stone crab, lobster and scallops with all the gourmet trimmings. Both were enjoying the evening breeze and anticipating a little romance when Mark Stein's call came in.

"Hello?" The tone was not friendly.

"David, it's Mark. We need to talk for a minute."

"This better be important. You know I don't like to be bothered with S&S business. I've got too much going on in other areas to have to get involved with how you make money for me. That's why I partnered with you."

Mark bristled at the aggressive tone of David's remark. Their partnership was distant and very impersonal. He knew that David provided vast amounts of capital which allowed S&S to flourish. It was also what made Mark Stein a very wealthy man in his own right. David didn't want details about the firm—only results. Even so, Mark knew that he was a controlling and manipulative tyrant, so every once in a while he needed to touch base. Mark Stein was one of very few business associates that had the freedom to operate without the normal oversight that David Sohlmann was known for and this simple fact kept him on edge.

"Our wonder-boy was given the offer tonight," said Mark. "I expect he'll give me his answer in the morning."

David softened a bit. "Good. Good," he replied. All David could think about was the increased stream of profits to his bottom line if things went as planned. And they always did.

"I'll be in touch with you as soon as we have his answer," said Mark. "He and I should be able to get things up and running in pretty short order—within the next month or so. Do you know how much of financial genius he's turning out to be?"

"Trust me, Mark. I know just about everything about Alex Coswell." David hung up without saying goodbye.

Chapter Four

Alex and Janey were lying in bed enjoying the thought of becoming parents. Both of them knew that the path toward parenthood they were now traveling on was one that presented challenges and opportunities. Janey was happy, but in her mind she believed that she was as unqualified to be a parent as any woman had ever been. She had nothing in her past to draw experience from that would make her a good mother. She had neither a positive mother figure in her life nor a grandmother figure to look back on. Her early life was filled with foster homes that not once fit the mold of what would be considered normal. She had never experienced a loving relationship like she now hoped she and Alex would provide for their coming child. Alex was having some of the same thoughts, though he would never share them with Jane.

"What were you coming home to celebrate?" asked Janey. She was gently caressing his chest and searching his eyes for a hint of his news.

"Oh, man! I completely forgot!" exclaimed Alex. "How could it slip my mind?"

He rolled on to his side to face Janey and propped himself up on his elbow.

"You're not going to believe the conversation I had with Mark Stein on the way out the door tonight. He called me in to his office and told me that he and old man Sohlmann want me to head up some new project at the firm. He didn't give me any details but said that they both felt I was the one for the job. I'm not sure how he expected me to respond, because he just kind of threw it out there and then walked away before I could say anything."

"What kind of project?" asked Janey.

"No clue."

"Do you think it will have anything to do with anything you've been working on lately?"

"He said he'd give me details soon, whatever that means. But I'm sure it has to have *something* to do with what I've been chasing."

"It sounds kind of mysterious. What are you feeling in your gut?"

"You know I don't like to let emotion influence my decisions. I need more detail. But to be honest, it sounds very exciting."

"Well, you have to have some feeling about it. Even without any details."

Alex grinned at Janey. "The only detail he gave me was that my salary would go up if I accept."

"That's always a plus," replied Janey.

"I guess so."

"How much of a raise do you think he'll give you?"

"Only about $100,000.00!" exclaimed Alex.

Janey was jumping on the bed faster than Alex could move to get out of her way. "Do you know what this could mean? I could afford to quit my job and take care of the baby when it comes."

"I've already thought about that. It would be great to have you at home. But let's see how things unfold for the first few months before we make any decisions. It's expensive to live in Manhattan and this would give us a boost."

Neither Alex nor Janey got much sleep. Both of them were silently playing out every possible scenario in their minds. Janey was thinking about motherhood—what if it's a boy? What if it's a girl? She preferred thinking in terms of a little girl. Alex was thinking about his work. What would this project be? What could possibly be worth an additional $100K? How would this opportunity affect his position at the firm? Would he finally be given an office?

Over and over, each of them analyzed their situations. Their methodical minds were playing out scenarios from as many angles as they could think of. It wasn't until after 2:30 that morning that Janey whispered, "Are you awake?"

"Yep," replied Alex. "I can't sleep. My brain is in overdrive."

"I think you should take the job, no matter what."

"That's what I'm thinking too."

"I love you, Alex."

"I love you too, Janey."

They drifted off to sleep. Both fully committed to the unknown. It was new territory for both of them. They were most comfortable when they knew where they were headed, or at least in control of where they were headed.

Chapter Five

Mark Stein was a brilliant man. After all, he'd built the firm from the ground up with very little assistance from anyone. He was the one that found all the talent and he provided the direction they needed to be as successful as they had been. He called the shots and was responsible for meeting the results their clients expected and the profits demanded by David Sohlmann.

He had been following the development of technology for the past several years. He knew that there would come a time when the ability to increase transaction volume would be the key to huge revenue increases. He just didn't have the technological knowledge, or the desire, to implement it. That's where Alex Coswell came in.

David Sohlmann had sent Mark a note 3 years ago about a student that was worth looking at, one with both finance and computer skills that were head-and-shoulders above any other short-term college prospects. Word on the street was that he had been approached by several Wall Street firms and that he would go fast. Mark acted immediately, and not surprisingly, Alex accepted the generous

S&S offer. It was exactly what David Sohlmann had expected. Another successful desired outcome.

No expense was spared in the recruiting of Alex Coswell. Sohlmann & Stein made it very clear from the first communication with Alex that they were very serious about having him join the firm. By the time Mark Stein finally met Alex face to face he knew that any offer he made to Alex would be impossible to match by any other Wall Street firm. Not only would the compensation be impossible to match, but the other perks provided would be too much for someone like Alex to refuse.

Now, with Alex solidly in place at the firm, it was time to take advantage of his idea. The new project that Mark Stein had offered to Alex was a new technology called Program Trading. It was a relatively new concept in trading Stocks and Securities. Simply put, it allowed for large dollar volumes to be traded through the use of computers via an ECN—Electronic Communications Network. These trades would be set up based purely on predetermined price rather than on the fundamental analysis that every firm spent huge dollars researching each month. Issues such as earnings, dividends or growth potential were replaced with speculative price movement. Interest rate movement, the fluctuation of currencies and governmental and political actions suddenly took a back seat to the opportunity to take full advantage of a market that was being driven by both price and the greed of those with the means to cash in.

Alex accepted the offer to head the new project. He told Mark about his decision early on the morning following the offer. Alex was excited about the opportunity to dig into something he had been studying for quite some time. It would allow him to have his feet firmly planted in both high finance and computer technology. Two things he loved.

Mark and Alex now spent a great deal of time discussing this project in detail. They talked about how his computer skills would play such an important role in the development of a completely new trading direction for the firm, one that no longer required physical presence on the trading floor. Both agreed that getting out of the blocks early on this project would be critical to long-term success. By all accounts, the prospects were very positive for significant growth at the firm and Alex was the key. His drive and expertise had proven to be the X-factor that Mark had been looking for.

Recent market conditions were in their favor. The Dow was up over 44% from last year and the stocks and securities they were *long* on would provide the necessary collateral for short-term cash. Bankers would stand in line to lend them money based on the recent performance of their portfolios. It was all about leverage, and right now they had all the leverage they needed.

"The ability to borrow money is the purest sign of a healthy economy," Alex said. "Our long-term portfolios are as solid as they've ever been. We can fund this project with very little, if any, of our own capital."

Mark agreed. He'd seen these conditions in the market before and they had served the firm well. The U.S. economy had started to surge under the current administration and it was time to begin reaping the benefits like never before.

"You're exactly right, Alex," said Mark. "I've already been hinting to some major banks that there might be some largescale deals in the near future for us. However, if we don't need to borrow any money to make this happen, then that will equate to even greater margin for the firm."

As spring turned into summer, 1987 was promising to be one of the best years S&S had ever had. Mark and Alex had come to a very comfortable understanding. Alex had free reign to grow the Program Trading project, as it was called and Mark gave him the access to firm assets to make it happen. The portfolio was steadily growing and outpacing any other account in the firm. Everyone was happy.

Alex was sitting in his new office eating lunch looking at the buildings across the street. He didn't have the same view as his boss, but it was a view none the less. Mark walked in and sat across the desk from him. He noticed the photo of Janey on the credenza and asked, "How's the pregnancy going?"

"Not bad, she has some bad days, but mostly they're what you might expect. She complains about gaining weight, she can't get comfortable in bed, she has weird cravings and her exercise routine is being interrupted," replied Alex.

Mark got right to business. "It's time to step things up with your portfolio," he said.

It wasn't really Alex's portfolio and they both knew it, but it made things easier around the office to refer to it that way. Everyone at the office talked about the project in those terms.

"We're up significantly this quarter," Alex said distractedly. He had reports spread across his mahogany desk that were piled as high as they would go without toppling over. His floor was covered with stacks of computer paper and he had installed two additional computers to continually track market conditions. He had a muted television in the corner that was tuned to one of the news channels so he could monitor the markets in real time.

He spent every day going over the reports, trying to understand every factor that was affecting the performance of his portfolio. He was consumed by the U.S. and foreign market activity. The New York Stock Exchange, Chicago Board Options Exchange, Chicago Board of Trade, the London Exchange and Hong Kong Exchange were constantly on his radar. He searched for any hints of opportunity to cash in on. He also found his own creative ways to grow the project. He was successful but it came at a price. His internal communication network was still solid, but his time to cultivate the relationships throughout the organization was now limited and he began to feel some tension. The amount of time he spent at the office was also becoming an issue at home, but there was just too much at stake. In reality, Alex felt he was reaching the limit of his ability to be productive. There just weren't enough hours in the week to get everything done.

Janey was working long hours too, but in the programming arena much of her time was more or less free. She longed for some time with Alex, but since he was working such long hours, she found herself exploring new things at work. She was thinking about the arrival of the baby. It was only a few months away now and they had not even begun to talk about a nursery, let alone what they would name the baby. Every time she brought it up, he would tell her that they had plenty of time. He had to focus on the project.

Mark said, "I know performance is up, but I want to show David that this idea has real merit, that it can start to generate some huge revenue for the firm. I want you to start funneling more money into the pool. We can cash in some favors from 4 or 5 bankers that have been eager to work with us.

"Let's leverage more of our long-term stocks and try to triple the portfolio volume for the next 6 months. If all goes well, we can easily repay the debt and diversify after the first of the year. If this goes as well as I know it will, it will mean really big things for the firm, and for you, Alex."

"It's your call, Mark. I'll make the phone calls tomorrow morning and get the money wired into our account as soon as the end of the week," said Alex. "It sounds like this will have the potential to generate a net increase of nearly 187% over last year. Maybe more...."

"You're being too conservative!" interrupted Mark. "I want to blow the doors off this thing. Take the ball and run with it. We have such positive market conditions right now that we can't afford not to exploit it." Mark was excited, but firm in the message he was delivering to Alex.

Alex went to work immediately researching the firm's long-term stock and securities portfolios. He drafted a list of his recommendations and had them on Mark's desk before the end of the day. Based on the analysis Alex pulled together, he would be able to provide Mark with two scenarios—one would add the requested increase to the project fund, the other would increase the volume by well over tenfold. He knew it was a bold suggestion, but their long-term portfolios had been performing so well, and the future prospects were so strong that it was worth the risk. Anyway, Mark wanted to repay the debt after the first of the year, so why not cash in now?

Mark reviewed the proposal with a cursory glance and gave Alex the green light. It was his typical response to the requests that Alex made over the past few months. He had gained so much confidence in his abilities that it never occurred to him to question Alex on anything. Everything was set in motion. His computer programs were in place and the trading parameters were loaded and the project was fully shoved into overdrive. Now, all Alex had to do was sit back and watch the money grow.

Alex paid full attention to his portfolio over the next 3 months. He was reporting to Mark almost daily about the gains they were making. S&S enjoyed a steady rise in the project portfolio from the beginning of June through the end of August. The portfolio was up another 14% and their clients were ecstatic. Mark was as pleased as Alex had ever seen him. The amount of overall S&S assets that Alex was now controlling was more than 85%.

What Mark did not know was that Alex had secretly tapped into a private Sohlmann and Stein account and was running a second Program Trading Account as a way to surprise the partners with a nice little bonus for their personal retirement funds. He had finagled access to the accounts from one of the administrative staff and promised her that he would include her in the accolades that were sure to come when the gains were announced in December. She was leery, but after Alex's smooth talking and charm, along with his track record and status at the firm lately, she gave in.

Alex had to keep this a secret from everyone. Even Janey would not know about this until it was presented to Mark Stein at the company Christmas Party. He hated the idea of keeping secrets from her but it was what he had to do.

In reality, Janey was keeping some secrets of her own.

Working long hours in the computer department of a large corporation allowed for a lot of unaccounted for time. Janey had befriended Tommy Gryskiewski, another programmer who never seemed to go home. His workstation was constantly filled with fast food wrappers and empty Mountain Dew bottles. His appearance was what you might expect, wrinkled, overweight and generally unkempt.

Janey recognized that his computing talent level was equal to her own. They were head-and-shoulders ahead of anyone else working in the department. From very early on it seemed that he was the only other programmer in their group that wanted to explore the outer reaches of what was possible.

One night, while hanging around the office well after business hours, Tommy called over to Jane, "Got a sec?"

"Sure, what do you need?" replied Jane.

"Come over here, I want to show you something that's totally awesome!"

As Jane approached his workstation, she bristled at the body odor Tommy was emitting. "You really should go home and take a shower, Tommy."

"Never mind that right now, look at this," said Tommy.

Jane was bending over to look at his computer screen, not sure exactly what she was looking at. The screen was covered with lines and lines of numbers. "What exactly am I looking at?"

Tommy was staring at her with a big smile on his face. It was a look of pride and shock all at the same time. "That, my friend, is the New York Metropolitan Life Assurance Company bank account! I finally cracked the code to access the bank's files!"

"Tommy, I'm pretty sure that's illegal," stammered Jane. "Illegal like, you could go to jail for that, couldn't you?"

"Yeah, yeah, only if you get caught, and I won't. I was just doing this for fun to see if it was possible. Besides, I developed a series of access points that would be impossible to trace. Even if you knew where the access point began you would never be able to trace it all the way back to me. I've got too many redundant routes and phone systems working on this for me. But even so, I want to ask you a favor. I want you to try to bust me on this."

"Why me?" asked Jane.

"Because, first of all, you're the only person I know with the talent to even understand what I've done and how I've done it. Secondly I know you won't rat me out on this. You're the only person I trust to look at this." Tommy was hoping he'd get the right response. "Besides, you've been spending lots of time here after hours with your husband working late all the time and I thought it would give you something fun to do."

After a short pause to think about her answer, Jane finally said, "Okay, Tommy. I'll bust you."

And so began Janey's entry into the world of hacking. She spent every free minute trying to bust Tommy's program. At each dead end, she became more and more determined to find the key to his access. She would ask Tommy for some hints and he would provide them, confident in his ability to hide. After about six weeks of failing to bust the program, she came to a startling realization; she had been forced to learn his skills for accessing remote computer systems and created many additional ways to access the computer systems of just about any company she wanted. Tommy had truly developed a top-notch program.

Soon, working secretly, Jane began to enhance Tommy's programs, making them even more robust and even harder to trace. Her computer technology skills along with her knowledge of Accounting and Finance allowed her to not only access the computer systems of banks and insurance companies, but also the systems of large and small companies alike. She could search any financial document or record that was kept on their system.

Jane continued spend time with Tommy after hours and together they explored this new frontier of hacking, simply for the fun of it. It was also a very satisfying challenge for them to target a company and gain access to their records. On several occasions, when they were both certain that everyone else had left for the day, Tommy and Jane would identify a company or a bank and race to see who could get in first. After a few months, she was confident that not only could she hack into any computer file she wanted, but she could get in and get out without leaving a trace.

Chapter Six

Janey sat in her cubicle looking at the work load for the week. What would take the average programmer a week to complete, she would finish in a couple of days, at most. The end of the year would be here before she knew it and annual reviews with her customers would be coming soon. One of the projects she was working on was for a large client that wanted to automate their financial transactions. They were also looking for ways to legally shelter their money. They had approached her on the side and asked if she might have any ideas worth exploring that might sidestep some tax liability. With her accounting and CPA background, this had really become one of her areas of expertise; she had been experimenting with the concept of how computer technology could allow quick and easy transfers of funds to numbered offshore accounts with a certain amount of anonymity, but that had only been in theory. Now, her relationship with this client was providing her with an actual test, so she agreed to take a deeper look into things for them.

With her secret hacking skills firmly established, she found herself doing a bit more than just accessing accounts. This client was asking her to actually manipulate the type of accounts she and Tommy had only been looking at for the past several months. What she found was how easily technology provided access and portability to money. This was exhilarating and stressful all at the same time. She was crossing a line that couldn't be uncrossed.

With her pregnancy progressing, she was finding it harder and harder to concentrate for long periods of time. She had the discipline to keep at it; that was never an issue, but she felt that she needed a break. Not just another walk around the block to enjoy the beautiful autumn weather that Manhattan was having, but a real break. She and Alex needed some quality time together. Her office phone rang and offered a welcomed distraction from the project she was plowing through and her newfound secret computer research project.

"Hello, this is Jane," she said.

"It's Alex, what are you doing right now, this very second?"

"Talking on the phone with you, but I'm trying to do some analysis for a rather demanding client," she said.

Alex picked up a hint of frustration in her voice. "Have you had your lunch yet?"

"No, I was hoping to get through some of this before I ate. Why, what's up?"

"I'll be there in 25 minutes, meet me at the curb. I'll have my cab honk twice for you," Alex said.

They found a little bar and grill a few blocks from Jane's office and ordered sandwiches and bottles of flavored seltzer water. The owner of

McGee's Pub was an old-country Irishman, who still spoke in a thick brogue accent. His restaurant wasn't fancy and would never be listed in any of the city's publications of where to eat, but it was good food. The wooden bar inside was highly polished and sparkling clean, there were ten dartboards hung across the side wall that looked very well used. The pub showed signs of a rowdy regular crowd, but was very welcoming at the same time. Certainly, the Irish liked their watering holes and made the most of McGee's warm hospitality. What the placed lacked in style McGee, himself, made up for in old-world service.

Since it was past the lunch rush, they had the place pretty much to themselves. Janey and Alex chose to sit at a table out on the sidewalk and enjoyed the early afternoon sunshine. They enjoyed each other's company while they ate and talked about the normal husband and wife things. McGee was very attentive to the young couple, but recognized when they needed to be left alone.

"Things are really rolling at the firm," Alex said after a while. "The project couldn't be going any better."

Janey smiled as she took another bite of her sandwich. Her piercing blue eyes seemed to look right through him. It made Alex think she could sometimes read his mind and made him a bit nervous, truth be told. She just had a way of looking at him.

He would never confess to what he was doing with the S&S private account. He knew Janey would go ballistic on him if she found out. He did, however, share many of the other details with her. Since both of them shared a computer science background, they found that they could easily talk with each other about things Alex was working on without the risk of boredom.

Janey felt the same way. There was no way she could ever let Alex know what she had been learning on the side. Computer technologies allowed her to access her client's money and move it without a trace. Neither the IRS, nor any private entity, could ever work through all the various portals that she directed money through before depositing it in a protected offshore account. It simply became untraceable. And with the banking privacy laws in other parts of the world, there would be an added layer of protection for her client. She was even learning how to access other people's money on an individual level. Hacking was what it was, pure and simple. In the circles of those that dared explore this new frontier there were a few that really excelled, and Jane Coswell was fast becoming one of the best. Her reputation was becoming that of legend in the underground world she was now a part of. Of course, she was not known as Jane Coswell in this world, but by an alias. Even Tommy wondered who this superstar of hacking might be.

So far, Janey had only been working with one client's money on a project like this. They were pleased with the results she was delivering and they were willing to pay handsomely for it. She knew that her client was the one on the hook if something went wrong, there was just no way she was leaving any trail that would lead back to her, but it still made her nervous. During slow days and slower nights while Alex was at his office, she began to wonder if this might lead to other opportunities for her to earn some additional income. Not that they needed it, but it could come in handy as the baby came.

She knew she was walking a very fine line. One misstep and her secret world would come tumbling down. She had gained access into so many bank accounts across the country over the past few months just to see if she could do it without getting caught, that she had lost track of the number. Big banks, small banks, credit unions, it didn't matter. It was really exhilarating, and now that she was actually proving her suspicions, that this could actually be done without leaving a trail, she searched for more complex projects to work on. She had to be careful and not let her guard down. So far, so good. She allowed herself to relax as she sat with Alex.

"So, what's up? You don't rush out of your office just to take me to a late lunch," said Janey.

"I have something for you," Alex said as he pulled an S&S envelope from his suitcoat pocket.

Janey put her sandwich down and wiped her napkin across her mouth. She studied Alex's face for a moment, trying to get a read on the situation.

"What's this?" she asked as she slid the envelope back and forth through her fingers.

"We're going on a vacation. Those are tickets to St. Thomas. Mark made all the reservations for us, we're staying at Frenchman's Reef Resort, and everything is taken care of. Mark will have William pick us up at the apartment and drop us off at Kennedy Airport. We leave next Sunday morning at seven A.M.

"We both need a week of sun and sand. It's a great time for you to go before the baby comes and heaven knows I need to come up for air. Mark said he'll keep an eye on the project for me and he wouldn't take no for an answer."

Janey smiled at Alex. Inside her mind was reeling. She would have to be sure to cover her tracks at the office before she left, just in case. She wasn't overly concerned about this, but with her being out for a week, she needed to clean a few things up.

"I can't believe this!" she exclaimed. "I think a vacation is exactly what you and I need, maybe more you than me, you've been working so hard lately. I don't really like the idea of spending a week in a bathing suit being pregnant, but the idea of sun and sand sounds very relaxing. I'll start packing tonight."

Jane made arrangements at work to take the next week off. She was a little concerned about spending a week away from the office and the extracurricular activities she had been working on, but she looked forward to the time away with Alex. Maybe they could finally decide on names. And who could complain about an all-expenses paid trip to the Caribbean?

Sunday, October 11th, was a blustery day in New York City. The high temperature for the day was only 52 degrees. It was a perfect day to get out of the city. William showed up right on time and the flight out of New York City was on time. Alex was exhausted and ready for a break. Jane was also ready for some down time. The past several weeks had been quite stressful with all she had going on. Everything was now in place, so she allowed herself to relax. They both quickly drifted off to sleep.

Chapter Seven

Mark was enjoying his third cup of coffee early on Wednesday morning. Things around the office were actually pretty quiet with Alex gone on vacation. He hadn't realized how much of his days were consumed with Alex and his project. He had to give Alex credit for one thing, he had this project so tightly put together that there really wasn't much Mark needed to do in his absence. Like Alex had said, "We just sit back and watch the money grow!"

The first phone call came from one of Mark's old friends and colleagues working in London. Bill Johnson headed an international trading fund for a major UK firm.

"Mark, how are things expected to play out over there today?" asked Bill.

"What are you talking about?" asked Mark.

"The International Market. How bad do you think this will be?" he asked in a very tense tone.

Bill obviously didn't have time for small talk. Mark quickly turned to his computer screen. It took a while for the bad news to appear on the screen, but there it was. Something was wrong, very wrong. Mark stared at his screen, then quickly turned on his television to find the business news.

Realizing that Bill Johnson was still on the line, Mark said, "Let me call you back, I need to do some quick thinking here."

Mark spent the next several hours trying to make sense of the day's developments. He knew this was going to be one of those rough rides. Business contacts were calling him all afternoon to get his insight. No one had answers. Something was causing the market to plunge and he had to find out why. Where was Alex when he needed him? There was no logic to the decline, nothing in the recent days had occurred that even hinted at this. Mark locked himself in his office and spent the rest of the day, and well into the night, trying to control the damage. What he didn't know was that the Program Trading project Alex had set up had predetermined trading parameters in place that saw the change in market price and started buying stocks that, for all practical purposes, were tanking.

Sure, the firm had experienced bad market days in the past, but today was record-breaking. It was the single-largest market decline in the history of the DOW—down over ninety-five points. Mark turned off his office lights and sat in the darkness. He stared at the city lights, but wasn't seeing them. He was counting the losses that had just been handed to S&S—those that he knew of.

The next two days would be more of the same. Thursday's drop was fifty-eight points and Friday cost the DOW an all-time record of over one hundred eight points. Mark was in panic mode for the first time in his career and hadn't left the office for two days. The market was sinking rapidly and Alex was nowhere to be found, or even contacted. The firm had lost hundreds of millions of dollars in the past seventy-two hours and Mark was completely spent. He stopped answering phone calls from angry clients before noon on Friday, but knew there would come a time in the very near future that he would have to return each and every call.

At least the week was over. They would put things back together on Monday morning when Alex returned. They would develop a recovery strategy for the firm, their clients, on the other hand, would have to accept the fact that investments came with risk, and that risk was loss.

Alex got the first bit of news about the market as he and Janey were having dinner at the hotel. The look on his face told Janey everything she needed to know. There was trouble, big trouble.

"I have to find a way to get to the office," said Alex. He knew there was nothing he could do, but it was his natural reaction to say those words.

"Alex, you know that's impossible. Besides, Mark is there to take care of things," Janey said, really not believing the words she was asking Alex to take comfort in. "He can handle this."

"No, he can't!" said Alex sharply slamming his hand on the table.

He had raised his voice and other guests turned to see what the commotion was about. He tried to calm himself, and whispered, "Mark doesn't know how to adjust the trading parameters I've set up. He doesn't know enough about computer technology to even understand how the program works. The program will be buying while the market is falling. We'll be overpaying for every stock we buy. This is going to cost the firm millions—hundreds of millions."

He stared out at the blackness that was the Caribbean Sea at night. They thought that a table by the window would make for a very romantic dinner. Reality was that it was so dark on the water at night that it looked like a black curtain had surrounded the entire resort. It reminded Alex of the complete blackness that was enveloping Sohlmann & Stein, especially the private account that David Sohlmann and Mark Stein had been protecting all these past years.

By Friday night, Alex was mentally exhausted. He'd spent all day Thursday and Friday trying to book an earlier flight home. No luck, everything was full. Mark wasn't even answering his phone. Alex was constantly worrying about the losses he was responsible for and it was consuming him. Janey was upset because Alex was upset. This had ruined the last 3 days of their escape. All Alex could think about was getting back to the office on Monday morning and fixing this.

David Sohlmann was also very much in distress over the recent market activity. His yacht was anchored in Nassau and he was on the front end of what was supposed to be a fun week of sun and scuba diving. He had 6 business associates with him and was forced to play host to them when what he wanted to do was cancel the trip, get to New York and put things back on track financially. The market downturn certainly qualified as one of the few things in his world that he could not control and David Sohlmann didn't like it one bit.

This bump in the road would surely hurt, but he knew that he had his safety net in place. The private account at S&S was large, and solid and protected. The conservative approach he and Mark had set up was put in place for situations just like this.

He forced himself to change his mindset and rejoined his friends on the sundeck. They finished their lunch and headed for the reef and some excellent diving. He would be sure that each guest enjoyed their time in the warm waters of the Bahamas. It would mean future business for him and that meant money. He *could* control them having a good time. Of that, he was sure.

The flight home from St. Thomas was stressful for both Alex and Janey. Alex was a complete basket case, he hadn't eaten anything since lunch on Friday afternoon and had said even less. He also hadn't slept a wink. Janey tried to talk with him, but he was too consumed with what was happening and what waited for him at home. He sat in his seat and stared at his lap. It was if he were rehearsing all that he would say to the people at the firm. People that were counting on him, that were relying on him.

Jane was starting to get mad. Not just mad that Alex had shut her out along with the rest of the world for his work, but mad that he had not prepared for this catastrophic turn of events. He was smarter than that and should have been prepared. He had allowed himself to be lulled into such a comfortable state of mind with the strong market, that he was blinded to the reality of preparing for "what-ifs." He knew better than that.

She had allowed herself to get sucked into the fray of his mistake and she didn't like it. She was usually more in control than this. Her whole life had been about remaining in total control of herself, no matter the situation. Being on her own for as long as she had been, she had developed an innate sense of mental and physical strength that had served her well. Now, she found herself a victim of his circumstances. It was causing a sick feeling in her stomach, one that she was unfamiliar with. Not queasy or a feeling of motion sickness, but something that felt very different. No matter how hard she tried to snap out of it, she couldn't overcome it.

They had over two hours left before they landed at Kennedy. It was clear that Alex wasn't in the mood to talk, so Jane tried to get some sleep. It wouldn't come, but it allowed her to set in her mind that she would take the necessary steps to avoid something like this from ever happening in her secret world. She used the time work out the framework of plans to provide her with a strong back up plan should anything go terribly wrong for her.

Chapter Eight

For the first time since he started, Alex wasn't the first one in the office on Monday morning. The time was 5:15 A.M. and Mark Stein was sitting at his desk with his sleeves rolled up and his tie already loose around his collar. He looked like he hadn't slept, and he certainly hadn't shaved this morning. Alex could only imagine what this day held in store for him. Depending on how the market recovered today, it always recovered after a disaster like Friday; he would have to come up with some explanation for what he had allowed to happen. He was nervous and rightfully so.

Alex dropped his briefcase in his office and went directly into Mark's office. Mark was on the phone and noticeably uneasy. This could only mean one thing—whoever was on the other end of the line wasn't happy. Either it was one of the firm's major clients getting their pound of flesh out of Mark for the losses they were hit with last week or it was something much worse.

Mark looked up as Alex walked in and motioned for him to sit down. He continued to listen to whatever it was that was being said in his ear. Alex could hear the faint sound of someone that was clearly unhappy. Mark began to rub the back of his neck in an attempt to ward off the oncoming thunderstorm in his brain, but there would be no luck there.

"Yes, he just walked in," Mark said into the cordless phone. "Okay, let me transfer the call to my other phone, I'll put us on the speaker."

"Alex! Welcome back. Do you feel rested and ready to get to work now that you're back from your vacation? I hope you and your lovely wife enjoyed the Islands."

Alex had never heard the voice before, but knew instantly who was on the other end of the line—it had to be David Sohlmann. The sarcasm in Sohlmann's comment was not disguised at all and Alex knew that he had no desire to do so. Mark stared blankly at Alex, not showing any sign of emotion. It was as if he had mentally checked out for the moment.

"It's nice to finally have the chance to meet you, sir," Alex said as he searched Mark's face for some hint of what was about to take place.

"Yes, well, the pleasure is all yours, it seems," retorted David. "Do you have any idea what has happened here while you were gone?"

Before Alex could respond, Mark said, "I'll fill him in completely. First we have to find out how deep this goes. There are questions that I can't answer yet."

Mark had started to pace back and forth behind his desk. Alex had never seen him in this state of mind and with everything that was going on, it was quite unsettling.

"Well, I plan to be in the office tomorrow morning," said David. "I want a recovery strategy in place and I want answers. Do I make myself clear?"

"We'll be ready..." was all Mark could get out before the line went dead.

Mark returned to the chair behind his desk. They both sat there and stared at each other.

After an uncomfortable moment, Mark said, "This is bad, Alex. Really bad."

"Who could have seen this coming?" asked Alex. His voice was calm, but it was hiding his true feelings of anxiety at the moment. "Wednesday, maybe. Thursday? Statistically off the charts. Friday's dive—completely one in a million, if that."

"That's not really our problem right now, is it? What's done is done. There's nothing we can do about whether we should have seen it coming or not. We have to fix it—right now." Mark was starting to show the signs of heavy stress. He was perspiring and couldn't stop fidgeting.

Mark and Alex had to come up with something to tell David Sohlmann. They spent the next three hours poring over research reports that interns had been working on for the past six months, but had essentially been ignored. They weren't making much progress, and when the market opened flat, Alex breathed a small sigh of relief. Every U.S. investor was nervous about what had taken place over the course of the last three trading days and what this day would hold for them. For once, Alex was very happy about a flat market, but his happiness didn't last very long.

They had decided to leave the Program Trading project parameters in place, hoping to pick up some incredible bargains as the market tried to right itself. Alex asked to move the meeting to his office so he could keep an eye on how things went today from his computer where he might be able to do something, if necessary. Mark needed a change of scenery, so coffee and rolls were brought into Alex's office and they told both their secretaries that they were not to be disturbed for any reason.

The intercom interrupted the silence. It would be one of those moments in life that seemed to unfold in slow motion.

Alex's secretary's voice said, "So sorry to bother you, Alex, but I think you and Mr. Stein might want to take this call."

"Who is it?" asked Mark.

"It's Mr. DeCamp," replied the secretary.

Jonathon DeCamp was one of the firm's biggest clients. S&S was controlling nearly one hundred and fifty million dollars of his money. He was one of those hands-on clients that wanted to stay in constant communication with his brokers. Everyone that knew DeCamp respected him for his intuition and insight. He seemed to be plugged in to information sources that were accurate and timely. He was one of the savviest private investors on Wall Street and commanded respect based solely on the volume of his net worth. He had relationships with four or five major firms and several other boutique shops. Rumor on the street was that he was worth several billion, but because he spread his wealth across such a wide range of mega-firms and others, no one knew for sure. When he phoned and asked to speak with someone, he was not to be denied. Today would be no different. In reality, today was very different.

Both Mark and Alex were aware of what was transpiring in the foreign markets and it wasn't good. In fact, it was very bad. The markets in Tokyo and Hong Kong were a mess. London was following the trend. Wall Street was beginning to show signs of yet another devastating trading day. All they needed right now was for a client like DeCamp to set off mass S&S client panic.

"Put him through," said Stein.

Mark answered the call on the speaker phone. They heard the devastating news together.

"What is Sohlmann & Stein doing to protect my investments? What's your strategy for getting me out of this? What's it going to take to cash out my account and cut my losses?" DeCamp was firing questions at Mark Stein like a raving madman.

Mark sat with his eyes closed as he listened. The overwhelming sense of urgency in DeCamp's tone, while understandable, was overtly confrontational. It was as if he personally blamed S&S for what was happening. It was more than Mark could take right now. His head was spinning, and all he could do was listen and make a lame effort at kissing DeCamp's billion-dollar butt. He tried to assure him that things would be okay.

"Jonathan, we've weathered storms in the past," said Mark. "We have to be patient here."

"Be patient!" screamed DeCamp. "Why? So you can lose even more of my money? You've got to be kidding me! I'm cashing out today. You'll get the paperwork by messenger later today."

DeCamp slammed the phone down and ended the one-sided conversation. Mark was pale. He was well aware of what the loss of a high-profile client like DeCamp would mean. Every Wall Street firm would know about this in a matter of hours, if not sooner. The ripple effect would be huge and Sohlmann would be out for blood.

As time would show, it was a lost cause. Both DeCamp and his money were gone, both figuratively and literally. Alex was sweating. His heartrate and blood pressure were skyrocketing and the caffeine from all the coffee he had been drinking wasn't doing him any favors. He was visibly shaking. He had to get a hold of himself. He tried to steady his breathing but the situation unfolding before his very eyes was just too much. He couldn't think clearly, he felt the onset of a migraine.

By mid-morning the market was down by over one hundred points. Alex and Mark were now scrambling to adjust the Program Trading's buy/sell parameters to stop the bleeding, but finding that making adjustments in real-time were much more difficult than Alex had thought. He never considered having to do this when he set up the program months earlier. Now, with the immense pressure of a market crash underway, his job was even harder, if not impossible. To make matters worse, with Mark by his side all day, he had no way to get into the "secret" program and make any adjustments. The private S&S account was in an unobstructed freefall.

After a slight rally just before noon, things got worse—much worse. Rumors were circulating among big investors that the NYSE would be shut down. This caused another knee-jerk reaction and plunged the market even further. The only solace, if there were any, was that S&S was not alone in all this. There were many firms from Wall Street to Main Street that were getting hammered. The only difference was that Mark and Alex had funneled so much volume into the Program Trading project and were so highly leveraged that their loss was much larger than most.

"We have to do something!" Mark was frantic. "Can't we just pull the plug?" In his mind he knew this wouldn't make any difference, but things were tanking so fast that the words just came out.

"I...I'm trying everything I can think of," Alex replied. "It's just that we don't have a real-time connection into the trading platform buy/sell parameters. I don't know how long it will take for our adjustments to take effect."

In reality he knew exactly how long it would take. Every change they were trying to make would be put into effect at the soonest possible opportunity. And that opportunity would come when the market closed. Not a minute sooner.

By the closing bell, it was a complete market bloodbath—a single-day drop of over 500 points. No one had ever seen anything like this. Foreign markets and the U.S. market were trashed. Both had experienced such a loss, that this day would forever be known as Black Monday. Fortunes had been lost around the world. One Wall Street analyst stated that this made the crash of '29 look like a kiddie-party.

Alex and Mark had nothing more to say to each other. Mark shuffled out of Alex's office and into his own. He needed some space. Alex put his head on his desk and tried to sort things out in his mind. He felt ill.

"We're ruined," said Mark to no one.

He was alone in his office staring at blank computer screens. The staff had gone home. Alex was not in his office, and quite frankly,

Mark didn't care where he was right now. He was mad at Alex. Mark wanted to blame most of this on him, but that wouldn't be totally fair. As managing partner, he was accountable, pure and simple. This had been the worst day of his career by far. Tomorrow would be worse, he was sure of that. David Sohlmann would see to it.

Banks had been calling all day demanding that S&S cover their margins, but Mark wasn't taking their calls. He knew what the rules were; either offer up more collateral or the existing collateral would be sold at fire-sale prices just to recover some of the loss. It's how they played the game. S&S had borrowed such a huge amount of money to fund the project, that there was absolutely no way that they could survive.

To make Mark's day worse, David was on his way to New York and he had no idea what he was going to tell him. David would want to dig into the details of what happened. What had been going on that allowed this crisis to so completely crush them? Why couldn't they cut their losses when it became obvious that things were so bad? He would be on a rampage, no doubt about it. There would be a price to be paid, and Mark feared what it might be. Mostly, Mark feared that David would assume control of the firm, or what might be left of it.

There was no way Mark could survive working directly for Sohlmann. Not now. Early on in his career, the two of them had spent a lot of time together getting the firm up and running, but now Mark had learned to enjoy the freedom of making most of his own decisions. He had become quite comfortable with the idea of running his life his own way and keeping David Sohlmann in the loop. As Sohlmann saw Mark's ability to generate wealth, he faded into the background and gave the appearance that he was hands-off. In reality, however, he was still very much in control.

Alex was in the men's room getting sick. Since the closing bell he had been trying to find a way out of the mess he was in. He was in serious trouble, and he knew it. The firm was sunk and he felt responsible. How many of his coworkers' lives had just been turned upside down? He couldn't help but think of each family that would be affected by his greed and stupidity. He beat himself up for not considering this turn of events and how to prepare for them. It wasn't like him. To make matters even worse, he thought about what would happen when Mark Stein and David Sohlmann discovered what he'd done with their private account. Who knew what they would do to him? Surely he would be fired on the spot, maybe worse. After experiencing the cold, unemotional demeanor of Sohlmann in a time of severe crisis, he knew he had no idea what the consequences might be. He literally began to fear for his personal safety.

Alex couldn't, rather, he wouldn't allow himself to go there.

He pulled himself up from the floor of the men's room and headed for home. He decided to walk home tonight in an effort to clear his head. The five miles or so he had to cover took him nearly two hours. He was wandering a bit, but it didn't matter. It was a cool October night and the crisp air actually felt good. It was almost refreshing. Under any other circumstances, he would be enjoying the walk.

He was in no hurry to get home to Janey. He'd ruined their vacation and hadn't even spoken to her since this whole mess started. He considered stopping in one of the many bars along the way, but figured that would only make a bad situation worse. He needed to find a way to make everything right and that included his relationship with his wife. That was where he would start.

When he walked in the door to their apartment he found Janey in the middle of her workout. She had stopped going to the health club when she started to show signs of being pregnant and began her workout routine at the apartment. She was always pushing herself, and had grown tired of the comments about slowing down now that she was expecting a child. She knew how to exercise, more importantly she knew her body and how to listen to it. She was still lean and very fit. He loved her dedication to fitness and admired her for it now more than ever. It was as constant a part of her life as breathing. It was another common thread that the two of them shared.

She knew something bad was happening again today, the news had been on the radio all day. She started to towel off, but Alex said, "Finish your workout; I'm going to get a bottle of aspirin from the bathroom. I think I need to take a short nap anyway. My head is ready to explode."

Jane finished her workout then showered while Alex slept on the bed. He was still in his suit.

Janey came out of the bathroom wrapped in her robe and sat on the bed next to Alex. Her hair was wet and as she bent to kiss his cheek, the coolness of her hair falling across his face caused him to stir.

"Feeling any better?" she asked.

"I'm in trouble," said Alex in a hoarse voice.

"What do you mean, 'trouble'? How bad are things at the firm?" asked Janey.

"They couldn't be worse. I really don't think the firm can survive. I don't think I can survive."

"It can't be that bad," said Janey as she towel-dried her hair.

"It's actually much worse." The look on Alex's face told her that he was quite serious about that last statement. "I'm not only responsible because I was stupid and didn't think about the project in a worst-case-scenario light, but I crossed an ethical line that can't be ignored."

"I don't like the sound of that," said Janey. As she said these words she thought about the ethical lines she had been crossing for the past several months. She thought about the lines she had crossed with her client. How could she pass any judgment on Alex after what she had become involved in?

Alex sat up, his breathing was shallow and coming in rapid spurts. "We need to talk."

Chapter Nine

David Sohlmann sat in the lush meeting suite of his private jet as they cruised at forty-two thousand feet. He wasn't a pilot, but an aircraft like this might just cause him to consider adding that skill to his lengthy list of expert capabilities. They were traveling at just under 580 miles per hour, well below the max speed the jet was capable of. The flight from Miami to LaGuardia would take just over two hours, depending on the prevailing winds. It was a brand-new Gulfstream G4 and it was the pinnacle of private aviation. He had it customized with a stateroom, complete with private master bathroom and shower, the meeting suite he was currently sitting in and a general seating area for six passengers to comfortably enjoy a flight of any distance.

The interior was finished with the finest leathers and burled walnut trim. The cabin chairs were designed to reline to a completely horizontal position for those wanting to catch some sleep while in the air. The lighting was customized with individual dimmers all throughout the cabin and a sound system that any dance club would be happy to have. There were two full-service wet bars and a fully stocked galley that his cabin crew would use to prepare gourmet in-flight meals.

He had taken delivery of the plane earlier this year and was quite proud of it. It was one of the first G4's off the assembly line and David had traveled to Gulfstream's Corporate Headquarters in Savannah, Georgia, to experience its maiden flight. He had been heavily involved with Gulfstream and Grumman since 1983 when the two aerospace companies began design on what would eventually become the G4. He provided not only business services through one of his manufacturing companies, but he was able to convince them that he could offer valuable customer input to the design team. David and Gulfstream's president were old friends and, up until now, distant business associates. Having been a Gulfstream customer for the past fifteen years, David's ego led him to believe that he deserved the right to throw his two cents in. No one disagreed with him.

He had already crisscrossed the country more times than he could remember in his new toy. This, however, was the first time he didn't allow himself to be pampered while in the air. No meal, not even a drink was served on this flight. He was too angry about the recent Wall Street events that had taken some measure of control away from him. His diving trip had been cut short and he had to leave clients on the boat with his crew to enjoy the warm waters of Nassau. He was forced to make an unscheduled visit to Manhattan; he was not in total control and it didn't sit well with him. He was on this flight alone. With no one to bark at, David grew more and more disturbed. He was consumed with the financial meltdown that was taking place at the firm in Manhattan and the fallout it would bring. At least he would have answers in the morning.

As the pilot circled the city on final approach, David stared out at the lights of the city that never slept. Anyone else would have been impressed with the way New York City looked at night from the air, but not David Sohlmann, certainly not tonight. He had only one thing on his mind and that was his money. He was losing it and someone else was responsible.

They touched down at just after midnight. He had a driver waiting for him on the tarmac in the private aviation hanger at LaGuardia and was quickly swept away to his Manhattan apartment. It would be a short night and there was much to accomplish at S&S tomorrow.

Chapter Ten

Alex started from the beginning to give Janey a clear understanding of his mindset. It was important for him to allow her to see where his logic had come from. She needed to understand that his motives were pure and that he was only trying to do something good for Mark and David. He gave her the details of the portfolio's performance and how the market had allowed the project to skyrocket. He was clear to point out that Mark was so taken by the gains the project was making that it was his idea to *super-fund* the portfolio.

"I know all this," Janey said. "What does any of this have to do with ethics?"

"S&S controls many different types of accounts. Mutual funds, private accounts, individual and municipal retirement accounts, you name, it we manage them all. The Program Trading project allowed us to pool these funds into a kind of super-account. As I saw the performance going up and up, I thought that maybe I could take advantage of this opportunity to do more.

"Mark Stein and David Sohlmann have this private account. It's jointly owned by both of them and my understanding is that they share it 50/50. It's been kept separate from all the other accounts that the firm manages for as long as anyone knows," said Alex. "To my knowledge, no one has even looked at it in forever."

"Please tell me you didn't steal their money, Alex." Janey was staring at him again with those steel-blue eyes.

"I wish I had," he replied. "I could return it and they'd never know."

Alex had regained some control over his breathing.

"I convinced Mark's secretary to give me the access codes to the account and set up a second 'project account' that would run parallel to my portfolio and really grow their money. It was going to be kind of a Christmas present to them." Alex laughed at the thought of phrasing it that way, given that both of them were Jewish and had never celebrated Christmas once in either of their lives. But it was nervous laughter.

"I not only put the entire account balance into the second project account, but I borrowed against it to make even more money. My plan was to cash out at the end of December and present them with an account statement showing the new balance. I'd return the account to its original conservative status and things would be fine.

"You have to understand that this private account of theirs was huge to begin with. Just last week it was up to over six hundred fifty million dollars. The problem is, I had it leveraged to the max with a new bank. Then Wednesday happened. Then Thursday and Friday. And now today. The bank called me to cover the margin."

"What can you do?" Janey asked this question more as a statement with a calmness that surprised Alex.

"Sohlmann is coming here tomorrow. To be honest, he scares me," admitted Alex. "I really don't think there's anything I can do at this point. I checked the account before I left the office tonight. With what we owe on the collateral, it's worthless. I'm completely upside down on it."

"We'll survive, Alex, won't we?" asked Janey.

"I hope so," said Alex.

He was doubtful at best. He knew his career at S&S would come to an abrupt end in the morning. He feared legal action taken by David Sohlmann for what he had done. He really didn't know what to expect.

"What's the worst they can do? Fire you?"

"I really don't know, Jane," said Alex. "I really don't know, but getting fired would probably be the best outcome. There could be legal action that could land me in prison for a long time."

He sat on the bed and stared at his wife. Even with all this going on, she seemed calm, but he could sense something churning beneath the surface of her beautiful façade. The stress of the last three days in St. Thomas coupled with what he'd just told her was starting to take its toll on her. But there was something else, he just couldn't put his finger on it.

When Jane rose to return to their bathroom to finish drying her hair, they both froze. The blood on the bed was pooling. She had started to hemorrhage.

The paramedics arrived in less than ten minutes. She was in the emergency room in less than twenty-five. She had two doctors feverishly trying to gain control of her situation. She had an IV in her arm providing the needed fluids to her system and they were giving her medication to stop whatever it was that was causing the bleeding. There were wires and monitors attached to her belly to try to get a read on the fetus, but they really didn't know how the baby was reacting to all this.

Alex sat in the empty waiting room. It was typical of emergency room waiting areas: cold, unfriendly, dimly lit and way too quiet. The magazines were all six months out of date and the muted television up on the wall was showing repeat after repeat of news anchors trying to explain the disaster he had lived through all day. The coffee tasted like mud, but at least it was hot. He was worried about Janey and the baby. He was scared about tomorrow and what would unfold in the morning. As he sat there waiting for an update he found he was becoming angry. Angry at himself, angry at Mark for the role he had played in all of this, angry at the market, and angry at the way David Sohlmann had so smugly confronted them with his demand for answers.

He thought about their future, about his future. What would he possibly do? Every firm on Wall Street would know about this by noon tomorrow. There wasn't a firm out there that would consider hiring him now. Even if S&S didn't press formal charges against him, he would be an outcast forever, one brilliant kid with a brilliant financial head that could never again be trusted.

He thought about all the work he'd put in at the firm building his reputation. He thought about the investment of his time and energy to develop the project. He was good at his job, maybe the best in a long time. And soon it would all be gone. All because the market tanked.

"Mr. Coswell?" asked the man in the scrubs. It snapped Alex back to the reality that was playing out at the hospital.

"Yes," replied Alex standing to greet the doctor, or whatever he was.

"I'm Dr. Farnelli. Your wife is stable and it appears that the baby will be okay. We want to keep her overnight for observation just to be sure, plus she needs some rest."

He had a calming effect on Alex. His apparent age represented experience and wisdom, and that was exactly what Alex needed at the moment.

"Thank God," Alex said.

The relief on his face was obvious as he slumped back on the old couch in the waiting room. He was unsure what his current state of mind was, still angry about the situation at work and relieved about Janey and the baby. He was conflicted and it must have shown in the features on his face.

"You don't look so good yourself," said Dr. Farnelli. "Why don't you go home and get some rest. You won't be much help to your wife sitting in here all night."

"I can't leave her."

"Well, it's your call, but I know from years of experience that this couch and those chairs are not the place to get any comfortable rest." Dr. Farnelli was speaking to Alex like a father. It had been a long time since he had anyone relate to him in that way.

Alex was torn. He wanted to be by Janey's side. He wanted to be in the room with her when she awoke in the morning. He wanted to be the one to bring her home and take care of her. At the same time, he knew he had to face the music tomorrow morning at work. He needed to be in the office no later than six o'clock A.M. What to do?

He allowed the anger that had built up inside him while has was waiting to hear about Janey to make the decision for him. He was going to take some control of his situation. He really only had one option. He rose from the couch, gathered his belongings and walked out of the waiting room.

Chapter Eleven

Mark Stein knew he was accountable to David Sohlmann for the loss of the firm. As Managing Partner, he would have to answer to each and every client, to explain their losses. He had no one else to blame, really. After all, he was the one to funnel more and more of the firm's money into the Program Trading project that Alex was working on. He was the one to approve the leveraging of firm assets, and the rampant borrowing of money to grow the portfolio. It would be him that would answer for the total destruction of Sohlmann & Stein. But that was a risk that he had always been willing to take. The fact that the firm was now basically insolvent as a result of his greed and poor foresight was a burden he would forever carry, but in reality he wouldn't lose any sleep over it. The investment game involved risk and everyone knew it.

What he would lose sleep over was what his eyes were reading right now. There had to be some mistake in what he was looking at because it just didn't make any sense. He had pulled a report off the computer system to look at the damages that yesterday's market crash had caused and he found a huge problem. He had anticipated catastrophe, but not this. He couldn't understand.

"How can this be?" said Mark to an empty office. He leaned back in his chair and stared at the ceiling. He felt the onset of a migraine. Risk was one thing, mismanagement was another.

His desk was covered in stacks of computer printouts. He had files of customer accounts scattered around his office and the printer in the workroom continued to churn out devastating reports that would have to be explained. Right now, none of them seemed to matter. The report in his lap was the only information that meant anything at the moment. The private account that he and David Sohlmann had put in place years ago was as good as gone. Worthless. As he studied the report, and as he crunched the numbers in his head, he realized that there was going to be even bigger trouble than he expected once Sohlmann arrived.

He wouldn't allow himself to mentally go where he needed to go to understand the situation and how it might have happened. There was no way someone would betray him from inside the firm. He had strict rules in place and they had always been followed. As he was rubbing his temples he was brought back to the reality of what this day would hold.

"Well, it's time to sift through the rubble. Are you ready?"

David Sohlmann was standing in the doorway to Mark's office holding a cup of coffee. It was just after six A.M. and he was ready for answers. He looked impressive in his Italian suit, shoes and silk suspenders, or braces as he liked to call them. He was the image of tranquility and control, but Mark knew that under the surface of that façade boiled a fiery rage.

"I didn't expect to see you this early," said Mark. "I was expecting Alex to be the next one in the office."

"Speaking of Alex, where is he?" David looked around and became noticeably on edge and didn't appear to be in any mood for small talk. "I have a few questions for him."

"He's usually here by now, and after yesterday I can't understand him being late," said Mark. He picked up the phone and dialed Alex's home number again. No answer.

Mark slid the Private Account report he was holding in his desk drawer. This was something he needed to get to the bottom of before he shared any of it with David.

Janey opened her eyes and looked out the window of her hospital room. She unconsciously rubbed her stomach as she relived the events of last night. She had slept well and felt quite refreshed given what she had been through. It must have been the sleep aids that the doctor had given her last night. She liked Dr. Farnelli, he made her feel like everything was going to be okay, though she wasn't sure. Maybe she had pushed herself too hard during her workout as he suggested. Whatever, her body reacted as it did and that was water under the bridge, she needed to be careful in the future.

She heard a stirring on the other side of the bed. As she turned to see what it was, a smile came across her face. Alex was slumped in the chair asleep, his head cocked in a very uncomfortable-looking position. He was still dressed in the clothes he had come home from work in. He looked a mess.

"Alex," whispered Janey.

Alex bolted upright, a bit confused by his surroundings. He saw Janey and gained his bearings. He moved over to the bed and put her hand in his. "How are you feeling?"

"I think I'll be fine," said Janey. "But I'm afraid for the baby."

"Dr. Farnelli said the baby would be okay."

Janey sighed with relief. Then a look of concern crossed her face.

"What's wrong?" asked Alex.

"Shouldn't you be at the office? With everything that's happened I thought you'd be there all night."

"Nothing is more important than being here with you right now. I'll take you home and get you settled, then go to the office and try to straighten things out. If that's even possible at this point."

Janey and Alex arrived at their apartment at 11:45. Dr. Farnelli had released Janey with strict instructions to take it easy for a while. No work for the rest of the week and absolutely no exercise. The light on the answering machine was flashing indicating that there was a message waiting for them. In fact, there were several. All of them were from Mark Stein asking Alex to please get to the office.

Alex showered and got dressed and headed to work. Janey assured him that she would be fine and sent him on his way. She would relax at home and get the rest that the doctor ordered. She told Alex that he needed to do what needed to be done at the office. She was sure that things would work out fine.

Mark Stein met Alex at the door as he entered the S&S office suite. He was visibly upset and ushered Alex into his office and closed the door before Alex had the chance to put his briefcase down. Mark's office was a mess, printouts, reports and coffee cups were everywhere. This was not like Mark.

"What happened in here?" asked Alex.

"Don't worry about it! What is this?" Mark slapped the Private Account report into Alex's chest. "And where have you been all morning?"

Alex stumbled backwards a step or two as he caught the printout in his right hand. One look at the report heading and he knew what Mark had handed him. It felt as though he were holding a ticking time bomb, a very heavy ticking time bomb.

"I spent the night at the hospital with Janey last night, she almost lost the baby," said Alex. He backed up to the sofa and dropped down. "I'm sorry for being late."

Mark didn't react to Alex's statement in any way. It was as if he didn't hear a word. "You know that Mr. Sohlmann is here, right? He's looking for answers today. Answers that we don't really have. You know we're sunk, Alex. The firm is gone. We lost everything yesterday!"

"I'm sorry, I knew it would be bad, but I had no idea."

Mark rubbed his temples again and said, "This business comes with risk, Alex. I know it, you know it. David Sohlmann knows it. I hope every one of our clients knows it." Mark sighed. "One of my responsibilities is to anticipate and prepare for events like those we experienced last week and yesterday."

Alex stared at the carpet.

"What I can't anticipate nor can I prepare for is that!" His emotions were on a roller-coaster. He was pointing at the report sitting in Alex's lap. "Can you tell me how that happened? Can you give me some understanding of how our most protected, conservative account got wiped out!?"

Alex spent the next hour providing Mark with the details of his plan to grow the account. He left out the part about Mark's secretary giving him the access code, rather telling him that he had hacked into the system to gain control. He tried to show Mark that his motives were pure, as pure as they could be while committing fraudulent activity. He told him that it had nothing to do with personal gain for himself.

"Sohlmann is going to erupt," said Mark. "You have no idea!"

He had calmed down a little, but was still visibly shaken. Alex had convinced him that he was only trying to help.

"This loss is going to impact him, us, in a huge way. That account was his safety net. It was his one insurance policy that covered the risk of all his other business ventures."

"I'll take full responsibility," said Alex. "No matter what, it was all my fault."

Alex sat silently in the main conference room and Mark filled David in on what had happened with their private account. As more and more details were brought to light, all Sohlmann did was give Alex an occasional glance. There was no outward emotion at any time during the meeting.

As things wrapped up, David stood and turned to stare out at the Manhattan skyline. Alex and Mark stole a glance at each other.

Without turning to face him, David said, "Alex, you know you're fired, right? You'd have to be an idiot to think otherwise."

No reply from Alex. He stared at his shoes.

"I'll be surprised if you ever work on Wall Street again. Have a nice life," said David as he turned to leave the offices of S&S for the last time.

Mark turned to say something to Alex, but kept silent.

"I'll clean out my office and be out of here before the end of the day," said Alex. "For what it's worth, I really am sorry."

He was expecting to be fired, but had actually hoped that David Sohlmann would have yelled at him or something. The lack of emotion in his reaction was, by far, more unsettling than any other reaction might have been.

Chapter Twelve

David Sohlmann was sitting in the office in his Manhattan apartment. He hung up the phone with an unemotional feeling of slight accomplishment. After the catastrophic events of the past few days, the least of his worries were the possible legal ramifications of the conversation that had just taken place with the person on the other end of the line. He was bent on revenge and would see to it that he got it. Right now, he needed to get back to his boat and some warm, sunny weather. He needed a change of scenery. Even spending less than 24 hours in the city had a negative effect on him. He had his flight scheduled and would be departing for Nassau within the hour. His first concern, though, was the simple call he had just made.

One of the many business holdings buried in the depths of the empire that Sohlmann owned was Prestige Properties, Inc. It was a multi-state real estate group that had boomed during the past several years. It controlled hundreds of commercial buildings, retail strip malls, hotels and apartment complexes across New York, New Jersey and Connecticut. While somewhat insulated from the market events of the past week, there was some speculation that even the real estate market might suffer some back lash from the crash. Sohlmann would not allow that to happen.

As it turned out, Alex and Jane Coswell were tenants of one of the buildings in the Prestige Properties, Inc., network. David Sohlmann called the manager of Prestige Properties and after a brief one-sided conversation the Coswell rent had been increased. Just like that. There were no questions. There was no hesitation by the manager to act on the direct order from Sohlmann. Orders like this were immediately and accurately followed.

This would be just the first step in the control that David Sohlmann would begin to orchestrate in the life of his newest adversary. Alex Coswell had no idea who he had crossed. Surely he would come to find out.

Chapter Thirteen

Alex walked into their apartment soaking wet.The rain had begun early in the day and hung over the city like an evil cloud looking to devour anyone that dared venture out. It seemed quite fitting that after the past few days of financial mayhem the weather would also conspire to make everyone's life miserable.

He held a cardboard box filled with his personal belongings from his office: photos, a coffee mug, a few books and other assorted items. This was all Janey needed to see to fully understand what had happened during the day.

"Are you serious? Did they just fire you on the spot?" asked Janey.

"It's what I expected, actually."

"I can't believe this is happening. What are you going to do now?"

"I really don't know."

Alex set the box on the table and headed out of the room. He needed to get out of his wet clothes and wanted to head down to the gym to work out some of the stress he was feeling. It was during his workouts that he was able to clear his mind. It was the only time he was able to sort through the chaos of life and regain focus and find his center.

Janey got up from the sofa and headed into the kitchen. The phone rang and she picked it up.

"Hello?"

Alex walked into the room and waited as Janey listened to the person on the other end of the line. She didn't say a word. She listened and then hung up the phone.

"Who was that?" asked Alex.

Janey walked back into the living room and sat down on the sofa. She had that look in her eyes that told Alex that she was not happy about something. It was rare that he could sense her anger, but this was one of those times. It was as if she were mentally preparing for some type of confrontation.

"He said he was the building manager, but it wasn't Frank."

Frank Adducci was their landlord. Alex and Janey had known him since the day they moved in to their apartment. He was a sweet old man that had come from Italy when he was about 35 years old. He was an old-world barber and had spent his career working in his small barbershop around the corner. When he retired, he negotiated a rent freeze for his little apartment by offering to handle the management and maintenance issues in the building and collecting the tenants' rent checks each month and making the deposits. Everyone in the building loved him.

"He called to let us know that due to the market events of yesterday, they are doubling our rent, effective immediately."

"They can't do that! We have a lease agreement through the end of April," said Alex.

"Well, whoever this was said if we didn't like it we could either move out, or sue him. Either way, he said it was a done deal. Then he kind of chuckled and hung up on me, which was weird."

Alex wondered if this day could possibly get any worse. Actually it would. Later that evening something happened inside Janey, she got the same cramping feeling she had felt while in the hospital last night, only this time it was much worse. She knew something was terribly wrong. She felt her pulse racing and her breathing became labored. The thought of Alex losing his job was causing her to get upset, an increase in rent without his income was going to be nearly impossible, and that was upsetting too. Their world was getting rocked and she didn't like it. She was stressed about last night at the hospital and now this.

They got a cab and went back to the emergency room. It was once again the typical ER room experience, too many people and not enough medical staff to handle them all. There were also too few medical staff who really seemed to care. Alex and Janey could only sit and wait for their turn. Even though she was obviously pregnant, and had been there that same morning as a patient, no one gave her any special attention. Alex made it a point to find two chairs out of sight of the television. The last thing he needed right now was to be reminded of the financial events the world was experiencing and that he was living. It was a long, long wait as they sat in silence.

After an hour and forty minutes, Janey was finally taken to an examination room, after a quick recap of last night's events, she was hurried upstairs for another full battery of tests. Dr. Farnelli came into the room and sat in one of the chairs. His mood was not what they were hoping for.

"Mrs. Coswell, have you been under a lot of stress lately?"

"You might say that," said Janey.

She and Alex looked at each other and decided that was enough of an answer.

"Stress plays an interesting role in the health of an unborn baby," said Dr. Farnelli. "If there are high levels of stress during the early months of a pregnancy, the brain releases hormones and other chemicals that are not healthy for the mother's body or for the baby. One of these hormones is called CRH, it stands for corticotrophin-releasing hormone. It's been found to be released in various parts of the female body, one of which is the uterus. It affects mast cells, which are best known for causing allergic reactions.

"There is an abundance of mast cells found in the uterus which is completely normal. The CRH causes these mast cells to secrete a substance that can cause miscarriage."

"Are you saying we are going to lose the baby?" asked Alex. He was beginning to have his own stress-induced breakdown. He walked to the bed and sat beside Janey.

"With what we have been able to learn from the tests we ran tonight, it is very likely that your high stress levels combined with the type of vigorous exercising that you do may have caused a negative effect on your unborn child. There is still a heartbeat right now, but I want to prepare you for what will most likely be a change for the worse over the next few hours."

Silence filled the room. Neither Janey nor Alex could find anything to say. They just stared at each other. Both were trying to find a way to fully understand what was happening to them.

"I'm sorry for your loss," said Dr. Farnelli as he turned to leave the room. "I'll let you have some time alone. If you have any questions, I'll be at the nurse's station down the hall. The nurse will check on you over the next hour or so. She can explain the steps that we will need to go through and schedule the…procedure. If you would like to speak to the hospital chaplain, please let us know."

With that, he left them in the room. Alex leaned into Janey's shoulder, placed his hand on her belly and began to cry.

PART TWO

Chapter Fourteen

1989

Alex Coswell sat at his desk trying to make himself look busy. He had the *Wall Street Journal* open but really wasn't finding it very interesting today. It was only mid-morning but he felt like he had been there all day. The past two years had certainly taken their toll on Alex's psyche. He was no longer as sure of himself as he had once been. From time to time he would think back to his days as the king of the hill at Sohlmann & Stein and wonder how it had gone so wrong. *Stupidity is how*, he thought. He knew better than to allow that to have happened. He was trained better than to allow that to have happened.

Business was slow at Rochester National Bank these days, especially for investment services at a small community bank. As the only employee of RNB Financial Services, Inc., located at the bank's main branch, Alex spent most of his days either researching investment opportunities that would never materialize or staying up to date on some of the latest IT developments available to the investment and banking industry. He had been trying to convince the top brass at the bank that they really needed to look into the development of some sort of technology that would appeal to the younger generation. It seemed this was where banking and investing were headed and without a solid base of young customers to rely on, the bank would continue to lose their share of that business. In the back of his mind, he was hoping for management to recognize that his computer skills would make him an excellent resource to head the development of a project like that. Alex was looking for anything to get him out of the tedium of being an Investment Broker for a small bank. No such luck.

His office was on the main floor in the front corner of the Rochester National Bank building, which was located on the corner of Main Street East and Gibbs, just across from the Eastman Theater. The theater was one of those rare gems found across America that showcased an impressive level of craftsmanship from a bygone era. Originally built in 1922 by immigrant European artisans, the theater was the pride of Upstate New York. George Eastman had proclaimed that the theater was "For the Enrichment of Community Life." In fact, his quote was carved into the façade of the theater at the main entrance. It had been living up to that expectation for nearly a century.

In recent years, the theater had undergone substantial renovations and now was in desperate need of more. The Rochester Philharmonic Orchestra called the theater home and was trying to raise money for a complete overhaul. The most recent attempt at this was a black tie gala event that Alex and Janey were able to attend last week thanks to free tickets from the bank. The theater had spectacular acoustics and the warm burgundy curtains and velvet seats, the beautiful murals on the walls of each side of the main hall and the grand chandelier created an environment that any city in the world would be proud to call their own; they just needed to be brought back to life—much the same way Alex felt these days.

The music was fantastic, the receptions before and after the concert spared no expense, and those members of Rochester's high society seeking to be seen were certainly in their element. The mayor and the theater manager made sure that every guest was having a wonderful time. Alex and Janey were enjoying a wonderful evening out, but knew that nights like this were few and far between.

They would like to have been regulars at the theater's events but as life would have it that just wasn't in the cards for them anymore. It reminded them of their early days of marriage in Manhattan when they had not only opportunity to enjoy some of the finer things in life, but also the money needed to do so. Now, however, things were very different. There wasn't enough commission generated at the bank to afford expensive theater tickets or black tie events of any kind. The reality of their financial situation was there wasn't room for many luxuries at all.

Alex looked at the calendar on his on his desk. He had only one confirmed appointment all day. Actually, it was rare that he had any confirmed meetings at all. The potential client was scheduled to come in at 2:00 P.M. and was expecting to talk about some high-level investment strategies. Whatever. Alex had heard it all before. Most of his customers wanted him think they were big players, but in reality they were all small-time investors that required about an ounce of his talent. Nonetheless, he looked forward to the prospect of breaking the routine that had become the make-up of his boring day.

Janey had found work in the one of the many IT departments of the Kodak Corporation. While she had plenty of work to keep her busy, she also found time to continue to explore the world of unauthorized access—hacking. After being forced to leave New York City because of the market crash, and leaving the client that had been willing to pay for her unique talents, she found herself interested in getting into remote computer systems outside the banking industry. She had also developed a program that could leave behind a hidden program that would alert her if an account had been accessed by one of its authorized users. How she would use this information wasn't really clear to her, but the challenge was exciting. The fact that she could do it at all was more rewarding than anything else she did these days. Maybe she could find a way to use this knowledge to earn some much needed income. In reality, Janey had no idea how to do such a thing.

She had lost all contact with her special New York City client. The Coswells' departure from Manhattan came quickly after Alex lost his job at Sohlmann & Stein and Janey was actually happy about that. After all, putting some distance between her and her very questionable activities was probably a good thing. She had heard through her underground network of hackers that there was word on the street that this same client was now seeking a new "partner" to assist them with special projects, but had not found anyone with her level of skills. Many times she considered contacting them, but had never followed through with it.

Andrew McNeeley entered Alex's office just as the clock on the wall struck 2:00. He was an older gentleman, looking to be somewhere in his late sixties. He had a rock-hard handshake and a spark in his eye that immediately caught Alex by surprise. His hair was white and neatly groomed; he was dressed in classic khakis and a white button-down oxford cloth shirt and wore boat shoes.

Alex smiled inwardly and introduced himself. "Mr. McNeeley, I'm Alex."

"Nice to meet you, son," said McNeeley. "I'm Andrew McNeeley. You can call me Mac."

They were both instantly at ease and things got off to a comfortable start. Alex suggested that they might be more comfortable chatting in the conference room down the hall and it would offer privacy and allow them access to the small kitchenette where they could enjoy bottled water or fresh coffee. As they settled into the comfortable leather chairs surrounding the long oak conference room table, Andrew McNeeley began the conversation with some background and a few questions for Alex.

"Alex, I've been around the investment block a few times in my life and have done pretty well for myself. So I think I know what I'm talking about most of the time. As I stated on the phone last week when we scheduled this appointment, I want to discuss some pretty lofty investment strategies. I have some ideas of what I want to get into and how I want to diversify my portfolio, but I'm getting too old to do it all myself. But before I get to all that, I'd like to learn a little about you and your qualifications."

Alex gave him the cursory overview of the licenses he held, Series 7, Series 3, Series 62 and 63, and his experience in the financial industry. He skirted the issues that led to him relocating to Rochester from Manhattan. It might have been an uncomfortable conversation if it had headed down that path of his history, but Andrew McNeeley seemed genuinely interested in Alex as a person and accepted his overview at face value. Alex explained that he had been married to his wife Janey for nearly five years and that she was a computer programmer and CPA. She was currently working for Kodak here in Rochester. They lived in the area and owned a dog named Daisy.

"Mac, I have to tell you that I don't usually get into this type of conversation with prospective clients after only fifteen minutes."

"I'm hoping I'm not going to be one of your usual clients," said McNeeley. "I have some unique ideas and I want to know that I'll be in good hands."

He looked at Alex with a sly grin and a twinkle in his eye.

"Well, all I can promise you is that I'll do my best to help you achieve your goals. If you are successful, then RNB Financial will be successful. My belief is that if we walk this path together and are open and honest with each other, we should do just fine," replied Alex with a bit of unexpected confidence returning to his demeanor. "I believe the market is in good shape for success."

"I couldn't agree more," replied Mac.

The rest of the meeting was spent discussing recent market trends, historical events that might signal change to look out for as opportunity and those to avoid, and how best they might be able to work together. Both Andrew McNeeley and Alex Coswell had sharp financial minds and seemed to play off each other very well. It was as if they had worked together for a long time and both were feeling comfortable.

As abruptly as McNeeley had begun the meeting by digging into Alex's background, he rose and said the meeting was over. He suggested that they meet for breakfast tomorrow morning at 6:00 A.M. at a local diner that had been in Rochester forever. He would be waiting for Alex in the corner booth at Smitty's. If it was okay with Alex, he would order Eggs Benedict and coffee for both of them and have them ready when he arrived.

"I'll see you in the morning," said Alex. He rose and shook hands with McNeeley. "I know exactly where Smitty's Diner is. See you at six."

The two parted company and Alex's best prospect in years eased his way out of the bank. When Alex returned to his office he immediately opened the phone book to search for Smitty's Diner. He had never even heard of it before five minutes ago.

Chapter Fifteen

David Sohlmann was just finishing up his afternoon walk on the beach when his cellular phone rang. He answered, listened and quickly ended the call without speaking a work. The message was clear—*Project underway. More to come.*

He returned to his yacht to shower and have some breakfast. *The Endeavor* could actually be classified as a ship at 165 feet. His personal crew and staff totaled 12 and he spared no expense on the lifestyle he lived. He was at the top of the food chain and was considered one of the wealthiest businessmen in the country. He held a U.S. Passport, but spent the majority of his time following the best weather climates in the world. Lately, he had settled in Grand Cayman because he preferred the mostly calm weather and favorable banking laws. It helped that the annual temperatures only varied about 8 degrees one way or the other. Maybe he couldn't control the weather but when he found himself in a climate like this, he could easily focus on the things he needed to control.There were other locations that he liked also, so there was never any lack of options for him to consider when it came to his time on his yacht.

At 57 years of age, Sohlmann defied the odds both in terms of his physical condition and sharpness of mind. He walked 5 miles every day—rain or shine—and in Grand Cayman it was mostly shine. *The Endeavor* was outfitted with a state of the art fitness center that he utilized 4 days a week to maintain his muscle tone and agility. Even at his age, he continually pushed his body. He never allowed himself to yield to the aches and pains normally associated with men of his age. He never slowed down enough to let age catch up to him.

His computer allowed him to read at least one magazine every day cover to cover just to keep up on a wide range of topics—everything from the latest business trends to skateboarding. Nothing was deemed unimportant to him. Staying current and relevant was critical to his ongoing success. His business holdings had grown over the years and he still maintained his desire to remain the silent behind-the-scenes type. He had become a master at controlling outcomes and working to ensure business results that were to his advantage.

Now he sat on the sun deck enjoying fresh fruit and juice and reading one of 4 daily newspapers that were delivered to *The Endeavor* every day. Sohlmann liked the feel of newsprint in his hands. Television and other media were fine, but the printed daily paper was the one link he held on to from a past era that was fast disappearing. His morning ritual did not vary much from day to day. One of the variables for him to decide upon was whether to dive on one of the many reefs in the area or spend a few hours trying to catch the fish he regularly swam with. Either way, it was how he decided on the menu for dinner. If he saw it or caught it, he would have his chef prepare it.

He thought about the phone message from earlier in the day. He allowed himself a small smile. Not because he was happy, it actually made him mad just thinking about it. He smiled because he had the ability to control his world and the desired outcome of his circumstance. David Sohlmann was a force to be reckoned with and he wanted everyone to know it.

He picked up his phone and thumbed in a number. "Proceed as planned" was all he said when the call was answered. He knew that things were in motion now. The planning had been meticulously developed over a long period of time and the end result would be exactly what he wanted. Nothing had been left to chance. His people had been selected for very specific tasks and would only know a small part of the master plan. There was no risk of anything hinting at his involvement. He would only reveal bits and pieces of his plan as necessary to the various people that would be involved.

He left the sun deck and headed to the ship's bridge. He spoke to the captain and set a course and travel schedule for Miami. They would depart at dawn. As he stared out at the calmness of the clear blue waters of the Caribbean Sea, David Sohlmann lost himself in the complexity of the plan he had created. For a moment, he allowed himself to think back to a time when he first realized that money was the driver when it came to controlling the events of life.

He was a just a young boy, but old enough to understand what was happening around him. His father was a typical working stiff trying to make ends meet in Brooklyn. It seemed that the Sohlmann family couldn't buy a break no matter what. Money was always tight and Sohlmann's father just never seemed to be able to rise above. On one sunny summer afternoon, a man in a fancy suit knocked on the apartment door of the Sohlmann family residence. Words were spoken softly but it was clear that there was tension in them. Young David wasn't sure what was happening but he very clearly saw the exchange of a large sum of money between his father and the man in the suit. David couldn't understand where his father could get so much money, but there it was. And why was he giving it away?

The man returned several times over the next year or so and before long things started to change for the Sohlmann family. They relocated to a much larger apartment and their quality of life become noticeably better. David never found out the reason for the frequent exchange of money or who the man in the suit was, but he did know that it was the money that somehow changed his life. When his father was gunned down on the family stoop on New Year's Day 1947, David Sohlmann vowed revenge. He wasn't sure who he would take it out on, but someone somewhere would pay.

At the early age of 15, Sohlmann vowed to himself that he would be the one to control the events of his life. He would never again allow other people to have any control on how his life unfolded.

It was now time to focus on the current plan that had been so long in coming—over two years. David Sohlmann would now begin to enjoy watching things unfold at a much faster pace. Things that he had planned. Things that he would control. The excitement of this control got his blood flowing, just like it did every time he was able to control the lives of others. He headed to the fitness center to take advantage of the adrenaline now coursing through his veins.

Chapter Sixteen

Janey walked in to Alex's office at the bank quietly. She still had a wet head from her shower at the gym. At age 26, she was now in the best shape of her life. She had been in the habit of working out 4 or 5 days a week for her entire life and never missed a session. Her employer provided a health club membership to all employees as part of the benefits package and she took full advantage of it. Recently, the club began a Cross-Training program that suited Janey to a tee. It reminded her of her improvised workouts of her youth when she didn't have any money to go to the local health clubs. Constantly changing the exercise routine allowed her to hone her agility, strength and endurance. She knew each of these to be critical elements of survival in today's world. Work and the stresses of a life filled with frustration could take their toll. Her secret computer activities also generated stress. Janey needed her exercise as a necessary release valve.

As she stood by the door, she saw Alex sitting at his computer completely lost in thought. He had several pages of handwritten notes surrounding the keyboard and the desk was stacked with many pages of information and figures. She hadn't seen him in this state of research in years. Something was up.

"Hi there," said Janey. "What's all this?"

"I've got a potential new client and he could be a huge deal," Alex absently replied. He didn't look up from the computer screen. His fingers danced over the keyboard as numbers flashed across the screen. He had several research sites open and toggled back and forth from each of them comparing data, looking at financial trends, researching various companies and reviewing historical data. He had a large glass of water teetering on the edge of the desk that spilled to the floor as he reached for another stack of pages. It brought him into focus on Janey.

"How long have you been here?" asked Alex.

Janey replied, "Only a few minutes, are you that deep into this? I just asked what you were up to and you said something about a new client."

Alex stood and gave Janey a warm hug. Looking into her eyes he could still see the sparkle that attracted him to her all those years ago. There was a hint of excitement. He could tell she was eager to hear about his afternoon. Even with all they had been through, most of which didn't turn out as they had planned, he loved the way she seemed to get excited about his work.

"Sorry, I'm really focused on this. I've got a meeting tomorrow at 6:00 A.M. with this new client. I think this could be a really big deal for me," said Alex. "I need to be prepared as best I can."

"Why don't you tell me all about it over dinner," she said. "Let's go home and I'll get something started while you finish what you're working on there."

Alex had spent the past several hours reading everything he could find about Andrew McNeeley. So far, everything he claimed was accurate. McNeeley had spent his entire career in the manufacturing industry and had bought and sold four different companies. Each of them had been turned into a very profitable enterprise. He seemed to have the Midas touch when it came to his businesses. His entire life had been spent in the state of New York and was highly respected in many business circles. He currently sat on three boards of directors—two for local charities and the Kodak Corporation—interesting. He currently lived in Rochester and was very active with his wife in the local social scene. He enjoyed sailing and buying and restoring classic automobiles.

Alex estimated his net worth at about $230 million, based on what he could find online. He knew that meant that he was probably worth closer to $400 million, maybe more. This would be something for them to discuss further as their relationship developed over the next few meetings.

Technically, McNeeley was retired, but when one created a successful business, or businesses in this case, as Mac had, retirement was never really an option.

As they ate their dinner of glazed salmon and rice, Alex told Janey about the meeting with McNeeley and how well things had gone. He shared with her the connection he felt and how comfortable both of them seemed to be with one another. He also mentioned that Mac was on the Board of Directors for Kodak.

"Have you ever heard of a place called Smitty's Diner?" asked Alex.

"No, should I?" replied Janey.

"Well, that's where I'm meeting this client tomorrow morning. He set up the meeting there like I should know about the place. I guess it has a very colorful history here in Rochester and I'll get to experience it first-hand tomorrow morning."

The rest of the evening was spent with Alex sitting at the table digging as deep into the life of Andrew McNeeley as he possibly could. Janey did her best to support him and keep him focused on the reality of the situation. She hoped he wasn't getting too optimistic with this one. They had seen it all before. Many times before. It was the typical "too good to be true" syndrome. But because Alex was desperate for even a hint of the success he once had, he couldn't help from getting overly excited.

It seemed that ever since Alex's fall from grace at S&S, they were both doomed to a life of disappointment and frustration. They had moved more times than Janey cared to remember. Each move seemed to drop them further and further from the pinnacle they had reached when Alex was the young hot shot on Wall Street. She watched him continually reach for the brass ring, but he always came up short. His confidence had been crushed and she saw him withdraw. The biggest of these blows came when he realized they would have to leave New York City. That was when he truly felt like he was a failure, like he had really let Janey down.

The past two years had taken their toll on Janey too. The miscarriage damaged her; she could no longer have children. The impact was devastating, as it would be to any woman. She willed herself to push through the anguish of her loss. Her career suffered when they left Manhattan, but not nearly as severely as Alex's. With each downward tumble of Alex's life, she found herself having to settle for positions that were less appealing than the last. Even the surprise offer from Kodak, while attractive, was mundane at best. But, she loved Alex. She was in love with Alex. Her devotion to him never wavered. So she did her best to try to protect them both from any further potential disappointment. Keeping him grounded was the best she could hope for these days.

She decided to take some of the negative energy that her life was filled with and use it to fuel her commitment to fitness. She thought back to the days of her youth when her only escape from the circumstances of life were a hard workout and the feeling of being in total control of her body. This was the driving force behind Janey Coswell. It had served her well over the years.

Now here they were in Rochester. They had been here for a year and lived in a small house. It was the most time they had spent at any address since the crash. Alex had accepted the job at Rochester National Bank after a recruiter had contacted him about a *great opportunity* in Upstate New York. The bank was looking to start up an investment banking department and Alex would be the perfect person for the job. His experience provided all the necessary skills needed to create a successful team of financial professionals. It would give him the chance to focus on getting his career back on the track to long-term success. Time proved that even this would be yet more career disappointment as the team turned out to be only Alex.

Rochester was a nice, thriving community surrounded by comfortable hamlets on the shores of Lake Ontario. Sure, it was in New York, but it might as well have been on another continent for Alex. He couldn't accept how far he had fallen. Gone was the energy that was New York City. Gone was the direct connection to the financial capital of the world. Gone were the subways, the local delicatessens, and the prestige that was the Big Apple. Gone was the comfortable income. Gone was the remote chance of restoring his dream.

Until now, maybe.

Chapter Seventeen

Alex arrived at Smitty's at 5:45 A.M. to find McNeeley on his second cup of coffee. The diner was a typical mid-century greasy spoon that reeked of bacon grease, stale coffee and burnt toast and syrup. The décor had not been updated since Eisenhower was in the White House and the waitresses had probably all voted for him. The walls were covered in framed yellowed newsprint recalling the headlines of the country's major events over the past 50 years. There were the usual photos of the owner, presumably Smitty himself, with celebrities, sports stars and other famous people. Alex recognized some of them, others he did not.

There were a few patrons scattered throughout the restaurant, each with their newspapers and coffee minding their own business and waiting on their meals. No one noticed that Alex had entered other than McNeeley. He settled into the red vinyl booth, not sure what to expect from this meeting.

"Glad to see you're early," said McNeeley. "It says a lot about your interest in our little partnership." Alex picked up on the word partnership and was surprised by McNeeley's choice of words. It made his optimism even greater than it was before he walked in the door.

"Not a problem," replied Alex. "I'm actually eager to continue our conversation. I've done a lot of research and I think there will be plenty of opportunity for us to do some creative things together."

"Good to hear. Breakfast should be here in about 5 minutes." Mac called the waitress over and she poured Alex a cup of piping-hot coffee.

Alex wasn't sure how to react to Smitty's Diner yet. It certainly wasn't what he was expecting given what he knew about the net worth of McNeeley. He was expecting that the restaurant would be much more upscale. He took a sip of coffee and decided to push it out of his mind and focus on the next 30 minutes. He pulled a file folder from his briefcase and opened it on the table.

"Let's not get too much ahead of ourselves, Alex," said Mac raising his hands. "I never conduct any business before breakfast."

Alex slowly closed the folder and placed it on the seat next to him. Breakfast came and the two of them dug into the tastiest order of Eggs Benedict Alex had ever eaten. They visited for about an hour and covered a wide range of topics. Nothing deeper than the latest car Mac was restoring or the summer weather they were enjoying this week. Alex had had his fill of coffee and was starting to get the feeling that things would not turn out the way he expected. Would this be yet another one of those deals that didn't materialize? Just another failure in a long line of recent career disappointments?

As the breakfast meeting was winding down McNeeley looked at his watch and said, "I need to run to my office for a while and take care of a few things. I'll grab my files and be at your office at noon. We can continue our conversation then."

"Okay, I'll have the conference room reserved," said Alex. "Do you want me to have some lunch brought in?"

"No, I don't think that will be necessary. I'm going to be ready to get down to business and don't want to be distracted. Pretty good breakfast, though, huh?"

With that, McNeeley was up and on his way out the door with a smile on his face. The waitress approached the table with the check and Alex paid the bill. It was 7:30 and he had some time to kill before he had to report to the bank for work. He decided to head to the gym. He still enjoyed a good workout and wished for the days when he and Janey would work out together. She was the one person he had ever found that could match his efforts in the gym.

One of the morning rituals David Sohlmann kept was to spend the early morning hours taking care of his boat. Whether he was in port or at sea, he was a stickler for attention to detail. As he was spraying the forward deck of *The Endeavor* his cellular phone rang. He knew who the caller would be so there was no hurry to answer. He finished with the hose, stowed his cleaning supplies and headed to the galley for some fresh fruit. Sohlmann enjoyed being on open water. It gave him a feeling of freedom that he had come to cherish. It was as if he were alone in the world. Alone, but controlling the events of his and others' lives. He got a rush of adrenaline as he considered what was taking shape.

As he ate his breakfast, he decided to listen to his voicemail message. The message was another simple one, only two words: "*On track*." This brought neither a smile nor any other reaction from

Sohlmann. He fully expected things to follow this path. After all, it was the way he had planned it from the beginning. Failure was not an option. There would be no surprises.

He returned to his newspaper and fruit. Nothing new in the news, which was a good thing for Sohlmann. Steady market trends and world events meant that he was about to concentrate on the things he was trying to manipulate. Things that no one outside of his circle would ever notice. And Sohlmann's circle was very small. At times, it was only him, but right now it was starting to expand. He needed to enlist the actions of a couple of other people to see this through. These people would be completely disconnected to anyone looking from the outside, but their roles were definitely connected to what Sohlmann was planning.

One of the things David Sohlmann had mastered was the ability to see the big picture and the importance of the long play. Patience was one of his greatest assets when it came time to construct a detailed sequence of events leading to a desired outcome. He was able to see beyond the horizon and control seemingly unrelated events that would eventually come together to deliver exactly what he wanted.

It was who David Sohlmann had become. His wealth allowed him to create ways to direct the actions of what looked like random people to be the ones carry out his plans. In his mind, there was always a script that had to be followed, and Sohlmann had become an expert at making sure that everyone involved in his plans was following his script to the letter.

His attention was drawn back to *The Endeavor* when a crew member interrupted his breakfast.

"Mr. Sohlmann, sir," said the crew member. "We just received a weather alert about a possible tropical storm approaching. Do you have any preference for where we relocate to?"

"Just find the sun." Sohlmann dismissed him with the wave of his hand.

The weather was one thing that Sohlmann accepted as uncontrollable. He was smart enough to know that complaining about the weather was useless. However, he could control where he guided his crew to take *The Endeavor*, so in his mind he was able to control the weather he experienced.

Chapter Eighteen

McNeeley arrived at the bank right on time. He carried a large briefcase that was overstuffed with files. Alex escorted Mac to the conference room and they began a detailed review of Mac's investment history. It was evident that he had done very well for himself over the years. In fact, he had survived the carnage of two years ago without much damage at all which was impressive in and of itself. McNeeley's diversification had given him insulation from the catastrophic damage that most others had experienced. As they talked, Alex came to realize that his estimated calculation of Mac's net worth was low, way low. McNeeley was so wealthy that Alex wasn't sure he would ever know the true extent of his personal fortune.

Soon, they were discussing Mac's desire to not only grow his portfolio, but how to capitalize on his knowledge of the market and leverage that knowledge by sharing it with others at a healthy price. If the two of them could create a successful investment strategy, why not try to sell that strategy to others? There was money to be made by selling success. Mac believed that the business of investments was no different from any other business—create a successful strategy and people will pay to get in on it.

Once again, Alex began to get excited about what he was hearing. This meeting with McNeeley was going well. It might actually turn into another shot at getting his career back on track. He would have to navigate carefully and this time, if given another chance, he would not make the same mistakes as he had made in the past. He would develop a strategy that took both a best-case and worst-case scenario into play and closely monitor daily events to ensure that he was continually tweaking his actions. He would build individual exit strategies into his overall strategy that would allow him to sidestep those hiccups in the market that could prove to be problematic.

Several weeks had passed with regular meetings between Alex and McNeeley. They soon began to see some of the gains they had expected in Mac's portfolio. They had scheduled daily phone conversations and a regular weekly meeting in the conference room at the bank to review the market and Mac's portfolio performance. Alex found himself spending nearly all his time every day working on McNeeley's account. There were no other significant customers at the bank that needed much of Alex's attention, so he was free to focus on his new project. It reminded him of the early days of his career.

"Just be cautious," Janey warned. "I know how attractive this must look to you, but I don't want us to get our hopes up too high. I don't want you to get your hopes up too high."

They were sitting on the patio in their backyard with iced tea. Janey had brewed sun tea and both were enjoying the late evening sounds of summer. The sun was setting and the colors of the sunset were beautiful. Daisy was curled up next to Janey on the lawn chair and Alex was thumbing through the evening paper.

"I know. You're right," replied Alex. "But this is the first significant commission check I've gotten in two years!" He was holding a check that was equal to 3 months of salary at the bank.

"And I hope there are many more to follow. I only want you to keep your head clear. From what you've said, McNeeley seems like a wonderful client and the bank seems very pleased at the business he's generating. Things are starting to look up for us. But don't let it cloud your thinking. We both know what happened last time."

Alex shot Janey a sharp glance. Even a slight hint at Alex's Sohlmann & Stein debacle stung. Neither of them really liked to discuss it. However, they both knew that it was caused by his poor decision making in the heat of the moment had cost them nearly everything. The only positive either could find was that Alex and Janey agreed they would never allow a situation like that to happen to them again.

"I know, I know," said Alex. "You don't have to remind me every time I bring up an opportunity."

Beneath the surface, the situation was tense. It wasn't talked about or acknowledged in any way, but both of them could sense it. After two years of disappointment it was like a wound that just wouldn't heal. Janey had developed a strong defense to guard her feelings and Alex had taken to the approach of completely burying it. Maybe if he didn't talk about it, it didn't really happen.

After some awkward silence, Alex looked at Janey and said, "Mac wants me to meet his lawyer on Monday morning, something about another strategic business opportunity. I have no idea where he's going with this, but he seems pretty excited about it."

Janey looked at him and cocked her head. "Again, just be cautious is all I'm saying."

Janey had done her own research on Andrew McNeeley. She knew about his holdings, his hobbies, where he shopped, where he vacationed, how much he spent on his latest sailboat, and where he parked his money. She also knew exactly how much money he had. This knowledge gave her every reason to be equally excited about what Alex was working on, but she knew they both had to be careful. She was also a bit edgy because she knew she could never hint to Alex that she had any of this information.

Chapter Nineteen

David Sohlmann and Andrew McNeeley sat on the rear deck of *The Endeavor*. The recent rain and cooler temperatures in Miami were welcomed by McNeeley but Sohlmann missed the more tropical weather he had become accustomed to. The dinner table had been cleared and they both enjoyed Cuban cigars and after-dinner drinks.

"How long are you planning on staying in Miami?" asked David.

"I'll be flying back tomorrow evening. My wife wanted just one day of shopping and I have the meeting with Alex and the lawyer scheduled for first thing Monday morning."

"Things with our little plan are progressing nicely. Now it's time to kick this in to high gear," said Sohlmann. "You're sure he has no idea what you have in mind for Monday?"

"I suspect he might have some suspicions, but how could he possibly have a clue about what we are planning?" said McNeeley.

"Then you've played your part quite well so far."

"As we both expected, correct?"

"Correct," said Sohlmann as he finished his cigar and crushed the ashes into an ivory ash tray. "I've put a lot of forethought and effort into creating this scenario especially for Coswell. Not to mention a large financial investment. This next phase will require that you are extremely convincing. I'm counting on you. Don't disappoint me. I'm giving you all the leeway you need to make this look real. Spend whatever you need to make it happen."

"You know, he really does have a brilliant financial mind. I'm enjoying some very impressive results in the short time Coswell has been in control of my money."

Sohlmann slammed his fist on the table, spilling the remaining bourbon in his crystal tumbler. "Don't tell me what I already know!" He stood and walked to the aft railing and stared out at the other boats in the marina. Turning back to face McNeeley, he calmly said, "He was great, he *is* great. Maybe the greatest financial mind Wall Street has seen in the past 25 years or so. I get that. But he cost me hundreds of millions of dollars! And he betrayed me. You know as well as anyone that I can't just let that go. I have to destroy him. It's the principle of the thing."

"I'm not saying you should let it go," replied a stunned McNeeley. "Or that he doesn't deserve to be destroyed, as you put it. But I don't think his destruction is a wise direction to take on this. We don't need any investigation into whatever you have planned. I only mention it to see if we want to allow this next phase of the plan to develop long enough to generate some sizable returns. We both stand to make some significant money here. You might even be able to recover some of your losses from— "

"I'm not going to physically hurt him, Mac," interrupted Sohlmann. "You should know me better than that."

McNeeley was not intimidated by Sohlmann in any way. He had known him for over twenty years and they had been business partners on several deals. Both had made huge profits with each other. He knew Sohlmann was a controlling, ruthless business tycoon that played for keeps, but he also knew that never in his career had Sohlmann ever resorted to any type of physical violence. Sure, some of his enemies had left this earth much earlier than they should have, but it was always a choice made by them, not Sohlmann. No, Sohlmann was content to simply ruin a person. But lately, he was noticing some changes in Sohlmann's intensity. He seemed to be obsessed with *this* project, as he constantly referred to it. McNeeley was becoming concerned.

David had regained his composure and returned to the table. He poured himself another drink and offered a refill to Mac. They sat in silence for a time enjoying the setting sun and watching the seagulls soar effortlessly above them. The clanging sound of mast lines on the sailboats was relaxing and the distant music from the Yacht Club Orchestra was soothing. More bourbon was shared and the mood on the ship mellowed noticeably.

It was dark now. The lights of the marina sparkled across the water creating a very serene setting. "It's not about the money, Mac. You and I couldn't spend all that we've made in five lifetimes. I have more exotic toys than I know what to do with and you have a warehouse full of old cars that are slowly rusting away. This is about winning. This is about letting Alex Coswell know that no matter how smart he might be or how smart he thinks he is, no matter how much insight he might have into the financial world, I am the top dog. I always will be. I will always come out ahead. No one gets a free pass if they cross me. It's about vengeance!

"So, fly back to Rochester with your lovely wife. Meet with Alex Monday morning and introduce him to your lawyer. Lay out the plans we discussed. Get him excited about this new opportunity and really build it up. I know he'll bite, he has to. I know exactly how he will respond. Then I'll have him right where I want him."

McNeeley left the marina to meet his wife at their hotel. The walk would take about 20 minutes—just enough time to allow him to reflect on things. This wasn't the first time that he and Sohlmann had conspired to get back at someone that had not met their expectations in a business deal. It certainly wasn't the first time that the two of them had worked to control the outcome of an opportunity. But it was the first time that he had seen David so completely obsessed. It was as if he was being controlled by his desire to make an example of Alex Coswell for anyone in the future that dared cross him.

Chapter Twenty

Jane Coswell was at the health club by 5:30 A.M. She hadn't slept well, knowing that Alex had his meeting today with his newfound client to discuss some plans that hinted at being very important. In the back of her mind she was concerned for her husband. He was spending every waking moment working on strategies for growing his client's portfolio. He had been researching the latest technology companies, looking for opportunities to invest in areas that promised a change in how the world economy worked, and anything else that would be useful in maximizing what he could do for his client.

But this was how Alex operated; it had been this way since they met. With Alex it was all or nothing. When he got his mind on something he became totally focused; nothing distracted him. His college classes, their courtship, his job at Sohlmann & Stein; each one completely consumed him. It wasn't necessarily a bad personality trait when things worked out as anticipated, but when they went wrong it was potentially devastating. Surely, the past two years or so had proven that to be very true. Now she feared he was once again locked in on the opportunity at hand. He was being a little too optimistic and possibly setting himself up for another fall. Maybe it stemmed from his upbringing. Being alone for most of his childhood, he had learned how to live his life alone, not trusting or relying on anyone but himself. Though he never talked about his youth in any detail, she thought she understood him quite well. She, too, had been alone most of her childhood and she would never talk about it either.

The health club was practically empty. There were a few early risers on the long row of treadmills walking too slowly to do any good and reading the morning paper, and there were a few muscle heads throwing barbells around but she had the place mostly to herself. Janey passed them without a second thought and headed for the empty aerobics room. She grabbed a few dumbbells off the rack, a jump rope and a medicine ball and began her workout. She needed to clear her mind and she had learned that intense exercise was the best way to accomplish that.

The next 90 minutes were spent working every major muscle group of her body. Improvising her workouts and constantly changing her routine with pushups, chin-ups, throwing the medicine ball, skipping rope, anything she could think of was a welcomed activity and delivered the desired effect. She enjoyed the feeling of pushing herself to the limit just to see how far she could go. It was part of who she was and it made her feel complete.

After her workout she was on her way out the door and nearly collided with Alex who was on his way in.

"I thought you might be here when I saw that you were gone when I woke up," said Alex. "I was hoping we could work out together this morning. What time did you get here?"

"I came at 5:30. I couldn't sleep thinking about your meeting today."

"Sorry I stayed up so late, I've had a lot on my mind all weekend. I'm actually surprised that I was able to sleep so well last night," replied Alex. "I need to work off some energy before I meet with McNeeley later this morning. I'm really pumped about whatever it is he wants to discuss. I'll call you later."

Alex gave Janey a kiss and headed toward the locker rooms to change for his workout. Janey walked across the parking lot to her car suddenly feeling a sense of excitement for Alex. For the first time in a long time he seemed genuinely happy with himself. She smiled and thought, *Maybe this will be a good day after all!*

Alex arrived at the bank just before 9:00 A.M. He had a little over an hour to get ready for his ten o'clock meeting with McNeeley and his lawyer but he really didn't know how to prepare. All that was said when McNeeley scheduled the meeting was that there were a few exciting things that he wanted to run by Alex and he wanted his lawyer to be there to help explain the details.

Alex spent a few minutes glancing at the *Wall Street Journal* and reviewing his notes on the performance of Mac's portfolio but found it hard to concentrate. He was anxious and restless. He walked to the breakroom and considered a cup of coffee, but decided against it. His nerves were already on edge and he didn't need the extra caffeine or sugar to make matters worse so he opted for water. He was glad he was able to get some exercise in before the meeting. It had certainly helped burn off some of the extra energy he had but for some reason he was still pretty wired. He decided to go back to his small office and just wait for them to arrive.

By 10:15 Alex was starting to develop that feeling in the pit of his stomach that reminded him of a visit to the principal's office as a kid. McNeeley had never been late for a meeting. Alex was fighting the inner demons that had developed over the past two years and were trying to convince him that once again he would be faced with yet another major disappointment. He was ready to make a phone call to Mac's office when he saw McNeeley enter the lobby with his attorney. He breathed a sigh of relief and tried to calm himself. *What has happened to me? Why am I so nervous about this meeting?* Alex was surprised at how much he really wanted this relationship to turn into something great for his career. He realized at that moment that he had done exactly what Janey had warned against, he had put all his hopes in this basket. He knew better! He had to put things in the proper perspective and he had to do it in the next 30 seconds. He closed his eyes and centered himself. *Deep breath in, deep breath out, Alex.* He stood and greeted Mac at the door.

Mac handled the cursory introduction of his lawyer to Alex as they headed to the conference room. Robert Mills was a middle-aged man that looked like the last time he exercised was in junior high gym class. He wore a rumpled suit and stained tie and his shirt was frayed at the collar. It was a stark contrast from how Mac always presented himself. Coffee was offered and declined and Alex set a pitcher of water on the table as they began the meeting. Mac started by complimenting Alex on the performance of his portfolio. So far, even in just a short period of time, the returns were quite impressive. Much more than Mac had expected. Alex relaxed and felt himself calming down. He thanked Mac and noticed the attorney taking a few notes.

"Alex, I'm more than impressed with how things are going so far. You truly have a keen eye for your business and unique ability to make things happen. I'm very comfortable with our relationship and although I never really thought I'd say this, I think you can do a much better job at growing my money than I ever could on my own." McNeeley was sitting forward in his chair with his elbows on his knees and facing Alex. "I want to run something by you. I've discussed this at length with Bob here over the past several months and we have agreed that it makes good business sense for me at this stage of my career. We both think the timing is now perfect for me to move forward. Also, I believe the market is primed for another round of sustained success. We've completed the due diligence and all the preliminary groundwork has been started. All the necessary wheels are in motion."

Alex's brain was in hyper-drive and his heart was racing. He was struggling to stay focused on where Mac might be going with this conversation. His mind was jumping from what he was currently hearing to past conversations about McNeeley's desire to… what was it? He couldn't remember exactly what McNeeley had hinted at several weeks ago. He had been too focused on making sure this client was successful. "Mac, can I interrupt you for a moment?" asked Alex. "I'm really sorry, but I need about a two-minute bio-break."

"Sure, not a problem," replied Mac with a confused look on his face.

Alex excused himself and hurried out the door. When he arrived in the men's room, he splashed some cold water on his face. His gut was telling him that something major was about to unfold here, but he couldn't figure out what it was. This made him feel very unsettled. He needed to be as sharp as possible for whatever it was that was coming and at this point he was just too keyed up. He leaned on the sink with both hands and stared into the mirror and willed himself to calm down and focus. After a few minutes he relaxed enough to return to the meeting. He wiped the water from his face, ran his fingers through his dark curly hair and left the men's room. He returned to the conference room to find it empty.

Alex rushed to the other side of the lobby to look out the window and scan the parking lot. He caught a glimpse of the back of McNeeley's car just in time to see it pulling away from the bank's lot. He slowly walked back to his office and slumped into his desk chair. Sitting in silence he stared up at the ceiling for several minutes. His phone was ringing but he ignored it. Suddenly, he angrily swept the stack of files, newspapers and everything else sitting there off his desk.

Chapter Twenty-one

McNeeley sat in his office at the garage sipping a fresh cup of coffee and thumbed through a *Hot Rod* magazine. He enjoyed keeping up to date with the latest trends in classic auto restoration. He was a purist, but some of these resto-mod cars were capturing the attention of the industry. Some of the more creative shops across the country were coming up with some wild designs and truth be told, he really liked the fresh aspect it brought to what could be thought to be a somewhat stale hobby. He would have to try one of these designs on his next project.

As he dialed the phone for the call he needed to make, he smiled at the fortunate turn of events that had taken place earlier in the day. He could not have scripted the meeting any better. It was too perfect.

"Hello?" David Sohlmann answered his phone with his usual tone of irritation.

"David, it's Mac. The gods are smiling on us today."

"I wasn't expecting a call from you so soon. Care to shed a little light on your overly optimistic comment?"

"Well, Alex did all the hard work for us," said McNeeley. "Bob and I were giving him the runaround about our plans, hinting at our idea without getting specific and trying to overwhelm him with double talk when he interrupted me to take a piss! He was visibly overloaded with what we were saying, or rather not saying. You were dead on. He couldn't take it all in, it was too much to process. He left the room and gave us our escape—handed it to us on a silver platter. We simply got up and walked out."

"How perfect is this?" replied Sohlmann. It was interesting how his temperament changed so quickly when good news was delivered. "Here's what I want you to do next. Let him sweat it out for a couple of days. Don't take his calls or return them until Wednesday afternoon. Don't go to your office in case he tries to come see you. Let him stew about this, it will drive him crazy. It's how his mind works, always has. He needs to be in control, or what he thinks is control. Go sailing for a couple of days on that new boat of yours to get away. Enjoy the last few days of good weather up there, just disappear from Alex.

"On Wednesday afternoon, late—make sure it's very late in the day, call the bank and make up some ridiculous story about Bob getting sick or something and schedule another meeting for Monday of next week. Coswell will jump at the idea of another meeting. That will keep him off balance. He'll be reeling trying to play out all the possible scenarios in his head of why you really walked out on him. I want him to be uneasy. Then we can take the next step in my project."

The phone went dead and Mac stared at the receiver. He rose and left his office. He had his marching orders from David Sohlmann and he would follow them. As he walked out to his car he thought, *I never want to become an enemy of David Sohlmann.*

The water on Lake Ontario in the late summer can be some of the most beautiful in the country. With the sun shining, the shallow waters are a bright blue-green, fading to dark blue as the water gets deeper. They provide for great sailing and when the wind blows out of the northwest, all is right with the world for accomplished sailors like McNeeley.

Over the course of his life, McNeeley had sailed in just about every part of the world worth sailing in. He particularly liked the southern Caribbean for the gentle breezes and the abundance of small islands to explore. He had sailed in the Mediterranean and all around the Greek Islands during one adventurous summer. He had also bought a Chinese Junk in Hong Kong just to sail in Victoria Harbor and around the Kowloon Peninsula for two weeks, although he vowed he would never return to Hong Kong due to the pollution. Sure, the Hong Kong skyline from the water was beautiful, especially at night, but the smog and water pollution were just too much. He spent three weeks in the North Atlantic, venturing up as far as the Arctic Circle, but learned that he really wasn't a fan of cold-weather sailing.

The marine forecast on Lake Ontario for the next several days was ideal for sailing and Mac actually considered calling Sohlmann to thank him for the forced getaway. He loved the water. He loved the freedom. He loved the solitude. He loved the sound of the sail when the wind snapped it crisply as he came about. The only problem lately was that he just didn't take enough time to enjoy these things. His sailboat was only a season old. He still considered it new because of how seldom he used it. But yet he felt completely comfortable aboard the boat. It was the one place where he could escape a life filled with the stress that comes with protecting immense wealth.

There were few things that McNeeley spent serious money on. His sailboat was one of them. His car collection was the other. Both of these indulgences were selfish. Everyone that knew him, including his wife, thought so. He couldn't care less what people thought; he worked very hard and wanted these things and all the enjoyment they brought him. The feeling of the wind in his face and the sunshine on his shoulders when he was sailing just couldn't be explained to anyone that had not experienced it. He got a very similar feeling when he was behind the wheel of one of his 50 or so classic cars. The powerful feel of the engine and the connection to the road were nothing short of pure joy. It made the life he lived worthwhile.

As he motored north away from his slip in the Southpoint Marina he was immediately lost in reverie. All the worries of life seemed to melt away as soon as he was able to cast off. As his thoughts slowed down and began to settle in the calmness of the afternoon, he actually began to feel sorry for Alex and what he and Sohlmann were up to. After all, Alex had never hurt him in any way. He had no personal beef against the young man. But his loyalty was to his longtime friend and if David Sohlmann needed him, he would be there. Mac wasn't sure the same would be true if the tables were turned, but why spoil the next few beautiful days on the water thinking about that?

He always had enough provisions for two weeks of sailing. His plan was to stay on the boat for the remainder of the week. He would return to the marina on Wednesday afternoon just long enough to call Alex and schedule another meeting, then return to his beloved sailing. In his mind, he was at peace. The feeling of the large wheel in his hands, the snap of the sails in the wind and the cadence of the 47-foot sailing vessel gliding through the water were all that mattered.

Chapter Twenty-two

Alex sat in his office in a state of shock. It was late afternoon and he hadn't moved in hours. Waves of emotion had been crashing in on him from every direction as he struggled with his past and how he was on the verge of repeating some of his darkest days. He could not allow that to happen again. At all costs, he had to get this client back on track, not only for himself, but for Janey. He didn't think he would be able to survive another failure and he feared how Janey would react when she heard about the way his meeting had turned out.

He had tried to reach McNeeley on the phone all afternoon, but his phone was never answered. He left a single message and even considered driving to his office to find him, but thought that would be inappropriate. The last thing he wanted was to appear desperate at this point. He replayed the meeting in his mind a hundred times trying to figure out what had gone wrong but couldn't make sense of their disappearance. He was at a complete loss. Their departure had caught him completely by surprise. He wasn't thinking clearly and needed help to sort this out.

Both McNeeley and his lawyer seemed very comfortable with Alex and what they were attempting to explain to him. Their plans had to be important. Why else would Mac need a lawyer present? If only he had been able to keep himself together. How stupid!

Several things were racing through his mind. What would he say to his boss when they met at the end of the day? More importantly, what would he say to Janey when he got home? He had ignored multiple calls from her since lunchtime. He considered not going home, but that wouldn't be fair to her. She knew about today's meeting and would be excited to hear what the big news was. He finally decided to face the truth that things had tanked and once again share bad news with his wife. At 5:00 he left his office for rush hour traffic. He skipped the meeting with his boss and headed for home.

Janey sat in silence as Alex explained the events of the meeting with McNeeley and his lawyer. She showed no outward emotion but inside something was beginning to stir. She didn't quite know what it was but it was there. It was undeniable and it was building. She was supportive and told Alex that there had to be a logical explanation for the two of them leaving while he was in the men's room.

"People just don't get up and walk out on a meeting like that," she said. "There has to be a reason."

"Yeah, well, they did today," said Alex. "I asked the lobby staff if anything was said as they were leaving and no one seemed to know anything more than me. So, apparently, there was no reason."

"You'll just have to call him in the morning and try to reschedule the meeting. What else can you do?"

They sat in their kitchen for the next hour trying to find some explanation. After hearing the details of how the meeting went for the third time, Janey saw no reason for Alex to blame himself. It just didn't add up.

"Maybe one of them got sick. Maybe they thought you weren't coming back," said Janey. She was really grasping at straws, but tried to be helpful.

"I wasn't in the bathroom for more than three minutes."

In her mind, Janey was struggling with her own issues. The events of today were stacking up on top of their past and she wasn't sure where things were heading. This made her uncomfortable. She decided that the best thing for her to do at this point was to force the thoughts to the back of her mind and focus on the positive things in their life. They were healthy and she had a loving husband. She stood, kissed Alex very affectionately and with purpose and led him into their bedroom.

As they lay in bed catching their breath, Janey realized that no matter what happened, she was happy. Her life with Alex was not defined by their circumstances. After everything they had been through, both good and bad, she loved him. She just had to channel all this emotion and energy. Besides exercise, her energy would be put into her work. She would dig deep into the life of one Robert Mills, Esq., to see if that might shed any light on the current situation. Maybe he had something in his past that she could uncover that would help them make sense of things. If so, she would find a way to get the information to Alex to ease his mind. But she would have to act quickly, she didn't have the luxury of time on this one. Knowing there was nothing she could do until she got to work in the morning, she drifted off to sleep.

Alex, on the other hand, couldn't sleep. He tossed and turned as his mind raced. There were so many scenarios playing out in his mind from the events of the day that he couldn't make his mind relax. Where did he go wrong? Was it something he had said? Was it something he failed to pick up on, something he missed? Had he somehow offended Mac during the meeting? He stared at the ceiling fan as it gently rotated above them. He listened to Janey's steady breathing as she drifted deeper into sleep. He envied her ability to shut out the world and sleep when she needed it. If he only knew.

Deep down he hoped Janey was right, there had to be a logical reason behind McNeeley's departure. After all, Alex was still controlling millions of dollars of Mac's money and McNeeley gave no indication that this ride was coming to an end; they were just hitting their stride. There were only positive trends unfolding with Mac's portfolio. Alex's projections were solid across every investment he was tracking. It was the S&S Project all over again. Certainly, Mac wouldn't need a lawyer to close an account, if that's what he had planned.

Alex forced himself to settle down. He would deal with all of this tomorrow. He gently leaned over and kissed Janey's forehead and tried in vain to get some sleep.

Chapter Twenty-three

By noon on Tuesday afternoon, all of the efforts of Alex and Janey the previous evening to make sense of Monday's bizarre meeting had been tossed out the window. Alex was a complete basket case as he tried to find some answers to what was happening with his client. His call to McNeeley's office was finally answered by a receptionist, but all she was able to tell him was that Mr. McNeeley had not been in the office since Friday afternoon of last week. She didn't know when he might be returning. No, she was not authorized to give out his cellular phone number. Calls to the law office of Robert Mills went unanswered, no voicemail.

To make matters even worse for Alex, his boss was on the way down to get the status report he had requested yesterday. Alex knew the meeting would be tense, he had never known the President of the bank to conduct a meeting anywhere but in his own office or executive conference room. James Williams was a conservative banker from the old school. At 60 years of age, he had spent his entire career at the bank, starting as a teller while attending school. He worked his way up the ladder of success by specializing in commercial lending after college. Having been the current President and CEO for the past 13 years, he was quite accustomed to getting what he asked for when he asked for it.

The fact that he was headed to Alex's cramped office to get information already spoke volumes about his mindset. There was nothing Alex could do at this point, so he had decided to focus on the success of the overall portfolio and how each of the investment accounts were performing for the bank's largest investment customer. He would highlight the income he was generating for the bank and provide the numbers that his boss could not ignore. He would also gently suggest that maybe the bank mirror these investments. This would be risky for Alex, but he wanted to show his boss that he might be more valuable to the bank than just a simple Investment Broker.

He would try his best to skirt the issue of the big plans McNeeley had and how yesterday's meeting went. He had also decided to completely avoid any conversation about why Mac's lawyer needed to be there. The fact of the matter was that Alex didn't know the answers to those questions. No matter how much he would like to be able to give that information to his boss, he simply could not.

The meeting with his boss went surprisingly well. After Alex gave him a detailed overview of the McNeeley portfolio, along with printouts of each investment account and their year-to-date gains, the president suggested that the two of them develop a proposal to restructure the corporation's investment strategy. They would present it to the board at the upcoming board meeting next month.

"How long will it take you to develop a detailed proposal with financial projections?" asked Williams.

"Well, depending on how much cooperation I get from Accounting, it could be as little as three weeks," replied Alex. In reality, Alex knew he could create a proposal like this for a small-time bank in his sleep in about 6 hours, but he wanted to make it seem much more complex than it actually would be. Besides, he already had all the research completed from his work on the McNeeley portfolio. He would simply plug in new numbers from the bank's investment accounts into his spreadsheets. He would run multiple scenarios with varying levels of risk and then place the entire burden on the board to decide which path they would want to take. He would be completely insulated from any negative outcome and, hopefully, praised for any positive results.

"Great, let's work together on this. I'll make sure you get all the cooperation you need from the folks upstairs. If you find you need anything, just let me know." Williams stood to leave and patted Alex on the back. He said, "Who knows, this might be a fine opportunity for a young man like you."

Alex had heard this before. Mr. Williams was no more willing to put any effort into the development of this proposal than to wash the cars that entered the bank parking lot at the annual bank carwash for charity. However, he was quite willing to take credit for Alex's abilities and efforts. Alex didn't really mind, he was just happy to have another project to focus on that just might distract him from the McNeeley account.

After Mr. Williams left the office Alex breathed a sigh of relief. He had dodged a bullet here and may have begun to pave the way for better things to come. Williams made no mention of McNeeley leaving the office after only a few minutes in the bank yesterday. He did not mention the pile of strewn papers and files in the corner of Alex's office. Nor did he bring up the fact that Alex had stood him up yesterday afternoon.

Alex called Janey at work to fill her in on the events of the day. He was feeling both deflated and uplifted at the same time. He explained the dead ends he had run into with McNeeley and Mills, how he was unable to get any new information about the whereabouts of either of them. Then he told her about his meeting with Mr. Williams and how he had reacted to the performance of the McNeeley portfolio; it was the detail of the numbers that put his mind to rest. Then Alex spent the next half-hour giving Janey the details of the conversation about the bank's investment proposal.

"That's how you got started at S&S, isn't it?" asked Janey.

"It's pretty remedial stuff, I know," replied Alex. "I can do this kind of thing in my sleep. But if it gives me an opportunity to get back into the game at even this level, I'll take it."

"I'm happy for you."

"See you at home. I love you."

"Love you too."

On the drive home, with the windows down and the late summer breeze coming off the lake, Alex found himself going back to the McNeeley issue. *Where had he gone and what was the reason for the Monday meeting? What were the 'big plans'? What did the lawyer represent? What would happen next?*

There were no answers to be found as he drove. He would have to play the waiting game and hope for the best. It was all he could do at this point. He cranked up the radio and looked forward a quiet evening with Janey.

Chapter Twenty-four

Alex was at his desk on Wednesday morning trying to catch up on the much neglected work for his other clients. Not that there was really much they expected him to be doing, but he had slipped into a rut of effortless guidance for them. Since he had spent the past month or so almost entirely on the McNeeley portfolio, and working it the way it should be worked, he realized that there was a whole lot more he could, and should, be doing to help each of his clients grow their wealth—even if it was small in comparison to what he might have been used to. The reality of his current situation was that with the daily calls and weekly meetings with McNeeley discussing strategy, various investment opportunities, emerging trends and the red flags to steer clear of, he had neither the time nor the energy to really focus on the small-time clients that made up his customer base. They just didn't seem to be worth the effort anymore. Now that his golden goose seemed to be slipping away, he was scrambling to find a way to make these small deals generate some level of commission. He felt he owed it to them and to himself. Just maybe he might find some renewed motivation in his now mundane work life.

The past two and a half days had convinced him that the McNeeley deal was dead. There had been no contact whatsoever. Six weeks of daily contact had ended with the disappearance of McNeeley and his lawyer from the conference room on Monday morning. Alex had decided during another sleepless night that he would quit trying to reach him. He would continue to work the portfolio and generate as much commission as he could before the plug got pulled and the huge portfolio was gone forever. He told Janey about his decision as they were eating breakfast this morning and she didn't seem to really have an opinion either way; she said she was preoccupied with a project she had to start at work.

Alex spent the rest of the day trying to rework each of the investment strategies for his client base. He decided that he would apply a scaled-down version of the Mcneeley approach to each client, prepare a new investment proposal for them, then hope they were open to the idea. The phone rang at 4:30. Alex turned away from his computer to answer the call and looked out the window of his office.

"FNB Investments, this is Alex Coswell. Can I help you?"

"Hello, Alex, it's Mac."

Foot traffic on the street was light, as it always was, there were a few cars and a cab or two, a city bus rumbled by, but suddenly everything seemed to fade away. Alex spun around to his desk and grabbed a pen and a yellow legal pad.

"Mac!" exclaimed Alex. "Where have you been? I mean, when you disappeared on Monday, I thought something must have happened to either you or Mr. Mills. Is everything alright?"

"Yes, well, I'm sorry for running out like that. Maybe I can explain later. I hope you haven't been too concerned," replied McNeeley. He knew his actions would have thrown Alex into a tailspin. Sohlmann had told him so. Now he needed to continue to keep Alex off balance with the rest of their plan.

"I'll admit, I was a bit worried, but I'm very happy that you called. I have a few updates on your portfolio that I believe you will be pleased with." Alex had regained his composure and was now projecting confidence in his demeanor. This wasn't lost on McNeeley. Even in the midst of this ruse, Mac was impressed with Alex and his level of professionalism.

"That sounds good. Very good. I wouldn't expect anything less from you. You've proven yourself to be very capable. Why don't we get together on Monday of next week and resume our discussions with Mr. Mills. I'll make sure he is available; see if you can clear your calendar and have the conference room reserved for 9:30. We can begin to talk about some specific ideas that I have and how you fit into the big picture."

"Looking at my calendar, there are a few conflicts, but I'm sure I can work around them," said Alex. He had an 8:00 meeting with Mr. Williams on Monday morning to discuss the proposal, but he would have it completed long before then.

"Fine, then it's confirmed."

"Perfect. Will you be wanting any updates between now and Monday morning?" asked Alex. He was hoping they could reestablish their regular communication schedule, just to make him feel better about things.

"No, I'll be out of touch for the remainder of the week and through the weekend. I can get all the updates from you on Monday morning. Maybe you can generate even more good news between now and then, huh?"

"You know I'll do my best. I guess I'll see the two of you on Monday then."

"See you Monday. Goodbye."

Alex hung up the phone and thrust his fists above his head in victory. Leaning his head back, he actually shouted, "YES!" For the first time in a long time, he felt things were going to work out for him. He swung around in his chair and picked up the McNeeley file. It was a thick file and Alex could almost feel success in his hands. He placed it in the center of his desk and quickly glanced over at the file folders of his other clients. While he was tempted to just ignore them, he knew he had to finish the work he'd started before the call from McNeeley came in.

For the next several hours, Alex worked like a man possessed on his other clients. He did research, made notes and scheduled appointments with his clients to discuss their financial goals, current portfolio performance and how he could help them grow their money. He had been rejuvenated—all thanks to a single phone call.

He walked out of the bank at 7:00 P.M. feeling good about himself and what he was doing. It was a rare feeling these days.

Janey sat at her desk staring at her computer screen and twirling a stand of hair in her fingers. She was confused and becoming angry.

What she was looking at didn't make sense, but that was only because she was trying to fit this information into the context of what she thought to be true. Clearly, the truth was not what she thought it was. Alex had been lied to.

It was a slow day in her department which gave her the time to do some digging into the life of Robert Mills. She had verified his personal information: date of birth, address, undergraduate education, law school attendance, etc. She was able to look at his financial history and other personal information that seemed to make sense. It was true that he had been a member in good standing of the New York Bar Association since 1974 and had never been late or missed a dues payment. He was registered as an Associate Member in several other states and had never been sued by a client for any reason. He had a clean reputation as far as the legal community was concerned.

What caused Janey to be concerned was his legal specialty. Robert Mills was a simple divorce lawyer. His entire career had been spent helping spurned, discarded and cheated-on wives rake their rich, mistress-doting husbands over the coals. His advertisements catered to the wealthy aging women of the medical community that had supported their husbands through the early days of med school and residency, long hours and tight finances and, in most cases, raising the kids. Once the money was plentiful these women were deemed useless. All his marketing efforts were aimed at exploiting the emotional trauma of the supportive wife being discarded and left all alone. He had never practiced any type of corporate law, tax law or any other type of law that might even hint at being valuable to an investor like McNeeley, certainly not one that might be needed at a meeting with her husband.

Janey faced a dilemma. How could she get this information to Alex without exposing her secret life? Even if Alex had known what she had been doing for the past several years, how could they expose Mills without raising a hundred red flags about where the information came from or questioning the trust between Alex and Mac? So many things were going through her mind that she couldn't begin to know how to sort them out or where to begin. After a long period of time, she made the decision to keep the information to herself. After all, the way things looked now, it might be completely irrelevant since McNeeley had disappeared. Also, maybe McNeeley had known Mills as a personal friend and simply wanted his input or maybe Mills had contacts that he could bring into the mix as things developed for McNeeley. Who knew? She would just sit on the information and only bring it up if necessary. But she would watch—closely.

Jane Coswell had become a master hacker; she could easily access just about any computer system now and could enter and exit without a trace. She had developed a way to receive notifications when files were opened by their owners, mostly just for fun to see if she was able to do it. At least this gave her some level of comfort that she would be able to gather more information when and if she needed to, but the burden of knowledge was sometimes quite heavy. Her ringing phone caused her to quickly erase any hint of her hunting expedition and exit the program she was in.

"Hello, this is Jane."

"Janey, it's me. Guess what I just got?"

"I don't know, what?"

"I got a call from McNeeley today," said Alex.

This took her by surprise. The timing was too close for her comfort level, especially with what she had just learned. She paused a bit and took a deep breath.

"Really?! To be honest, I didn't think you'd ever hear from him again. What did he have to say about Monday?"

"Not much, now that I think about it. But he apologized and said that he would explain it more when we meet again. We have another meeting scheduled for Monday morning at the bank. He wants to get into the details of his big plans."

Janey's mind immediately began spinning even faster. With the knowledge she had about Mills, she was now really struggling with what, if anything, to say to Alex. Her instinct was to try to protect him, but after the mental argument she had had with herself just before the call, she decided not to say anything yet.

"That's great! I'm so happy that you can try to get this back on track. Did he give you any idea what those plans might be?"

"No, but just the fact that he called has to be good news, right?"

"I guess so." There was a slight hesitation in Janey's answer.

"You don't sound so sure about that. Is there something wrong?"

"Alex, I don't know. It's just that we've had more that our share of disappointments. . . ."

"We have to be positive about this, Jane," interrupted Alex. "After all the time I've put into this, and the results of his portfolio, my gut is telling me that this is a good thing. A real opportunity for me to do what I do best, what I'm the best at doing. I really don't need you bringing me down right now!"

Janey was hurt by Alex's scolding. Maybe she knew he was right, but it was rare that they ever yelled at one another, and she wasn't used to his anger. Had she not gotten the information about Mills, she would be excited for Alex. But she knew what she knew. Now, she would just have to live with it.

“I'm sorry, Alex. I've had a busy day and didn't mean to throw a wet blanket on you. Will you forgive me?”

“Yes, I'll let it go. But it would be nice for you to support me like the old days. Especially after the history we've had. I have to go now. I'll see you when I get home tonight. It will be late. I'm working on my other clients' portfolios. I'm creating proposals for each of them and I need to get them completed before I leave tonight.”

“I do support you, honey. I'm sorry. I love you.”

“Love you too. See you later. Bye.”

Alex was frustrated when he hung up the phone. He didn't think the conversation with McNeeley could have gone any better than it did. After all, things seemed to be getting back on track with the prospect of more to come. Why couldn't Janey see that? Why throw all the negativity on it? There was something with her lately that seemed a little different, like something was bothering her all the time. Not in their relationship, things were as normal as they had ever been. It was something else, but Alex couldn't put a finger on it.

Chapter Twenty-five

Sohlmann was sitting in the restaurant at the Fort Lauderdale Marina enjoying a late lunch of Caesar salad with grilled chicken and sparkling water as he looked out over the intercoastal waterway. The restaurant was nearly empty, the lunch rush having ended nearly two hours ago. There were a few hardcore drinkers at the bar, but then they never really left or so he had been told when he entered the dining area. There was a small party of six finely dressed elderly ladies celebrating the ninetieth birthday of one of the members of their group. The wait staff had thinned considerably, with only two waitresses on the floor at the present time. Sohlmann knew neither of them. He also knew that he would not be recognized here. He had been here a few times before, but not enough to make any impact on the employees. This was by design, as far as Sohlmann was concerned. He needed this little get-together to be as discreet as possible. He would normally meet on his boat in his slip at the Miami Yacht Club, but wanted an extra layer of anonymity today. This would be a key element of his plans for Coswell and he needed this part to be totally controlled and contained. There would be no possibility for this meeting, or anything about this meeting, to be made known to anyone other than those that Sohlmann had invited to be here.

The short cab ride up from Miami to Ft. Lauderdale was tolerable, Sohlmann couldn't remember the last time he was in a taxi. To him, taxis were for a class of people well below his. The weather was close to perfect and the afternoon sun was warm, but not hot. The only irritating thing that David Sohlmann was dealing with so far was the fact that he had not heard from McNeeley yet. He had been quite direct when he told Mac that he was to call Alex Coswell today and set up an appointment for Monday to continue discussing their deceptive plans. Mac had acknowledged his instructions and seemed to be clear on what was expected. There had also been a very clear understanding from the beginning that Mac was to report in immediately after each step in the plan, even if his report were only two or three words. This was something that Sohlmann would need to address as soon as possible.

Seated at the table with Sohlmann were two men who couldn't have been more opposite of each other if they tried. One Sohlmann knew of but had never met, the other he had never heard of before. Bill Davis was a struggling realtor from Rochester, NY, that had never really lived up to his potential, if he ever had any. He was complacent and lazy to the core. He eked out a meager living by scouring the real estate listings in his office, then working hard to coattail on the success of the listing agent to bring buyers and sellers together. Every once in a while he scored a hit and earned a partial commission. No one ever called Bill Davis to list a property; in fact, he wouldn't know how to list a property on his broker's computer system if the opportunity presented itself. This would soon change, however. Davis jumped at the opportunity to take an all-expenses paid trip to Fort Lauderdale when he received the call from a real estate broker friend. It promised the opportunity to make a quick listing and sale in one fell swoop in the Rochester market.The best part of it was that Davis would be entitled to 100% of the commissions available.

He showed up wearing the typical wannabe boater attire that caused him to stick out like a sore thumb. Cheap khaki slacks with boat shoes, no socks, a nautical print silk shirt with several pastel colors and a pair of gas station sunglasses. But the best part of his get up was the gold chain and matching bracelet that weren't gold. If Davis were 75 years old with a deep Florida tan, he might have been able to get away with this look. But being in his mid-forties and fifty pounds overweight and having not seen the sun in years made it obvious that he was very much out of place. Sohlmann bristled at this at first and shook his head in disgust, but then realized that this would play to his advantage—if anyone was asked about any meeting that took place in the restaurant today, no one would remember Sohlmann; they would remember the ridiculous-looking guy in the cheap resort wear.

Jack Cline, on the other hand, fit in to this environment perfectly. He was wearing a navy sport coat and a white shirt with tan slacks and Italian loafers. His watch looked expensive and his Ray-Ban sunglasses completed his desired look. He was from Los Angeles and was loosely associated with one of the Sohlmann Manufacturing companies; at least that was how he was paid. He wasn't a business man, nor was he involved in any way with the business that Sohlmann controlled. Jack Cline was an actor, a player in the many schemes that Sohlmann had orchestrated over the years. He had never met Sohlmann before and wouldn't be meeting him today, or so he thought. This was just a necessary step in the development of a role that Jack Cline would play, facilitated by a third-party director. He had brought himself up to speed on this acting role as he flew from LAX to Ft. Lauderdale. Bill Davis, on the other hand, would believe this to be a legitimate real estate deal, and would handle all the details of bringing Cline, a California business man relocating to Rochester, in touch with sellers of a house in the Rochester market. The transaction would be a cash deal and there would be no problems with the financing nor would there be a problem with the appraisal of the property to be purchased.

"Gentlemen, thank you for coming to meet with me this afternoon," said Sohlmann. "As you know, I'm sort of brokering a deal as a favor for a family friend for Mr. Cline here. The only problem is that I don't have a license to sell real estate in the state of New York. That's where you come in, Bill."

"Thanks for the opportunity," said Bill. "It's nice to get away from Upstate New York to meet with you both. But, I really don't understand why we didn't just meet in Rochester. We could have taken a drive to look at some houses that might be what you're looking for." He was looking at Jack Cline as he tried to sound as competent as possible.

"I suppose we'll get to that in a few minutes," said Jack to Bill. Looking at Sohlmann, he continued, "My dad sends his best. Thanks for helping me out on this, Joe."

Sohlmann had assumed the name of Joe Carlson for this meeting. Already he was satisfied that Jack Cline would be worth every cent he was being paid for this charade. He was assuming his character role perfectly.

"Don't mention it, Jack. I'm happy to help any way I can." Looking at Bill Davis, Sohlmann said, "Bill, here's the deal. Jack has been to Rochester on several occasions. Prior to his decision to relocate, he became very acquainted with the area. He and I have driven the market many times, both separately and together, and we believe we have found a great place for him to raise his family. The school system is solid, the commute to his office is manageable and the houses are far more affordable than what he's leaving in Los Angeles.

"We have the selection narrowed down to two or three houses at this time and we will need you to assist us with scheduling the walkthroughs, etc. The only problem at this point is that one of the houses is not for sale. Yet."

Bill said, "That shouldn't be a major problem. I've sold many houses that weren't on the market. If the price is right, you'd be surprised at how many people will drop everything and sell. Mostly, it's the husbands that will take the money and run. The wives and children might tend to put up a bit of a fight, but it usually doesn't last too long."

"Well, to ease the pain, I'll be offering a cash deal. The equity in my LA house will hopefully be more than enough to pay for a house in the Rochester market. No offense, but we've enjoyed a pretty favorable real estate market that Upstate New York will probably never see." Jack could have played this part of his role as a complete southern California snob, but chose to try to come across as likable. It seemed to work.

"Hey, you don't have to tell me about the market in California. I'm always asking myself why I don't relocate out there and get my hands on some real commissions," said Bill. "If the amount of work is the same, why not get paid bigger bucks, right?"

David Sohlmann found it hard to stomach Bill Davis. He knew what his reputation was and knew what his earnings were. He knew where he lived and how he lived; none of what he was hearing right now was matching up with the reality of who Bill Davis was. But he let it go because this was part of the plan. He needed Davis and was willing to accept his lies and the façade he was erecting to achieve his overall plan.

"Bill, Jack will be coming to Rochester two or three times over the next month or so to finalize his plans to relocate. I'm asking that you make time in your schedule to accommodate his availability to look at these houses. Most of his availability will be somewhat last minute, but you'll just have to deal with it," said Sohlmann. He was studying Bill Davis to see how he reacted to this request. If there were any issue at all, Davis didn't show it. He simply nodded in agreement. So far, so good.

Jack looked at Bill Davis and said, "I'm going to need about forty-five days before I can really get things rolling. I'll be ready to spend a few extra days in Rochester at that time and maybe we can meet at your office to get things underway. One thing I might need to lean on you for is an estimate of what local real estate taxes look like."

"Not a problem. I can begin pulling those numbers together before you come out," replied Bill. He was making some notes in a folder he had brought with him to the meeting. "Can you give me some idea of where you're considering and what size home you're looking at? It will help narrow down the tax range so I can be as accurate as possible for you."

"I'm looking at the east side of the city in the Scottsville area. About 2,500 square feet."

"Got it. I'll get on it as soon as I return home. Anything else you might need?" asked Bill.

"The only thing I need is for this to kind of remain quiet. I mean, if people start to hear that a family from California is coming to town to buy a house with cash, all my negotiating power will evaporate." Jack looked at Bill with a shrug as if to convey that this was more important than maybe he thought.

"I hear you. My lips are sealed until you tell me to schedule some visits."

Sohlmann tapped the table and said, "Well, looks like everything is in order. Bill, thanks for coming. Your hotel room bill is covered through Friday night. I'm sure you can get a cab to the airport on Saturday morning. Enjoy the rest of your time in South Florida.

"Jack, glad I could help. Please tell your father and mother that I send my best. I hope to see them both soon. You and I will be in touch in the next week or so."

With that, the meeting was over. The three of them stood and headed for the door. Bill excused himself as he headed for the men's room; Sohlmann and Cline boarded the elevator and headed down to the main floor.

"Interesting meeting, huh?" said Jack Cline.

"Kind of weird, but then I never ask questions. I just do what I get paid to do, and say what I get paid to say. That keeps everything nice and neat," replied Sohlmann. He was making it look like he was an actor, same as Jack.

"Well, whatever old Bill is in for, I think he's completely clueless."

Sohlmann only nodded and smiled as the elevator doors opened and they exited. Each said their goodbyes and went their separate ways once in the lobby of the building. David Sohlmann loitered a bit to be sure that Bill Davis also left the building. When he saw him exit and head for the hotel that had been reserved for him, he headed to the street to look for a cab and the return trip to Miami.

Mac McNeeley spent a couple of hours tending to some unexpected business after he made his call to Alex. He was able to get a vacant office at the Rochester Marina that had a desk and a phone, which served his purposes well. There were a few fires that needed to be put out with one of his newer companies and he was able to address them in short order. The bigger issue was dealing with his wife's ailing mother. She had been in a nursing home for the past 8 years and her health was failing fast; the end was not far now. While this upset his wife, Mac was even more distraught by the thought of losing her. She had been a wonderful mother-in-law, accepting him wholeheartedly from the very beginning. He loved her and would miss her greatly. Now, he was the one that had to make the decisions that were painful. End-of-life decisions should be decided upon when everyone was healthy. It was what he had always said, but no one wanted to take his advice. Now, with emotions running high, these decisions would be much more difficult to make and his wife just couldn't face them. Mac was very troubled and he was in no mood to deal with David Sohlmann and his coldhearted schemes when his cell phone rang.

"Hello, David," Mac said as he answered his phone. His tone was almost unfriendly.

"Is there any reason for you not calling me? I've been waiting on your call for hours," said Sohlmann.

"David, I am in no mood to be scolded by you at the moment. I have had an afternoon that I would really like to forget, and calling you to let you know about the outcome of something that you already know was not very high on my priority list today."

Sohlmann was not accustomed to this kind of treatment from anyone. His initial reaction was to explode and unleash his fury on Mac, but given their long history, he knew there had to be a very good reason for Mac's delayed call, so he let it go.

"Mac," David said. "Let's not go down this path. If you can tell me that you were successful with your call to Coswell and that things are on track, then I'm fine."

Mac was silent, he really didn't want to be having this conversation at all. After a moment, he said, "Our meeting is scheduled for Monday morning. I will call you afterward. It might not be from the parking lot, but you'll get your update." With that Mac pressed the "end" button and hung up on David Sohlmann.

Chapter Twenty-six

The meeting with Mr. Williams on Monday morning lasted less than an hour. Alex had been able to satisfy his boss that he was completely in control of the proposal they had been discussing. In fact, it would be Alex that would attend the board meeting as a guest and present the idea. Now, he sat at his desk and prepared for his meeting with McNeeley and Mills. This time, they were on time.

After some small talk about the weather and other completely meaningless topics, Mac said, "Alex, let's start by laying some groundwork. My experiences over the past several years have taught me a few very important lessons. One is that while I might think I know everything I need to know to achieve success, the reality is that I don't. I've learned that it is usually in my best interest to find partners and associates to help me get to where I want to go. I have to allow my ego to be set aside and rely on others if I want to continue to enjoy the success I'm accustomed to. At this point in my life I can no longer handle every detail required to manage my money effectively. To be truthful, I'm not sure I have the energy even if I had the desire.

"Secondly, to build upon the success I've created over the years, the formula for that success has to be repeatable. If it is, then I can save considerable time and money as I look to grow my businesses in a similar fashion as what I've done in the past. There is no reason to reinvent the wheel when I've found a business model that works. I've seen this play out many times over the years and you'd be surprised by how many business leaders don't understand this simple concept." McNeeley paused and looked at Mills, who had a blank stare on his face as if he were a thousand miles away.

"Thirdly," said Mac, "I've learned that timing is everything. There are limited windows of opportunity in life. I know this to be very true. When they are open they must be exploited, because once they close they're usually closed forever."

Alex sat and listened intently to what Mac was saying. Nothing he had said so far came as much of a surprise to him. He had learned these same lessons early in his career and was well aware of how valuable each of them was. Hearing Mac outline them now, however, caused Alex to wonder where he might be going with all this. He was jotting some notes on his pad, but was waiting for the meat of the conversation to make its way around.

"Before we go any further there is a small legal matter we need to address," said Robert Mills. "We need to ask you to sign a nondisclosure agreement for us." He was pulling a single-page document out of his briefcase and slid it across the table to Alex. This was the first time that Mills had shown any level of interest in the meeting. It had appeared to Alex that he was completely bored with the conversation and that his mind was elsewhere. "If you will read our agreement and sign it, we can proceed."

Picking up the document and scanning it, Alex said, "Don't you think that this is something that I should run past the bank's legal counsel? I mean I don't have any authority to enter into agreements for the bank that extend beyond my financial planning responsibilities."

"This doesn't have anything to do with the bank, Alex," said Mac. "What we are about to discuss is between you and me. In all likelihood, your acceptance of partnering with me in the plans I have will require you to sever your ties with Rochester National Bank."

"That's probably enough information to share right now," Mills interjected. He was making this comment to McNeeley. "Until we have Alex's signature on the nondisclosure, we cannot get into any further detail of your plans or how they might impact him or his future or the bank. You may have already gone beyond what I'm comfortable with."

"It's alright, Bob, I'm not overly concerned with what I've shared so far," said Mac. Looking at Alex he said, "Take your time and carefully read the agreement, Alex. I want you to enter into this arrangement completely at ease." McNeeley eased back in his chair and crossed his legs. He cradled the back of his head in his hands and stared up at the ceiling. He almost had a content smile on his face.

Alex spent the next several minutes carefully reading the agreement. As he was doing so, his mind was racing. He was finding it hard to concentrate and focus on the document in his hands. *What could Mac have in mind that would require me to leave the bank?* After going through the document a few more times and seeing nothing that would obligate him to anything other than confidentiality, Alex pulled the Mont Blanc pen from his shirt pocket and scribbled his name across the bottom of the agreement and dated it. He spun it around and slid it back to Mills who also signed his name to the bottom of the page, as did McNeeley .

"Thank you, Alex," said Mac. Turning to Bob Mills, he said, "Bob, I'm going to ask you to leave the room now. I don't believe I need you to be a part of this meeting any longer. Thank you for your assistance. Please see that both Alex and I receive a copy of the fully executed agreement by the end of the day today. Also, please be sure to have it notarized."

Bob Mills stood, gathered his things, and quickly left the conference room. He didn't say a word to either Mac nor Alex. There were no handshakes nor any other sign of common courtesy normally associated with parting company. It was almost as if he expected this and was happy to be leaving the room. In reality, Robert Mills, divorce lawyer for the wealthy women of the medical community was, in fact, very happy to be leaving. The entire past two weeks had been almost more than he could handle. He was unaccustomed to this kind of stress in his professional life. Never before had he been so intimidated by a client. If he only knew....

He had been approached in the parking lot outside his office by two large and rough-looking gentlemen. Both were dressed in fine suits but they looked like they would be much more comfortable wearing prison jumpsuits. They forcefully escorted him to his late-model Porsche where they explained how the next two weeks would unfold for him. He was being "hired" by an anonymous client for a very easy assignment. He was to make contact with a Mr. Andrew McNeeley, attend two meetings with him and produce a single pre-printed document when the time was right. Memorize and deliver a short script when kicked under the table—only a few sentences. Then, he was to sign the documents and make them legal, and then disappear. He was given a manila folder which contained two sheets of paper and an envelope. The first sheet of paper was the nondisclosure agreement that Alex would sign. Mills was familiar with them, but hadn't seen one since his days in contract law class many years ago. The second had a name and phone number on it along with a very vague overview of how he was to handle himself over the next week. It was very clear that during the next two weeks, he was not to answer any phone calls from anyone. The envelope contained nothing but a note that instructed him to check his glovebox after the second meeting.

The two men made it clear to Robert Mills that he had no option whether he would accept the assignment or not. They would not be happy if they were contacted by the client and had to come back and "visit" with him again. Mr. Mills certainly would not be happy if another visit were required. They also told him that he would be watched closely and if he gave any indication that he was sharing any details of this assignment with anyone, there would be unpleasant consequences. The two men were very convincing and Mills knew immediately that they were serious. He would follow the instructions to the letter. He immediately looked in his glovebox, but found it empty of anything that had not been there since he purchased the car. This made him even more uneasy than he already was.

Now, sitting in his car in the bank parking lot, he began to feel the full weight of his involvement in all this. He actually started to hyperventilate and was almost sick. He sat in the parking lot for what seemed like an eternity trying to calm himself down. Finally, he reached over and unlocked the glovebox. He wasn't sure what he would find there, if anything. He reached and pulled out an envelope that was identical to the first he had received. He slowly opened it to find crisp one hundred dollar bills totaling $15,000.00. He breathed a sigh of relief and realized that he had stopped breathing all together. It was probably the easiest $15,000.00 he had ever earned in his life. He contemplated heading directly to the airport for a spontaneous and much needed vacation, but decided against it. He reasoned that it might draw unnecessary attention to him, and if he were still being watched, like the two visitors had said he was, then it might cause things to unravel. He thought for a moment about how the envelope even ended up in his locked glovebox, then quickly decided that the best thing he could do would be to let it go, pocket the cash, and simply drive home and lay low for a while.

There were a few moments of awkward silence after Bob Mills left the conference room. Mac had expected this and seemed to allow them to linger a bit. Alex sat in his chair and had a confused look on his face that hinted at his inability to process what had just taken place and why. In his mind, he was trying to understand why a lawyer would be asked to attend a meeting only to present him with a nondisclosure agreement, and then depart. Maybe Mac and Mills felt that they needed a witness to his signature. Mac stood to stretch his legs and poured himself a cup of coffee. He offered one to Alex, who accepted. McNeeley was now in complete control of the meeting, just as it had been planned. He had spent an entire career controlling meetings and this was no different. As he walked over to the window and stared out at the street, he said, "Okay, now we can get down to talking about some real business."

Mac returned to his seat and began to lay out his plans for Alex. "Alex, you have proven yourself to have a very bright mind for high finance. Your insights, depth of research and instincts are the best I've ever experienced. Over the course of my adult life, I have worked with dozens of investment bankers and none of them have had the combination of skills and instinct that it is very clear that you possess. The luckiest day in my recent life was the day I called you to schedule our first meeting."

"Thank you. That's a very nice compliment," replied Alex.

"Your ability to take control of my portfolio and generate the results that you have delivered over the past few months has been astounding. I couldn't be happier. Your demeanor and professionalism, and your ability to handle the pressures of an up-and-down market are exactly what I've been seeking for a long time. With market trends now showing long-term promise, I want to begin to explore some very new territory for me.

"First, I'm going to be increasing the dollar volume of my investment portfolio. I want you to take control of a much larger percentage of my money. There are sizeable investments that I have been sheltering within various corporate entities that I control. There are other family-owned investments which I haven't shared with you and that you couldn't have known about. Finally, it appears that my mother-in-law will be passing soon and my wife and I will be inheriting her estate, which in and of itself is quite substantial. You and I can work on the details of this over the next few weeks. We will need to sit down and review the scope of all my investments, both here and abroad, and determine how best to consolidate them into a package that will enjoy the same results as what you've been working on for me recently.

"Next, I want to explore what I hinted at last week when I said that I wanted to exploit my knowledge. This is where your acceptance of my offer will require you to terminate your employment with the bank."

"Okay, I'm all ears," said Alex. "You have my complete attention. However, given the nature of your last statement, would we be better served by taking this conversation elsewhere? I don't want anything we discuss to be overheard by anyone. Maybe we can go to your office and continue?"

"That won't be necessary, Alex. Let's just stay here. If I feel that things are getting uncomfortable, I'll let you know."

"It's your call. Please continue."

Alex was reeling. His mind was spinning so fast that it was hard for him to keep up with all that was being talked about. He did his best to settle down, but was finding it very difficult.

"As I said, I have become convinced over the past month or so that your ability to successfully manage an investment portfolio is unmatched. I also believe that there are a lot of investors out there that are being duped by their investment bankers or brokerage firms into believing that everything in their individual portfolio is being maximized for the best results possible. You and I both know that this simply is not true. Too many brokers out there are happy with mediocre results. They are lazy and don't want to put in the time to really generate wealth for their clients. If they have enough clients, even average results can earn them a very comfortable living. I see something different in you. I see your drive, your commitment to excellence. It must be from your upbringing.

"The other thing I want to share with you is that I'm very tired of paying large sums of my money out as transaction commission. Every move made with my money costs me money; it's just the nature of the game. Don't take this personally, Alex. You're earning every cent of your commissions, but I think it's time to look at another alternative for me. I have been trying to find a way to sidestep this and have finally found myself in a position to do so."

Alex was fully engaged now. McNeeley had done a great job at baiting the hook. There were still a few enhancements that needed to play out over the next few weeks so Mac pressed on. "I want to open my own brokerage firm, Alex. I want the commissions generated by my money to be paid to me. I want to take my knowledge and your expertise and generate commissions from other people's money that will be paid to me. Is that greedy? You bet it is! And I want you, Alex, to run it. I want you to be the one that controls the direction of the firm, where the money is invested. I want you to be the one that makes my firm a success."

Mac let this last statement linger. He knew that this would knock Alex off balance, Sohlmann has promised it. He was right.

Alex was caught off guard by this. At first he didn't know how to respond, or if he should respond at all. He immediately started thinking about all the ways his life would change and the impact an opportunity like this might have on his life with Janey. He thought back to his days at Solhmann & Stein and how he felt about his skyrocketing career back then. They were all good feelings. He gathered this thoughts and said, "Mac, I'm sure you know you have me interested. Let's press forward."

"Great, why don't we get together over dinner on Wednesday night and talk some more. Better yet, why don't you and your wife come to my house for dinner? I'd love to meet her and I'd like to introduce you both to my wife."

Chapter Twenty-seven

Mac realized he may have made a mistake inviting Alex and his wife over for dinner. As he thought about it on the drive home he realized that he had gotten a bit caught up in his own ruse. The money Alex was generating was real and the growth of his personal portfolio was certainly real, but that's where reality was supposed to end. At least according to Sohlmann and the plan.

Bringing both wives into the scheme complicated matters greatly. It meant that he was going to have to lie to his wife and try to control the impact on the plan that Alex's wife would now have. More importantly, it meant that he would have to lie to David Sohlmann—something that he was very much afraid of. If Sohlmann were to find out about Mac's deviation from his plan, there certainly would be a high price to pay and he did not want to know just how high that might be. McNeeley decided at that moment that this little sidestep in the plan would never be made known to David Sohlmann. He gassed the pedal on his red 1965 Ford Mustang convertible and headed back to his warehouse. Hearing the roar of the powerful 289 engine and the feel of the open air with the top down allowed him to momentarily enjoy the crisp weather and forget about his error.

Bill Davis was sitting at the desk in his cubicle eating his fourth or fifth jelly-filled donut of the day and drinking a cup of coffee while reading the local paper when his phone rang. It was a slow day and the afternoon was dragging on. It was very unusual for him to receive a phone call at work. He slurped a quick mouthful of coffee to wash down the donut and answered the phone.

"Bill Davis," said Bill.

"Bill, Jack Cline here, from Los Angeles."

Bill sat up quickly and cleared away the newspaper to find his note pad and a pen. "Yes, Jack! How's it going? Nice to hear from you. Are you in town?"

"No, I'm in LA. I'm working on a few things today and wanted to clear some stuff off my calendar before the day gets away from me. I have you on speaker, if that's okay?"

"Perfect, what can I do you for, buddy?"

"I think I'm ready to start looking at the houses we discussed when we were down in Florida. I'll be coming to Rochester in the next week or so and want to get some house tours lined up. My availability will be limited and the sooner I can book a few dates and times with you, the more in control of my schedule I'll feel."

"Great," said Bill. "Do you know when you're coming to town? I need to check my calendar and make sure I move some things around to make time for you." The reality was that Bill didn't keep a calendar.

He wasn't even sure he could find one if he needed to. This was the shyster salesman approach he had always used to make it seem like he was more important than he really was. Right now, even Bill thought it sounded phony.

"Well, here's what we need to do. I talked to my wife and she wants to look at the house that's not for sale yet first. Remember? We talked about this one at the meeting."

"Sure, sure," said Bill.

"I took some photos of the houses I was interested in during my last visit. After seeing them, my wife thinks the nicest-looking one is the one that's not listed."

"Isn't that how it always goes?" Bill was scribbling on his pad. "What is the address? I need to do a little detective work and make contact with the homeowners."

Jack gave Bill the details of the house and promised to fax over a photo to be certain that they were talking about the same house. They spent another thirty minutes discussing three other properties that were listed for sale as a backup plan in the event that the first house didn't work out. Bill was feverishly making notes trying to mentally determine how he would make all these visits fit into Jack's schedule.

They spent another half-hour talking about real estate taxes in the areas that Jack had identified. While Bill was intently focused on the detail of the call, making notes and mental reminders, Jack was sitting by his pool enjoying the warmth of an LA fall morning and not listening to a word Bill was saying. His girlfriend Kara was half listening to this while adjusting her bikini and getting comfortable in her lounge chair and laughing to herself. She had been with Jack for a couple of years and had heard some of his phone calls in the past. This one was at least comical, given that Jack had filled her in on Bill Davis and some of the details after returning from Florida. Jack's "acting jobs" paid well and afforded her a comfortable life with him.

There was a time when Kara wanted to live the Hollywood dream—move to LA as a teenager, find an acting job, get discovered and soar to stardom. She waited tables and tended bar, got all the necessary surgeries and dental work to "enhance" her chances of landing a role, and waited. She was beautiful, but so were all the young girls that had the same dream. She found the cheapest agent possible and went on hundreds of auditions. She landed a commercial here and there but those paid nowhere near enough to cover the rent. She finally came to the stark realization that the competition was way too high and the dream way too elusive.

She found a job working for a small production company and completed her degree at night. The pay was actually very good and she had done well rising through the ranks. It was here that she came to meet Jack Cline. They enjoyed each other's company and the freedom that Jack's lifestyle offered. The past couple of years were very comfortable for them both.

After Bill finished his lengthy overview of the real estate tax landscape in Rochester, Jack informed him that we would be out week after next. Bill made note of the dates and promised to get back to him to confirm the times of each of the visits. Jack took a final look at the script package he had received in the mail from the Sohlmann Group and noticed he had missed an important part of the role he was playing. This act required a critical element to be presented and Jack had almost let it slip by. That would not have been good. Jack was very clear in understanding the fact that any future acting assignments with the Sohlmann Group were based on him following each script to the letter. There could be no deviations in any way.

"Bill, one more thing," said Jack. "When you reach out to the homeowners of the house that's not for sale, you might need to be persuasive to get them to allow me to talk with them. Be sure to mention that I'm coming in with a cash deal and that I'll make it worth their while to consider my offer. Use exactly those words."

"No problem," said Bill. "I've done this many times. I know how to convince a homeowner to let me show their house. All I need to do is turn on the Bill Davis charm!"

Jack was rolling his eyes as Bill was saying this and shrugging at his girlfriend. He had to make one or two more trips to complete this assignment then he would be done with Bill Davis forever. It couldn't come soon enough for him. The pay for this acting job was by far the most he had ever earned and he looked forward to maybe taking a few months off to enjoy life.

When the call ended Jack looked over at Kara with a grin and said, "Maybe I like the idea of having a wife to buy a house with. What do you think about that?"

She just looked at him with a coy smile on her face then turned away. She slipped out of her bikini top and closed her eyes. She allowed the late morning sun to warm her and knew that Jack was enjoying the view that she had just given him. What Jack didn't know was that she was also an actor playing a role. She had been hired by the Sohlmann Group three years ago and was told only to get close to Jack Cline—very close.

Bill Davis certainly had his work cut out for him. As he sat at his desk and thought about all the things he had to do for his new client Jack Cline, he quickly became overwhelmed. He really didn't know where to begin other than to go search for the house that Jack wanted to see first. He could pull the other listings from the computer and schedule those visits with no problem. That's all he ever did. But the showing of a house that wasn't for sale was completely new to him. How would he make contact with them? How would he list the house if there were a cash offer that was accepted? Would he even need to list it? How would he earn commissions if there were no listing? What would his broker say about all this? The questions went on and on in his mind. He looked at his desk and realized he was in a bit over his head.

He decided that the best thing to do was to leave the office and call it an early day. He grabbed the fax off the machine and headed out. He would spend some time working at home and trying to figure out a strategy for satisfying his client. Even a fair market value price for a house in the Scottsville area would pay a nice commission for him. If Cline had to pay above market value to get the house his wife wanted, his commission would only go up. He liked the sound of that a lot.

Chapter Twenty-eight

Alex and Janey were in a great mood Wednesday evening as they were driving to the McNeeleys' house for dinner. They had spent the past few days talking about every possible scenario that Mac's plan could offer them but couldn't come up with any concrete answers to the one question that kept surfacing—*What does all this mean for us?* Opening a private investment firm wasn't as simple as printing some business cards and finding real estate to lease. There were Securities and Exchange Commission filings and approvals that needed to be completed, there were insurance policies for Errors and Omissions that would need to be put in place, there were secretarial and support staff that would need to be hired. They would need to purchase furniture, equipment, computers.... The list went on and on.

As they pulled into Mac's driveway, Janey said, "Alex, let's take this nice and slow. I know how you can get excited and rush things. Just try to ease into this with Mr. McNeeley."

"You're right. It's just that this whole thing has my mind racing at a hundred miles an hour trying to figure out all that's going on here.

I mean, this really came out of nowhere." Alex was looking out the driver's side window at the sweeping manicured lawn and the small pond with a miniature waterfall to the side of McNeeleys' home. "I'm finding it hard to keep myself calm. I mean, this is a huge opportunity and I don't want to—"

"Alex, look at me." Janey reached over and physically turned Alex's head toward her. She placed her hands on his face and looked deeply into his eyes. She said, "You deserve this. You know you're capable. You have one of the best financial minds out there. You need to relax and let this evening happen. It will be what it will be. If there are details that need to be discussed, I'm sure Mr. McNeeley will cover them. You've told me over and over that he's a very successful businessman. You don't last as long as he has and build a fortune like his without being able to take care of all the details.

"And look at this place!" She, too, was admiring the house and landscaping. "If you think for one minute that he hasn't thought through his plan, you're very wrong. A place like this doesn't just happen. It takes planning. A lot of planning. And if the McNeeleys' plan like this for their yard, just imagine how they plan for the things that are really important!"

Alex leaned his head back on the headrest. He let out a long sigh and closed his eyes. "Again, you're right. Remind me, how did I get so lucky to have you in my life?"

Janey leaned over and kissed Alex, lingering just enough to make it more than just any kiss. "That reminder will have to wait until we get home tonight." She winked at him, grabbed her sweater and purse and got out of the car.

If what Alex and Janey could see of the McNeeleys' front yard was beautiful, the backyard was even more spectacular. The stone patio, pool area and seemingly endless flowerbeds were something right out of *Landscape Architecture* magazine. There were many different types of plants, flowers and design features that encompassed several seating areas—some small, some large enough to seat up to twelve or more. One table had been set for four, complete with candles, gentle outdoor lighting and soft music playing in the background from speakers that were not visible.

Mac and his wife were wonderful hosts. The evening was very comfortable and the food was everything that Alex expected it to be. Mac had to have a personal chef on staff to deliver such a meal. But it was his wife that was the family chef—she took great pride in the creations that came out of her kitchen and she spared no expense when it came to cooking. Her kitchen was her sanctuary and she was quite proud of it.

The conversations were easy and filled with a combination of laughter and interesting stories from both Alex and Janey and the McNeeleys. After dessert had been served and the dishes cleared, Mac suggested that they move indoors to talk business.

"Would you like Janey and I to stay in the kitchen and enjoy some coffee while the two of you move to your den, Mac?" asked Mac's wife.

"Nonsense! I'm comfortable with all of us talking openly about this. After all, we'll be seeing a lot of each other going forward, so let's just stay right here and talk. I'm sure that as we get into the details, Janey might want to ask some questions. I would expect that and I encourage her input," replied Mac.

"Thank you," said Janey. "It makes me feel valued by your offer to be included in this conversation."

"Don't mention it. It's my pleasure to have the chance to get to know you." Mac smiled a genuine smile and looked Janey in the eyes, then turned to Alex and said, "You realize how lucky you are, right?"

Alex shrugged and said, "I keep reminding myself of that all the time." What he didn't say was that Janey had been the glue that had kept him together through all the struggles of the past few years. He hoped that his true feelings hadn't been showing on his face. For most of the evening, he had been battling negative thoughts that this just sounded too good to be true. Yet here he was, getting ready to begin the detailed discussions of how to get a boutique investment firm off the ground.

Mac spent the better part of two hours laying out his plans for his firm. Several times he solicited input from Alex about operational details, strategies for attracting the attention of prospective investors, whether or not to approach corporate clients and how best to leverage their combined knowledge to maximize their effectiveness. It seemed as though the two of them had worked together for years. They were able to build off one another's ideas and create a solid outline of the initial direction they would take over the next several weeks. Alex had been taking detailed notes on his pad as they talked. He filled several pages with their ideas on initial staffing projections, furniture needs, computer and phone systems, timelines, etc. He was feeling very comfortable with how things were progressing.

Alex could tell by Janey's reaction to the conversation that she too was becoming more and more comfortable with how things were developing. He was always able to read her eyes and right now they were giving him a strong signal to keep pressing forward. Mac and his wife were equally at ease, or so it appeared.

"Alex, I have made arrangements for you and I to fly down to New York next week to look at some real estate," said Mac. "I've been working with a local broker to keep his eye out for some Wall Street space, and received a call just this morning that some leasing opportunities have surfaced that have caught my attention."

The look on Alex's face must have said it all. Mac asked, "Is there something wrong, Alex?"

"No. I mean, all this time I've been thinking that you would be opening your firm here in Rochester. I had no idea that you meant Manhattan."

"The big leagues play on Wall Street, Alex," said Mac. "That's where we'll be setting up shop. Is there really any other place in the world to operate from?"

"Actually, no," said Alex. "Okay, when are you thinking of heading down there? I'll need some lead time to allow me to cover my responsibilities at the bank."

"We are scheduled to fly out on Tuesday morning and should return mid-afternoon on Wednesday. I have arranged for my flight service to take us directly into JFK."

"Is there anything specific that I need to prepare for?"

"No, I'm mostly interested in your assessment of the physical space. Whether it will work for what you'll need from a employees perspective, both administrative support and research staffing needs. You've done this before when you were working on Wall Street, right?"

At this, Alex bristled a bit. He had not really gone into any detail with McNeeley about his past other than to let him know that he had enjoyed success on Wall Street prior to the crash. Again, demons from the past were starting to surface. He quickly brushed them aside and as he was about to reply, Janey spoke up, "Alex was very instrumental in directing the growth of the firm while he was there. He was able to provide his HR department with personnel requirements for administrative, support and research staffing needs. I know because I helped him with it."

"Doesn't surprise me one bit, Janey," said Mac. Turning to Alex, he said, "I don't suppose there is any chance we can hire her to help you, is there?"

The mood was light and all of them understood that this was said in jest.

"My heart lies in the computer science area, Mac," said Janey. "Working with numbers and other people's money is not for me."

The evening came to a close with Mac letting Alex know that he would pick him up at his office on Tuesday morning at 8:30 before heading to the airport. All the accommodations were taken care of and he would deliver a package of legal filings, documents and other partnership agreements first thing in the morning. He suggested that Alex review them prior to the trip. They would be discussing them on the plane ride to JFK. Lastly, he handed Alex a sealed envelope.

"This is your personal compensation package. Please don't open this until we have an opportunity to discuss it together. Maybe while we are in New York," said Mac.

This was a sort of test for Alex. Mac wanted to see how much Alex was trusting him and how much he could be trusted.

The ride home was quiet. Alex and Janey were mentally and emotionally spent. Neither of them wanted to admit it but they were both wanting this more than they realized. For Alex, it was not a real surprise. However, for Janey it came as a very big surprise. She had come to realize during the course of the evening that the lifestyle they enjoyed while living in Manhattan was once again within reach. Not that she gauged her happiness by any financial or social status measure, but this opportunity seemed to offer her a comfortable enhancement to what she was currently enjoying. As they drove, the envelope sat prominently on the dash board begging to be opened.

Chapter Twenty-nine

Alex and Mac arrived at the airport very early.The private terminal was nearly empty, with only employees visible. McNeeley stretched out his hand to Alex as if expecting something. Alex grabbed his hand to shake it.

"Don't shake my hand!" said Mac. "Give me the envelope."

Surprised,Alex quickly reached into the pocket of his suit jacket and pulled out the envelope. "Sorry!" said Alex. "Here you go."

He handed the unopened envelop to McNeeley who pocketed it in his jacket. It was immediately noticed by Mac that the envelope was still sealed.

The flight to JFK went very quickly. The time was spent reviewing the legal documents outlining the relationship between McNeeley and Alex. Alex had seen papers like this before with clients he had worked with. There was nothing out of the ordinary and he felt very comfortable with how Mac had structured things. It was very clear that this partnership had been created in such a way to offer both Mac and Alex an equitable position in the firm. Each would provide what their individual skills afforded and they would be compensated accordingly. As the firm grew and assets were increased, there would be incentives for Alex, which was to be expected. What Alex didn't expect was the offer to provide him with escalating profit sharing that would be immediately applied to a coownership position, if they achieved anticipated levels of success.

The other documents in the package were the standard legal filings for the creation of the firm, SEC approvals, etc. Alex was a little surprised by the fact that it appeared Mac had made so much progress on this end of things. In the back of his mind he knew that SEC filings and approvals took forever to complete, but he dismissed those thoughts quickly. He just assumed that this had been in Mac's mind and in the works, for a much longer period of time than he might have alluded to.

"Our first stop this morning will be with a commercial real estate broker that I've been talking with for quite some time," said Mac. "There are some properties that we have identified that I think will work out nicely. We just need to work the right deal on rent so the numbers make sense for us."

Alex said, "Okay, I have limited experience there, but I can offer my thoughts on whether the space will suit us."

"That's what I'm expecting from you. I'll deal with the cost negotiation. I hold some other properties here that should give us some leverage. We can use those properties as a backup plan, but I think we should be in a strong position to drive the price we want."

Alex and Mac had just finished the initial meeting with the commercial real estate broker and were headed out to take a look at the property on Wall Street when Alex literally bumped into Mark Stein on the sidewalk. There had been no contact between the two of them since the day his employment ended at Sohlmann & Stein. Alex's first reaction was to apologize, but he stopped when the recognition hit them both.

"Mark?" said Alex.

"Alex. Funny seeing you here," replied Mark with a quizzical look on his face. "What brings you back to Wall Street?" There was hint of contempt in his tone that was not lost on Alex.

"Sorry for bumping into you. I'm here with a business partner working on some new opportunities. Mac, Mark Stein. Mark, this is Mac McNeeley."

The two shook hands. It was a normal cordial introduction and there was no recognition between them. Not that there would be. The two had never met before. McNeeley knew of Mark Stein and his relationship with David Sohlmann, but that was the extent of it. Mark Stein had no knowledge of McNeeley nor his relationship with Sohlmann.

"Pleasure to meet you," said Mac. "How do you two know each other?"

Feeling very uncomfortable, Alex quickly said, "We're former colleagues from my days here on Wall Street." He looked at Mark and said, "Nice running in to you. See you around."

Before Mark could reply or Mac could ask another question, Alex began heading in the direction they had been walking and steering Mac along with him. Mac was looking back at Mark wondering if this chance meeting was coincidence or another one of Sohlmann's doings. Either way, it planted yet another question in McNeeley's head about just how far Sohlmann was willing to go with this plan.

That was entirely too close for comfort for Alex. Within seconds, the crowds separated them and they were forever lost to the streets as if the chance meeting had never happened. Alex had no desire to enter into any conversation with McNeeley about Mark Stein. There was too much risk associated with heading down that path.

"Seemed like there was some tension between the two of you," said Mac.

"Well, you know how things can get on Wall Street," replied Alex. "Someone gets burned a little and they seem to remember it for a lifetime. Mark and I have some history, but I'd rather not go into all the ugly details."

Mac seemed satisfied with Alex's answer and let it go. The reality was that it didn't really matter anyway. Nothing seemed to matter these days. Sohlmann was controlling things and had everything orchestrated to the most particular detail. Mac thought for a moment that if Sohlmann had planned for Mark Stein to bump into Alex on the street there was nothing he would be able to do about it. Then he began to wonder how his reach could extend that far. That would be impossible for even Sohlmann to pull off unless he was literally watching every step Mac and Alex were taking.

At that point, Mac's mind began to drift to a place it had never been before. He felt a cool chill run down the length of his back. *Is Sohlmann that obsessed with this deception that it has completely consumed his every waking thought? Has he become a man to be really and truly feared?* Mac considered these thoughts running through his brain and decided at that moment that he needed to start being very cautious where David Sohlmann was concerned. He had never been afraid of David Sohlmann, but maybe some healthy fear might be prudent about now.

The remainder of the day was spent looking at multiple office spaces on Wall Street. It was clear that all but one of them were junk sites offered to make the target location look as good as it possibly could. The broker was just going through the motions at each of the first three offices. He had been trying to point out features of each that would provide some level of benefit, but in reality would never work for the type of space that Alex and Mac had discussed.

Neither Alex nor Mac showed any sign of frustration in the properties that were presented. They looked at each with a discerning eye and politely pointed out the shortcomings of each space once the broker had completed his tour and explanation. It was a time-consuming process, but one that was necessary—at least in Alex's mind. He knew that with commercial real estate, the key to success was to look at as many locations as possible before making any decisions. Only then could you be certain that the best property would be found. The day was exactly what Alex had been expecting and he knew the game well enough to expect nothing different.

They were scheduled to arrive at the last property of the day after lunch at a local landmark restaurant. Minetta's Tavern had been in the city since the mid-thirties. It had been a hangout for many of New York's elite over the years, the least of which were the likes of Hemingway and other contemporaries from the Greenwich Village scene. It was clear that Minetta's knew how to take care of their best customers and over the years they made many long-lasting friends by seeing to the wellbeing of those patrons that enjoyed more than their fair share of the place.

The broker promised them the best lunch they could get and he did not disappoint with Minetta's. From the moment Alex and Mac entered the restaurant, they were impressed. The black-and-white tiled floor, offset by the highly polished bar with its red-topped bar stools, a full-length mirror behind the bar and a tin ceiling all made the first impression that this was a place where a meal was to be enjoyed, and it had been that way for a long time. Alex also noticed that the place was packed. There were professionals and tourists alike filling every seat available. There was an electric feel to the place without it being overly loud. The shelves behind the bar were well stocked with the finest collection of booze anywhere in the city. Minetta made sure that not a single customer ever went away disappointed.

As they were escorted to their booth in the back, Alex had been wondering how he had managed to miss out on the experience of Minetta's until now. He knew that he would have to bring Janey here as soon as they arrived back in Manhattan. The booth was also finished in red leather to match the bar stools, or maybe it was the other way around. Either way, it was very comfortable. Even the caricatures of well-known celebrities on the wall felt very high-class. White linen tablecloths and napkins with fine silverware and crystal drinking glasses completed the overall dining experience. The wait staff were dressed in black vests with starched white aprons and knew exactly how to take care of their customers. Nothing was overlooked at Minetta's. Lunch lasted for over an hour and the time was passed with easy banter and light conversation about the state of Manhattan commercial real estate.

As they walked into the lobby of the final building they were to look at, Alex was immediately taken by the two-story waterfall that demanded the attention of everyone that entered. There was a small pool at the base and the entire lobby was finished in gleaming granite and marble. There were small trees and plants positioned throughout the lobby giving it a very tropical feel and the artwork also reflected the same overall theme. They were greeted by a young lady seated at the Information Desk, which looked like a NASA Control Center station.

"Good afternoon, gentlemen. May I be of assistance to you?" she asked.

"We are here for a 2:00 viewing of the vacant space up on 43," replied the broker.

The young lady checked her calendar, then picked up the phone and dialed a number. After a brief conversation in hushed tones she turned to the three visitors, smiled and said, "Yes, sir. Everything is ready and waiting for you. You may take the bank of elevators on the right and go directly to the 43rd floor. My associate Marie will be waiting for you to unlock the door. May I offer you something to drink?"

"Thank you very much, but we just came from a late lunch," replied the broker.

"My pleasure. Have a wonderful day," she said with another genuine smile.

As the elevator doors closed, Mac said, "That was certainly impressive."

"It was impressive even without the waterfall," replied Alex. "These folks know how to take care of visitors. Imagine how they must treat their tenants."

As they entered the space on 43, Alex knew right away that this would be the perfect location for the firm. He felt his pulse quicken and he impulsively began to imagine the operations of the space.There was a reception area, private offices with fabulous views of Manhattan, a large conference room, spacious filing rooms and administrative work areas. There was a very comfortable kitchen area with a full complement of amenities.And most surprising of all, it was completely furnished, there were even telephones, fax machines and computers throughout the entire office. Alex did not expect to see any furniture in this space, yet here it was.

"Mac, I didn't expect to see any furniture in here," said Alex.

"Neither did I," replied Mac. Looking at the broker, Mac asked, "Are we in the right space? I was under the impression that this location was recently vacated."

"This is the correct location. No doubt about it," said the broker. He seemed a bit confused as well. He checked the listing printout he carried with him in his portfolio and confirmed his notes that the space would be empty. "When we get back to my office I can make a few phone calls to clear up this confusion."

Alex and Mac spent the better part of the next two hours going through each area of the office. Mac seemed genuinely interested in Alex's assessment of the layout and how he envisioned the work to flow.They talked about staffing needs, computer programming needs, security and every other element that might impact the operation of the firm.Alex found he was quickly slipping back into the mindset that had served him so well during his prime at Sohlmann & Stein.

His speech was quick and sharp and he felt a level of adrenaline coursing through his blood that he had not felt in years. He was about to get back into the game at the highest level and he couldn't wait. This time, however, he would be able to avoid the pitfalls that took him down. He had the benefit of experience and promised himself right then and there that this time it would be different.

As they were leaving the space to head back to the broker's office, Alex took a final look around and committed every detail to memory. He wanted to be able to describe it to Janey in such a way that she, too, would be able to feel it. Their dreams were starting to come true, again.

Chapter Thirty

The broker hung up the phone and headed to his fax machine. The revised lease agreement was waiting for him. As he entered the conference room where Alex and Mac were waiting, he smiled and said, "Well, this just keeps getting better."

Mac stood and faced him. "What news do you have for us?"

"It seems the leasing company is experimenting with a new approach to filling vacant space more quickly. They have confirmed that what we looked at this afternoon is what they are offering—furniture and equipment included. I have a revised lease document here which outlines all the same details as the previous lease, but with the added sections for the furniture and equipment. It's ready for immediate occupancy, requiring only proof of insurance and the standard down payment."

Mac looked at Alex and gave a shrug. "What do you think, Alex?" asked McNeeley. "I've never not selected my own furniture and equipment before. But I know quality when I see it and that office was filled with some quality furniture. I have to admit, I can't comment on the computers, I just don't know much about them. And the phone system looks like the same one I have at my office."

"I think I have to agree with you," said Alex. "I might have selected a different style of furniture, but the layout was almost perfect. It's as if it was designed knowing exactly what this firm would need. The computers are state of the art and the phones are new. We'll have to take a look at the service contracts, but I can't see any reason why either wouldn't be satisfactory for the term of the initial lease agreement. Also, this really saves us a lot of time on the front end trying to get things up and running. Furniture delivery can take a long time, then planning the layout of the space can get tricky without actually seeing the furniture in place. This will allow us to focus on the hiring of staff and hit the ground running right out of the gate."

"Those are all very good points, Alex," replied Mac. "But before I move forward with this lease, I want to make sure you feel it's all going to work. That there are no glaring issues that jump out at you that would cause either delays or setbacks."

Alex said, "I can't see any, Mac. I'm going over the space in my head and struggling to find anything that I wouldn't be able to adjust with a few simple tweaks. Again, it looks like it was set up with our firm in mind."

Mac, Alex and the broker finalized the details of the lease paperwork and Mac made a phone call from the broker's desk to his secretary. He faxed the lease to her and had her forward the lease to the legal department to review the lease on the spot, then fax the required insurance documentation and other necessary legal paperwork to the broker. After the lease was signed, Mac phoned his bank to have funds wired that would cover the first year of rent. This all took Alex by surprise, but then he convinced himself that everything else about this opportunity was unfolding at the speed of light, so why should this be any different? Mac then made another phone call. Alex only heard one side of the conversation, but understood that there was another appointment that the two of them would need to get to.

It was getting late in the day and Alex was wondering what Mac had planned next. After Mac got off the phone, he and Alex left the broker's office and headed down to the lobby. They caught a cab and headed a few blocks north.

"Alex, there's one more thing we need take care of. That last call was to a residential realtor. We need to go look at another property before we finish up here." Traffic was heavy and the cab ride took nearly 30 minutes to cover just 6 blocks; they could have walked faster than the cab was moving. There was little conversation during the ride, Alex sensed that Mac wanted it this way. He sat there in the back of the Yellow Cab and stared out the window. He watched as the New York City hustle and bustle passed by completely unaware of where or why he was heading to their next destination. He was not uneasy about this at all. In fact, the energy of the city passing by just beyond the window of the cab was causing his spirits to soar in anticipation of all that was in store for him, and for Janey.

The cab stopped in front of an old hotel that had been recently renovated. It was clear by the new windows and doors and the fresh paint that this building had been converted into something other than its original design as a hotel. Mac and Alex exited the cab and stood on the sidewalk as the sun was beginning to set. In the steel and glass caverns of Manhattan darkness can come fairly quickly and the evening was fast approaching. Mac looked up and down the street then turned to face Alex.

"Alex, there's something that I've kept from you about this partnership. It's probably based on my own selfish motives for wanting things to move forward, fast. Which means that you get to start working your financial magic at this firm, fast. Which means that the firm starts making money, fast. Which ultimately means that *I* start to make money, fast.

"I don't want you to have to waste any time on things that don't make a positive impact on the success of the firm. I want you to be focused on running the business and turning other people's money into money for us. Are you with me?"

Alex was unsure where this was going. He trusted McNeeley and the events of the past several hours had him completely convinced that Mac was a man of action. No, *fast* action. But this had him at a loss. He decided to let it go and see where Mac wanted to take it. He replied, "I totally agree, Mac. I'm not certain where you're going with this but you know I'm on board."

"Well then, let's go inside and take a look," said McNeeley.

Mac led Alex into the lobby of the building as the doorman held the door open and greeted them. Once in the lobby, Mac shook hands with a striking woman dressed in a business suit. He introduced Alex to the woman and they nodded at each other in a cordial manner. Mac let Alex know that she was a residential realtor that he had worked with on various projects over the past 5 years. At this, Alex's mind once again began trying to figure out what the purpose of this meeting might be. This seemed even more unexpected than the way the earlier meetings had unfolded. What could Mac possibly need to talk to a residential broker for? This trip was all about finding a Wall Street location for the firm and that had been accomplished.

The three of them entered the elevator. It was an ancient contraption that had gold gilded grates, buttons and levers and exposed cables and an open view of the large lobby as they ascended into the elevator shaft making their way up to the top floor. The elevator attendant was an elderly black man wearing a red velvet uniform and spats. He had probably worked in this building for 60 years or more, but looked as fresh as if it were his first day on the job. His nametag read "Grady" and he was as pleasant a man as one could ever encounter. Clearly, his main goal in life was making the 3-minute elevator ride in his car as enjoyable as possible. Grady had a full repertoire of stories about the history of the building and the notable characters that had either visited or lived there over the years. Today he shared a quick story of the time he met the great Louis Armstrong and what a friendly and engaging follow he was. Clearly, Grady was a polished storyteller. He held their attention for the entire ride up to the Penthouse on the 27th floor.

The elevator lobby on 27 was a spacious area with antique gas lighting and a tall mirror against the opposite wall. It looked to be as old as the building itself. On either side of the lobby were large leather couches and side tables with current magazines and newspapers neatly situated upon them. There was a single door to the left of the elevator. It was an intricately carved mahogany door with a very large brass knocker in the center just below the eyehole. Yet another relic from the building's original glory days.

The realtor reached into her purse and pulled out a skeleton key that fit snugly into the door's lock. With a quick twist and a turn of the brass doorknob, the large door swung inward. Alex found himself in a magnificent New York apartment. It had been recently renovated with every amenity one could imagine, but what really caught his attention was the view of the city out the wall of windows in the living room area. This was a truly amazing place. After a quick tour of the living room, dining room, den, kitchen and 4 bedrooms, each with its own bathroom and large walk-in closet, they gathered in the living room area again to take in the view as lights began to twinkle on in the many buildings spread out in front of them for as far as they could see.

"Quite a place, huh, Alex?" asked Mac. "How about that view?" He walked over to the windows and looked out across the city. Even McNeeley had to appreciate the splendor of the view.

"It's amazing!" replied Alex.

"Glad you like it. I recently purchased this place and the renovations were just completed last week. Got it for a steal, really. I love the city and all the energy that it offers. It seems like there is always something going on and things to do. Most of them good, some not so good, but hey, that's life in any big city. When I decided to open the firm, I started to get excited about spending more time here. The problem is I can't convince my wife that she would come to love the city the same way I do.

"So, here's the plan. I've made arrangements with Mills to transfer ownership of this apartment to the firm. It seems to me that it only makes sense for you and your wife to call this place home when you move back here. No charge. Look at it as a perk, company benefit, whatever our accountants will want to call it.

"Alex, I want you and Jane to be comfortable. I don't want you to be distracted by the tedium of trying to find a place to live when you need to be focused on running the firm. And who knows how long it would take to find a place? You don't want to rent a seedy apartment while you're looking, do you? No, of course you don't. Plus, it's close to everything you'll need. Restaurants, shopping, the office, everything."

Alex stood looking out the window at the city that would soon become his home again. Truth be told, he was speechless. As he turned toward Mac, the realtor handed him the keys to the apartment. Before he could say anything to Mac, she smiled and said, "Feel free to start moving in any time you want. I think you'll find this apartment fully stocked with linens, dishes, flatware, just about everything except your clothing. Mr. McNeeley was very specific with what he wanted when he outlined the renovation project."

Alex looked at Mac with a look of astonishment on his face. "I don't know what to say, Mac. This goes way beyond what I could have ever imagined. Are you sure you want to do this? I mean, don't get me wrong, this is an amazing place. I know Janey will love it to death! But really? You're giving this to me as part of my compensation package?"

Mac smiled and said, "No, Alex, I'm confident that you'll earn this place as you run the firm. Now, let's go. We have dinner reservations."

The three of them left the apartment and rode the elevator down to the lobby listening to Grady tell a story about Teddy Kennedy just before his political career really took off. He wasn't nearly as complimentary of Teddy as he was about Satchmo.

At dinner, Mac was clear that he preferred to enjoy the meal and not discuss work. Alex agreed, although he now had so many questions that he was bursting at the seams. He was also very eager to look at the sealed compensation package that Mac had given him at dinner last week, although he was much less concerned about it than he was this morning.

The dinner was served at a very comfortable pace. They would be spending the night in the city so there was no rush. After a few drinks and the house specialty appetizer of shrimp cocktail, they each enjoyed a surf-and-turf dinner. They chatted about everything from cars and Mac's obsession with classic American muscle cars to sailing on his sailboat. Alex realized that besides physical fitness he really didn't have any hobbies worth talking about. He mentioned that he might have to try to change that as he and Janey got settled in the city. At 11:00 P.M. they headed to the hotel and agreed that they would meet in the lobby at 6:30 the next morning to head to the airport for the trip back to Rochester. Alex couldn't wait to call Janey and share with her the events of the day. He wasn't sure where he would start, there were too many things to talk about, but he knew it would be a great conversation.

Chapter Thirty-one

David Sohlmann was sitting at his desk in his New York apartment, alone. That in itself was a rare thing. He had a very strong desire to be surrounded by people. Mostly because those people would bend over backward to meet any need he might have. But tonight he found himself alone. He was reviewing a stack of financial reports from his various interests around the world. It seemed to Sohlmann that it was becoming increasingly difficult to keep track of things. His attention span was also not what it once was. He remembered a time when he could sit for hours and pore over numbers from multiple companies and keep track of all of it. Maybe he was feeling the onset of age, but he quickly pushed that thought out of his mind. He firmly believed that a mind would stay sharp as long as it was exercised regularly. No different than any other muscle in the body.

His office was massive. His desk was an antique from some castle in Scotland, or was it Spain? He couldn't remember and he didn't really care. All he knew was that it was expensive and came at the recommendation of some designer that had been hired by an assistant that worked for one of his companies that handled his properties.The other furnishings were an eclectic collection of leather chairs and sofas, tables and lamps and artwork that cost him more than he wanted to consider at the moment. She probably earned a nice little commission on the sale of these furnishings, but that was not his concern right at this moment. He needed this time alone to give attention to his businesses, which he had been ignoring over the past several weeks.

The ringing of his phone actually startled him. He snatched it up and growled, "Sohlmann!" He looked at the old grandfather clock in the corner of the dimly lit office, it was nearing midnight.

"David, it's Mac."

Mac was sitting in his hotel room only 2 miles from where Sohlmann sat at this very moment. He had contemplated making this a personal visit, but due to the late hour and his fear of ever showing up unannounced in Sohlmann's private residence, he decided to make a phone call. In hindsight, that would prove to be a very wise decision.

"It's a bit late, don't you think?"

Sohlmann's tone made it clear to Mac that this would not be a pleasant chat. He knew instantly that this would be one of those conversations where he passed along information and did so in a very efficient manner. He and Sohlmann were friends, but he also understood that there were times when David's personality could put a strain on even the best of friendships.

"I just finished a very long day here in Manhattan with Coswell. Almost everything went as planned, and—"

"What do you mean 'almost everything went as planned'? Where was the deviation?" demanded Sohlmann.

"Well, we literally ran into Mark Stein walking down the street when we left the brokers office this morning. I knew who he was but I don't think he knew who I was.Alex played it off very well and Mark seemed to let it go as coincidence. I'll tell you,Alex is quick on his feet. He was pretty smooth about the whole encounter."

"Hmm, interesting. But you know I don't like surprises."

"It couldn't be helped, could it?" Mac again thought about whether Sohlmann had anything to do with that chance meeting. "Anyway, your decision to furnish the office space was brilliant. Everything about it was top notch and spot on.Alex spent over 2 hours walking through the space and pointing out how the operation of the space would flow; it's clear he knows his stuff. The apartment twist was also a very smart addition. He's fully engaged at this point," said Mac.

"I know it's brilliant! I don't need anyone, including you, especially you, patronizing me.This is costing me way more money than I anticipated,but I promise you it will be worth it in the end when I see the look on his face!

"Movers are already emptying that office space. Do you have any idea what a hassle it is, and how expensive it is, to rent furniture, equipment and computers for a single day? It's ridiculous! But worth every penny." Sohlmann let out a sinister laugh as he hung up the phone.

Mac started to reply, but heard the line go dead before he could speak. He was once again starting to feel just a little bad for Alex, but quickly put that thought aside. He had an early morning and needed to get some sleep.That was wishful thinking. He had so many thoughts running through his head about this plan of Sohlmann's that it was becoming increasingly difficult to allow his mind to relax. He was also starting to see a darker side of Sohlmann than he ever knew existed. That alone would be keeping him up at night.

Sohlmann sat in his office suddenly unable to concentrate on the numbers he was working on. The only sound was the gentle ticking of the grandfather clock and the crackling of the fire in the huge fireplace. His mind had been derailed by the McNeeley call and now all he could think about was Coswell. He was so deep into this plan and spending so much money that every time he thought about it, he became just as angry as that day back in '87 when this whole thing started. Slowly, his mind began to shift from the anger that fueled his plan to what was to come. He began to imagine the day when the joy of all this planning, controlling and directing, spending and manipulating would finally arrive. He would look Alex in the face without showing a single emotion and bask in his victory. He would watch as the reality set in of how completely destroyed Alex was.

Sohlmann realized at that moment that he was now driven more by his overwhelming desire to crush Coswell than his desire to win at business. Crushing an adversary was not a new experience for Sohlmann—he had been down this path many times in his career, but never had he gone to this extreme. He found that it provided him with a kind of evil adrenaline rush like none he had ever felt before. He started to wonder if he could draw his original plan out further just to make the feelings he was now experiencing last longer.

He walked over to the bar and filled a crystal tumbler with some of the best single-malt Scotch whiskey he owned. He stood in front of the fireplace and stared into the flames, allowing himself to be transported back in time to when he first discovered that he could control events and deliver an outcome that served his interests. It was nearly thirty-five years ago and he was working as a silent business partner that financed a distribution company in Philadelphia. His partner had been found skimming profits and was altering the books to cover it up. Circumstances aligned by sheer luck and Sohlmann was able to gather some valuable information from three of their main suppliers that brought everything to light. Sohlmann decided to keep things quiet and take matters into his own hands. As it turned out, the three suppliers, all of whom had also been cheated by this same individual, were looking for a way to get even.

Sohlmann quickly made plans to set up another similar company operating in the same market. He sold his interest in the first company to his partner at a very healthy profit and promised to introduce his now former partner to other investors. This would never happen. He also made arrangements with the suppliers to give them partial ownership in the new company, which solidified their loyalty to Sohlmann. The plan was that after three months, all the suppliers had agreed that they would use their union connections and blacklist Sohlmann's former partner from not only receiving any merchandise from any suppliers, but also from access to any of the Philadelphia teamsters' services. This quickly drove him into bankruptcy court, allowing Sohlmann to come in and take over his operation at pennies on the dollar. Sohlmann made no attempt to hide his involvement in the acquisition of his former company and immediately fired his former partner. He never gave him a direct reason for being fired, but made it very clear that he should think twice before cheating the wrong person again—consequences can be uncomfortable.

And so David Sohlmann learned that with the right amount of money, a little luck and the drive to come out on top, that he could orchestrate events to his benefit. The chimes on the grandfather clock striking 1:00 A.M. brought Sohlmann back from his visit down memory lane. He looked around at his office and at the views of the city and for the first time in a long time felt some measure of satisfaction. He *had* been able to control events. He *had* been able to manipulate people and direct outcomes. They *did* serve his interests. This Coswell plan would be no different.

Chapter Thirty-two

Janey had finished her workout at the club and was eating her dinner in the living room of their home when Daisy began to bark at a stranger approaching the house. When the doorbell rang Janey was a bit startled. She wasn't afraid to be alone when Alex was out of town, but having a stranger show up unannounced was unsettling. She set her TV tray aside and cautiously went to the door to see who might be visiting at this hour of the evening. Not that is was late, but it was fully dark and Janey was street-smart. She noticed a sedan parked in the driveway. She couldn't make out the license plate number but could tell the car was white and had four doors. That might help if anything went awry.

As she got to the front door, she peeked through the sidelight glass and noticed a middle-aged man holding a notebook. In a loud voice she asked, "May I help you?"

Bill Davis was dressed in casual slacks and a light jacket. He held up his business card to the glass and said, "Ma'am, my name is Bill Davis. I'm a realtor here in Rochester and was wondering if I might be able to talk to you about your house? I know you haven't listed it, but I have a client that is interested in buying it.

"He's relocating here from out of state and happened to pass through your neighborhood a few weeks ago while exploring the area. Your home caught his attention and he has asked me to see if you might consider selling."

Janey's initial reaction was to send him away without a thought so she could get back to her dinner. Instead, she replied, "My husband is not at home right now and he would need to be part of this conversation. Can you leave your card on the porch? I'll talk to him and if we have any interest, we'll give you a call."

"That will be fine," said Davis. "I'm sorry for showing up unannounced, but didn't know any other way to contact you other than sending a letter. My client's timeframe is rather short, so that didn't give me enough time to wait on the mail service. I'm sorry for disturbing your evening. I really hope I hear from you. I think you'll like what I have to say." With that, Bill set his card on the doorstep and left.

Janey watched him leave and made sure he was gone for good before she opened the door to retrieve the card. Daisy was no longer barking and had curled up on the sofa so she felt at ease. She would look into the validity of Bill Davis when she arrived at work early the next morning. With her finely tuned hacking skills, she knew that she would learn everything there was to know about Bill Davis - Realtor in less than an hour.

As Bill was heading home, he felt that this initial contact had gone about as well as it could, given the unique circumstances of this opportunity. After all, what else could he have done? A true cold call was his best option. His only fear now was that they wouldn't call him back. Then he realized he failed to get a name. There was still a lot of work to be done by Bill Davis. He was hopeful he could have it done before his client Jack Cline called back. Actually, he wanted to be the one to make the next call.

Janey was lying in bed as she talked to Alex. She didn't know how to process everything the two of them had just been talking about. First, Alex's news about how the day had gone had completely floored her. She never expected things with the firm to progress as fast as they were. Add to that, his running into Mark Stein made the day even more eventful. When he got into the fact that the final property was furnished and that McNeelely had signed the lease and paid the first year's rent, she was completely floored.

She told Alex about her unexpected visit by the realtor and what he had told her about an interested buyer. They would talk more about it when Alex returned home.

There was a moment of silence on the other end of the line. Alex had not mentioned anything about the apartment to Janey yet, he was saving that for when he got home. But now he had to tell her.

Alex said, "Okay, there's one more thing I have to tell you about our day in Manhattan. It's huge!"

"What more could there possibly be?" asked Janey.

"After we left the broker's office having signed the lease and paying the rent, Mac took me to his new apartment. Well, it's not new, it's actually pretty old. But the building was just renovated and his apartment was completed last week. The building is about six blocks from where our office will be.

"Janey, it is amazing! It has a doorman and an elevator attendant. The unit is on the top floor and has these incredible views of Manhattan. You would love it. Anyway, Mac told me that he can't convince his wife to live in the city, so he transferred ownership of the apartment to the firm and gave me the keys! He wants us to live there! For free!

"We'll be responsible for utilities, but can you believe that?"

"Alex, this is all too much for me to take in right now," said Janey.

"How do you think I feel? I expected to look at some properties for the firm and come home. Now, not only do we have space for the firm, but the lease is signed and paid for, the furniture is in place along with computers and phones. And, we have the most awesome place to live. Did I mention that the apartment is furnished?"

"Well, I won't be getting much sleep tonight. My head is spinning. I guess we need to give this local realtor a call when you get home, huh?"

"Yeah, I'll reach out to him from my office tomorrow afternoon. I really think things are lining up for us, Janey," said Alex.

"Okay, I'll do some research on this Bill Davis first thing in the morning and pass any information to you when you get to the office."

"Janey, who do you know that would know anything about some local realtor?" Alex had been ignoring some of Janey's recent comments about "research." He thought he knew what it meant, but didn't want to press it right now.

Janey let the comment go. It was best to keep Alex in the dark for as long as possible. In her mind, she knew that her skills gave her untraceable access to any computer system out there. The hours she had spent learning her craft and the "test runs" she had made gave her complete confidence that no one could follow her trail, not even her colleagues that taught her these very valuable skills. Especially for something as mundane as confirming the employment of a small-time local realtor.

They were about to end the call when Janey asked, "Alex, did you and Mac open the offer letter yet?'

"Actually, no. With all that's happened today, I kind of forgot about it. I'll ask him if he wants to go over it on the plane ride home."

They ended the call and both struggled to get some sleep. Their minds were racing. Though they were 350 miles apart they were experiencing the exact same feelings as if they were in the same room.

Chapter Thirty-three

The private jet charter flight from JFK to Rochester was delayed due to a major storm that was blowing in from the northwest and hammering the Rochester area. It had moved in quickly overnight and was expected to bring a large late-fall snow. This was not unusual for Rochester, especially with the effect that Lake Ontario had on their weather. Snow accumulations of several inches was becoming more common than not leading up to Thanksgiving. Alex and Mac were the only passengers sitting in the private terminal waiting area, sipping coffee and wondering how long of a delay they would have to endure. The space was comfortable with leather sofas and plenty of fresh coffee, but still, a delay was inconvenient. Especially for Mac. He wanted nothing more than to get home and allow his mind to relax. The past week had been stressful for him, beyond what he had expected. What made their delay even tougher to endure was the fact that the weather in New York City was sunny and clear.

There were two female employees quietly chatting at a reception area. They were quite skilled at blending into the background and only making themselves known when a passenger needed something. They understood very clearly that travelers in this terminal expected to have their privacy. Today was no different. Mac asked them when they arrived to give them some space and to be sure that the coffee did not run out. The pilots of the private jet had their own small waiting room and were waiting out the delay watching the early morning news on their TV.

"So, Mac," said Alex, "my mind has been racing since last night. I can't help but to allow my mind to start putting things in motion for the firm. The next big hurdle will be to start searching for staff. I've been trying to figure out the best approach for us to take and can only come up with one feasible solution. And trust me, I was up all last night thinking on this.

"My thought is that we get started with whatever help I can find short-term and I'll bear the burden of the admin and research part until we can grow the team. I'm thinking that we need to engage a Wall Street search firm to help us find the best people out there. That might take until after the first of the year, if things go without a hitch, maybe longer."

Mac nodded and said, "That's up to you, Alex. You're the one with the responsibility for getting things off the ground. The sooner the better as far as I'm concerned. Besides, you're the one that will be working with these people on a daily basis. I don't feel the need to get involved in this level of detail."

"Alright, I'll continue to work through this in my mind. I'll also start researching some search firms in the city when we get home. I'll have a plan put together for you in the next few days."

"Alex, let's go through the envelope I gave you last week. Since we have some extra time here it seems like the perfect opportunity to discuss your compensation package. Are you ready to go through it?" asked Mac.

Alex's heart began to race and he felt his entire body flush with adrenaline. Mac reached into his briefcase and pulled out the envelope. Mac set the envelope on the sofa between them.

Alex looked at Mac and said, "I don't know what's in there but I'm sure, based on everything else, I won't be disappointed."

"Let's go through it. There are a few things we need to talk about given the events of yesterday. First, I want you to start your formal employment tomorrow morning. No sense in waiting. I want to get things moving just as quickly as we can. I know that this puts some strain on you and your relationship with the bank, but I don't think you'll be needing them as a reference." Mac smiled at Alex after making this remark. He hoped that Alex accepted it as sincere. They were at an important junction in Sohlmann's plan and much of the rest of it hinged on this detail.

"I've asked my attorney to draft a letter of resignation for you that covers all the legal separation language you'll need that will release you from your current obligations with the bank," said Mac.

He reached over and picked up the envelope, opened it and pulled out a stack of documents. Thumbing through them, he found the one he was looking for and handed it to Alex.

"This is the resignation letter. Take a look at it. It's basically a standard resignation letter, but with some additional language included that negates your need to provide any length of notice. The bank probably won't like it, but they'll get over it."

He handed the letter to Alex, then picked up the remaining stack of documents that had been sealed in the envelope.

"This is the formal employment agreement," said Mac. He pulled out his pen and entered tomorrow's date on the first page and handed the stack to Alex.

"To summarize quickly, it outlines your role as Managing Director of the firm, your responsibilities and everything else we've talked about. There is a section at the back that outlines your equity position that will develop as the firm begins to generate profit—it's an escalating formula that grows as you grow the business.

"There is also language that talks about the apartment. You will have unencumbered access and use of it for as long as you like, at no cost. There is also a provision that will transfer ownership of the apartment from the firm to you and Janey over time, if the firm is as successful as I think it will be, and if you think you might want it. It would carry some personal tax liability, but could prove to be a valuable asset in the future. If you'd rather just live in it, that's fine also. Your call.

"Finally, there's the matter of your pay, benefits, vacation and firm perks. You'll see that I want to continue to be generous with you. Your base salary will be $450,000.00/year with full medical, dental and vision coverage for both you and Janey through one of my other interests. You will receive four weeks of vacation and a company car—your choice. I would suggest a German sedan, but you can select whatever you are most comfortable with. We discussed the profit sharing and equity, but you will also have access to creating a 401(k) program for you and the other firm employees. We will have a matching program for them, but your equity position prohibits you from participating in the matching program.

"Other than that, I think we've covered everything else. Any questions?"

Alex held the papers in his hand and looked at them. He could see his dreams coming true right before is eyes. His heart was pounding but he managed to keep himself calm. He looked at Mac and said, "Let me read through this and I'll sign it. I can't see any reason why we can't get started tomorrow."

Janey was at the office early, the commute in was slow and quite treacherous due to the snow. What normally took her twenty minutes took over an hour. She saw several cars in the ditch—the first major snow of the season always took its toll on those drivers that seemed to forget how to drive in bad weather from year to year. Or maybe it was the ones that were too clueless to know that a storm like this would require a slower commute. Either way, they would now pay the price.

Her research on Bill Davis only confirmed that he was a legitimate realtor working the Rochester market for the past several years. He was a local resident and other than some high credit card debt, she found nothing noteworthy about him. This made her feel much more comfortable with the exchange that had taken place last night. It also got her excited about the fact that someone was interested in buying their house. *That would be very convenient, wouldn't it?* she thought.

At 9:30 she received a call from Alex letting her know that he would be delayed getting home due to the weather in Rochester. The pilots were not being allowed to take off and he didn't know when that might change. She let him know about the snow that was piling up and asked him to be careful when he got home.The roads were a mess and according to the news reports there were several accidents all across the Rochester area.Alex mentioned that he and Mac had gone over the employment offer and he would talk with her about it when he got home.

Janey sat back and allowed her mind to wander.A smile came across her face as all the feelings that had surfaced since the dinner with the McNeeleys began to warm her soul. She felt change coming and it was going to be a good change. She was so happy for Alex and the new life that awaited them both.

Chapter Thirty-four

The afternoon did not go as Alex had anticipated at all. If fact, he was very surprised at the quick turn of events that took place once he got to his office.The flight from JFK finally landed at the Rochester airport at 3:30 P.M. during a very brief break in the storm. Once he got into his old Jag and started heading to the bank the snow started again. It was really coming down and traffic was still a mess.The city and county plow trucks were struggling to keep up with the storm, but they were fighting a losing battle. It was coming down too fast.

He walked into the bank at 4:20 and tried hard to organize his thoughts. His desk was covered with work that was waiting for him, but his decision had been made at 30,000 feet that this would no longer be his place of employment when he woke up tomorrow morning. He had accepted Mac's offer and signed the employment agreement while they were flying home. He was totally pumped at the thought of getting started with Mac on this next chapter of his life. But first, there were four very important things that he needed to do. He needed to communicate his decision to his clients, call Janey and let her know what would happen tomorrow and he also needed to give the local realtor a call. Finally, he needed to talk with his boss. Other than that, nothing else here mattered, really.

He drafted a simple form letter that he would send to his clients. It would inform them that he was leaving the bank, effective immediately, to open a new firm on Wall Street in New York City. If they wished to keep their business at the bank, a new Investment professional would be in touch with them soon. If they preferred to keep their business with Alex, they could reach out to him after the first of the year to transfer their business. He made copies and printed mailing labels for his client base and gave the stack of work to one of the ladies in the administrative pool for mailing.

His call to Janey was quick and was about the only part of his afternoon that went as expected. The call to the realtor was not what he expected. The realtor pushed to set up a meeting for Saturday morning for the buyer to look at the house. They would come by at 9:30. The realtor was certain that this buyer was legit and that an offer would be made, he was very motivated to move quickly. Alex had limited experience with real estate but it seemed a little weird that the realtor would push for a showing so quickly. Maybe the buyer was really in a big hurry. Either way, it was something that Alex was able to push out of his mind; he had other things to focus on.

The meeting with his boss, Mr. Williams, was what really shocked him. He expected an amicable conversation about his opportunity to head back to Wall Street. What he got was the exact opposite. Mr. Williams erupted in anger. He blamed Alex for betraying him. What about those plans we just discussed with the board at the last meeting? What about loyalty? Where is the gratitude for taking you in when you were basically unemployable? What about all the current clients you are working with? How can you leave me in a position like this? The barrage of confrontational questions went on and on. It seemed unending, and all Alex wanted to do was finish this conversation and return to his office. What he got instead was an escort by security to his office with a single box for his personal belongings. He was told that he had 10 minutes to clear out. His final paycheck and commissions would be mailed to him.

He loaded his box into his car and started the engine and sat there for a while. His initial natural reaction to getting thrown out of the bank was to be angry and upset. Then the reality of his current situation settled in. He blew out a long breath and leaned his head back. A large smile spread across his face. Tomorrow he would be starting the actual creation of an investment firm on Wall Street. Sure, there would be a few weeks of preparation work before they actually moved to Manhattan, but it all started tomorrow. Mac had promised to advance Alex some money to survive on in the interim period between working at the bank and getting the firm's payroll system up and running. They agreed that Mac would have the money to Alex by the first of December. No problem. With accrued vacation pay and his final check from the bank, things would be fine.

As he drove home, he didn't notice the weather, nor did he notice the congested traffic that usually frustrated him. He was allowing his mind to think of the things he and Janey would do once they got settled in the city again. As he drove, his mood was improving with each mile. As he got closer to home he was looking forward to some time away from the bank to clear his head of the tedium of his small-minded clients, allowing him time to mentally prepare for his new endeavor. Tonight, he and Janey would celebrate with a quiet evening at home. Maybe one of their last in Rochester.

Bill Davis called Jack Cline as soon as he got off the phone with Alex Coswell. He was so proud of himself for getting a viewing set up for Saturday morning that his hands were shaking as he held the phone. Jack Cline picked up on the third ring.

"Hello?"

"Jack, it's Bill Davis in Rochester, New York. Did I catch you at a convenient time?"

"Sure, Bill. What's up?" asked Jack.

"Well, as promised, I got all our viewings scheduled. You know that house in Scottsville that you like? The one that's not on the market? Well, we have a 9:30 appointment to look at it on Saturday morning. I think we can knock them all out by mid-afternoon. What do you think of that?"

"That sounds great. I'll arrive in Rochester on Friday evening and stay at a hotel near the airport. You can pick me up from there on Saturday morning. I'll fax you my hotel information as soon as I make my reservations."

"Sounds like a plan. See you then," replied Bill.

Jack Cline hung up the phone and called his travel agent to make his flight and hotel reservations. This would be his first and last trip to Rochester and he was happy about that. He had seen on the news that Upstate New York was getting hammered with an early winter storm that showed no sign of letting up any time soon. He would have to purchase a winter coat for this trip. In fact, he would have to get two. The most recent package from his employer informed him that this trip would include his lady friend acting as his wife—an important element of the acting role he was playing. They were to be very convincing of their desire to purchase the home in Scottsville, NY. Under no circumstances were they to leave New York until the deal was done. Money was not an issue. Simply make it happen.

Jack completed the reservations and went to inform his girlfriend that she'd be making an unexpected trip to New York with him. They needed to go shopping right away for some winter coats and boots, not something easily found in southern California. After Jack shared this news with her, she seemed genuinely excited about the idea of making a trip back east, especially if it included adding to her wardrobe. The reality was that Kara Wilson, Jack Cline's girlfriend, had also received a recent package from the Sohlmann Group with new instructions for the role she was being paid to play. She was already aware of the upcoming Rochester trip and had made plans accordingly.

Kara Wilson had also been given some very specific instructions about what was to take place when they arrived back in LA from this trip. It appeared that her current relationship with Jack Cline would be ending. The Sohlmann Group would be terminating the current role she was playing and another would be presented to her in the near future. She had been an "actor" for the Sohlmann Group on and off for the past 4 years. Her first role came right after she started with the production company and she had been earning a very comfortable living ever since. She earned a degree from UCLA which was a great safety net, and once the "acting" assignments began, she no longer was required to keep regular business hours with the Sohlmann Group. They offered her a unique employment opportunity; in her first acting role she would be playing the role of a homewrecker and would be paid handsomely for a successful performance. At first she was leery of what she might be asked to do in this performance, but was quickly assured that there would be no expectation of inappropriate activity. This role would be one of simple deception and altered perceptions of others to affect a desired outcome. The role lasted for nearly a year with regular packages being sent to her with clearly defined directions of where to be and how to play her role. She had been told to alter her appearance on several occasions—color her hair, buy a wig to give the appearance she had long hair, acquire a wardrobe to appear filthy rich, rent an exclusive condo and drive a luxury automobile, look like a homeless person and don't bathe for a week, look like a haggard soccer mom, look like a college coed. It no longer surprised her when she was asked, or rather told, to make a change. The details were always surprisingly well thought out and the money was always there to make it happen. She also had access to very skilled makeup artists that provided the necessary assistance when needed. One thing that was clear from the very beginning was that her employment details were to be kept very confidential. Any hint of sharing even the slightest detail would result in immediate dismissal from the company.

The best part of employment with the Sohlmann Group was the money, it was as consistent as the sun rising in the east. There was also the expense account that seemed limitless. She was sure that somewhere someone was tracking the money she spent on her acting roles, but never had she been asked to give any accounting of it. She would just fax an expense report to an 800 number and money was deposited into her bank account the next day.

Another comforting part of the relationship she had with the Sohlmann Group was that every contact she ever had was via the U.S. Mail or some overnight delivery service. She hadn't met with her employer face to face since the day she accepted her first role, and she had grown to like it that way. In the back of her mind she knew that they had an address for her which was only a P.O. Box number, but unless they had been watching her closely, they no longer knew what she looked like. Even if they did, what did it matter? They left her alone to do her job and that was fine with her.

All she really cared about was her lifestyle and the easy money she was earning. Now, however, she was being asked to sever her long-time relationship with Jack Cline. This had been the easiest role she'd played since her employment with the Sohlmann Group started. She really had a great life with all the trappings of the wealthy southern California elite. She also realized that she had actually developed a strong fondness for Jack, which surprised her. She knew he was an actor playing a role and hired by the same company that was paying her, but that was about it. Her employment was to be kept "very secret" from Jack Cline. She was living a lie but her feelings for him were anything but a lie. Then the other day his comment about liking the idea of having a wife to buy a house for... where did that fit into all of this? She needed to sort this out and fast.

Was it time for her relationship with the Sohlmann Group to come to an end? Was she ready for it to end? She quickly realized that, no, she didn't want it to end. It was the best job she could imagine. She had some friends that were trying to make a living in the entertainment industry and they weren't even coming close to making the kind of money she was making. Besides, Jack Cline was not a real person, Kara didn't even know if Jack was his real name. Nor was the life they were living real. They were just actors in a real-life movie. Plain and simple. She would follow her instructions, continue to collect her pay and see what came next.

She had managed to save lots of money over the years since almost everything was paid for in this role she was playing. Jack provided the house, the cars, the lifestyle expenses, all Kara did was her job and put money in the bank. But that wasn't what concerned her now, it was her feelings for Jack. She decided that she would delay making any long term plans until she received her next assignment from her employer. Until then she would enjoy the ride, see part of the country she hadn't seen before and see what tomorrow brings.

Chapter Thirty-five

The Coswells agreed to sell their house to the couple from California after spending the entire morning with them. They were a very likable couple and were offering a cash deal that was just too good to refuse. They recently sold their house in Los Angeles and needed to invest the proceeds back into a house here in Rochester to avoid the tax liability. With the vast difference in real estate values between Los Angeles County and Monroe County and the sizable amount of equity in their home, they were in a position that allowed them to pay cash. They talked at length about the transition from the west coast to Upstate New York, Jack's new job here with a division of the Eastman Kodak Corporation along with a variety of other things. They talked about Alex's plans to open an investment firm in Manhattan and the excitement of moving back to New York City. Janey and Kara both felt that they could become friends if circumstances were different and talked about trying to get together in the city sometime. But like any other relationship that didn't have any depth, they both knew that it probably would never happen.

The Clines' biggest struggle would be dealing with all the snow. These two clearly had no experience with what an Upstate New York winter could be like, their coats were stylish, but not suited for this weather. Jack and Kara made no attempt to hide the fact that they had a lot to learn about life in the north, as they called it. They also asked how long it might take them to adapt to driving in snow, something that neither of them had ever done before. Given the current weather, both were very happy that Bill Davis had been doing the driving today. Alex and Janey looked at each other, then at Bill Davis and smiled, the reality was that it could take a very long time to get comfortable with driving in snowy conditions, but decided to encourage them by saying they would be driving like locals in no time.

As the conversation was coming to a close and the snow continued to pile up outside, Jack and Kara hit them with the last little detail that was not little at all. They needed to take possession of the house immediately. Part of the reason for a cash deal was so that they would be able to get in and paint, replace carpeting, etc., before they moved in. Their timeline was to move in in less than a week. This took Alex and Janey by surprise, but they rolled with it quite well since the offer was so attractive. After a few minutes of conversation about not being able to vacate the house that quickly, they decided that they could accommodate this request.

Jack and Kara and Alex and Janey were well aware that they were offering a purchase price that was well above market value, but that was part of the motivation to get Alex and Janey to act quickly. Jack and the realtor had a purchase contract already drafted and ready to present to the Coswells.

After reviewing the contract, they accepted the offer. Once the papers were signed, Jack arranged for his bank to wire the money to the Coswells' mortgage holder first thing Monday morning. He presented them with a Cashier's Check for $10,000.00 as earnest money to seal the deal. Everything was falling into place.

Alex and Janey spent the rest of Saturday afternoon making plans for their relocation to Manhattan. Their emotions were high and it seemed that they were running on pure adrenaline. Their lives were about to change dramatically, and these changes were happening very quickly. They didn't have time to stop and think about all that was happening and that's exactly what Sohlmann had hoped for. He wanted to hit them with such overwhelming positive stimuli that they couldn't help but lose sight of reality, at least temporarily. He only needed them to make a few decisions at this stage of his scheme that were real and not reversible, and as it was turning out they were doing exactly what he expected they would do. Sohlmann was a master manipulator and once again he was successful.

Alex spent hours on the phone arranging for a moving company to come and pack up their belongings and deliver them to the storage facility he had leased earlier in the day. The moving company would be at the house early Tuesday morning and there was a lot of work to do between now and then. Both Alex and Janey were surprised that the moving company was available so soon, but being the week of Thanksgiving it made sense. Not very many families choose Thanksgiving week to move.

The two of them decided that they would spend Sunday and Monday packing up personal things like valuables, jewelry and the sentimental things that they didn't want the movers to handle, then gather some of the essential items that they would need when they checked into the hotel on Tuesday afternoon. They would be staying in a hotel for the next two weeks while things in Manhattan came together. Alex left a message for Mac about their decision to remain in Rochester for the next two weeks so Janey could give proper notice to her employer—she didn't want to experience the same thing Alex had experienced with the bank, and she felt she might need a reference so she wanted to be polite. Alex would begin the process of searching for his staff from Rochester and begin to schedule interviews for the month of December once he arrived in Manhattan. He would also take care of the administrative details like ordering stationery, business cards, office supplies, etc., from Rochester.

Alex and Janey were spending money that they didn't really have to put everything in motion. The hotel reservation was expensive, the storage facility required a minimum of six months' rent up front and the moving company required a 50% down payment to reserve the date for the movers to come and load up their house, then payment in full prior to unloading the moving van at the storage facility. This wasn't a concern for Alex, the earnest money and his advance from McNeeley would be coming before the credit card bills were due and his new salary would allow them to pay down all their debt in a matter of months. All this spending activity had maxed out their credit cards but neither he nor Janey was concerned about it.

Bill Davis received a phone call late Saturday afternoon from Sohlmann. It was a very matter of fact call and Sohlmann only identified himself as the family friend of Jack Cline that he met down in Florida. He was told to fax the purchase agreement to an 800 number and also to provide the details of the outstanding mortgage on the Coswell home. He was also instructed to provide his bank account information for the transfer of commission funds into his account. Sohlmann already had all this information, of course, but needed to protect his image with Davis. The sale of the property would be finalized by noon on Monday and Davis would have his commission by the end of the day. Sohlmann also instructed Davis to hand deliver the equity from the Coswell house to the sellers on Monday evening. The bank would have a Cashier's Check ready and waiting. Bill Davis was elated by this phone call. He was already trying to calculate how much commission he would be earning but decided that it really didn't matter. It would be more that he'd ever received before, since he wasn't sharing it with his broker. He left his office and headed home. Bill Davis smiled as he drove through the snowstorm. He thought this was turning out to be very good deal for him. He considered getting in touch with Jack Cline once he moved to town and got settled and try to connect with his friend to see if there might be more real estate opportunities for the two of them to work on together in the future. This was another thing that would never happen. Sohlmann would have to come up with other plans for both Bill Davis and Jack Cline once this scheme had run its course. He couldn't afford for there to be any loose ends. He knew he was in much deeper that he originally planned, but what did it matter at this point? What difference did it make if he ruined two more lives? The ripple effect was an unavoidable consequence, and all of it was Alex Coswell's fault anyway. This all would point back to him.

Sohlmann sat in his office and considered how things were escalating. He was still every bit as angry with Coswell as he had ever been, and he couldn't wait to deliver the news to him that his life was basically worthless. That alone would make the past several months, maybe even years, worth the effort and all the time and money he was spending. This was the plan from the beginning. He would make Alex Coswell pay and pay big. Only now he had involved others in this plan of vengeance that he had not originally intended to include. The problem was what to do with them.

He picked up the phone and called McNeeley.

"Hello?"

"It's Sohlmann here. We're ready to schedule the final act. Everything is in place and it's coming together exactly as I planned. I want you to get in touch with Coswell and schedule a meeting for Wednesday morning at your office. I'm coming to Rochester to personally destroy him.

"I don't want you to do anything at this meeting other than to be present. We'll discuss the details when I arrive at your office. All I want from you now is for you to call me when the meeting is confirmed," said Sohlmann.

"I'll call him first thing Monday morning. I don't see any reason why there should be any problem getting the meeting scheduled."

"Perfect. I'll wait for the call."

Sohlmann again hung up on McNeeley before he could reply. He called his flight service and booked his private jet to Rochester for Wednesday morning. He then scheduled an afternoon flight to Kingstown, Jamaica. *The Endeavor* was moored at the Royal Jamaica Yacht Club and he had plans to enjoy his Thanksgiving dinner aboard his ship as he traveled to Tortola, BVI. He let his crew know of his plans and his desires to have the Thanksgiving Day meal be one of the finest that they had ever prepared for him. He would be traveling with a new female companion and wanted to be sure she was impressed.

He called his latest lady friend and made sure she understood the new schedule for the holiday. The slight alteration to their travel plans included a very quick trip to Rochester, NY, but it wouldn't last more than half the day. She was excited to escape the New York weather and if that meant spending a few hours on his luxury Gulfstream parked in Rochester before they headed to the Caribbean, then so be it. She had been told about the airplane and the ship and was very eager to experience both of them. It's not like she would be complaining about anything to David Sohlmann. She didn't know much about him, but she knew he could throw a party, and that was all that mattered. The fact that this party would last for a week and be in the Caribbean was more that she could ask for.

Now Sohlmann had to wait. It was something that he was not very good at. Until now he always had parts of the master plan to coordinate, people to manipulate, events to control. Now, however, all the moving pieces were in place. Each of his actors, both those that knew they were actors and those that didn't were where they needed to be and had performed as expected. The only remaining scene to play out was his grand finale.

He sat back and started to think about the few loose ends that were hanging out there. First, he never intended to pay any commission to Bill Davis for coordinating the sale of the Coswell house. That didn't really matter to Sohlmann because Davis had already fulfilled the service that he had been expected to provide. He decided that Bill Davis would receive a visit from the same two thugs that dealt with the divorce attorney in the parking lot of his office when he was hired.

He was also not concerned with how the equity from the sale of the house got delivered to Coswell. He'd let the mortgage company deal with that detail.

What he was concerned about was what to do with Jack Cline. For the first time ever, he had actually met with one of his actors face to face. Looking back, that had been a mistake. He should have spent the money to hire another actor to deliver the message down in Miami. When he scheduled the meeting in Florida he never thought about this detail. Jack had always been a great actor/employee for the Sohlmann Group. He had always performed his roles to the letter and was very good at what he did. However, Jack Cline could now identify Sohlmann. He had to find a way to correct that. He had Kara Wilson terminating her relationship with him right now, which was necessary. But he needed to remove any risk of Jack Cline coming back to haunt him. This needed more thought and now was not the time to worry about it. He needed to focus on the meeting with Coswell.

Chapter Thirty-six

Alex was tired as he drove across town for the meeting with McNeeley. Traffic was heavy and barely moving due to all the snow. He didn't like sitting in traffic, especially when there was snow, and there was a lot of it today. It agitated him and he was already dealing with the stress due to all the work required to prepare for the move. He and Janey had spent the past three days working nonstop on emptying their house, trying to organize the storage facility so they could get to their clothing, finding a temporary home for their dog Daisy, deciding what to keep and what to donate to charities, and everything else associated with leaving town. They had to cancel utilities, cable TV services, get change of address forms from the post office. It seemed like an endless process, but at least it was complete now. Finally, Alex could focus on recruiting for the firm and getting the first step of the administrative details underway.

Added to the stress of all the work of moving was this winter storm. It had been snowing on and off continually for the past five days, and more was expected. It had taken a toll on both Alex and Janey. She was going to work every day and fighting the snow and the traffic while Alex stayed at home working on the move. She was getting her workouts in during her lunch hour and then coming home already exhausted. She and Alex were working until nearly midnight to get the house cleaned out and the storage facility in order. It was tiring and their emotions were frayed, but they were excited for what the future held for them.

Janey was trying to stay focused at work, but the reality was her heart was no longer in it. She knew she was leaving so she had already checked out mentally. There was no one to train as a replacement for her position and her workload had immediately been reduced in anticipation of her departure, so she didn't have much to do. This left a lot of free time for her to tinker with her hacking activities. She was getting more and more confident every time she ventured into this realm of what they were now calling cyberspace. She was experimenting with the idea of creating hidden alarms that might alert her if someone accidentally stumbled on to her presence in their site. So far, it seemed to be working well. She was testing it herself by acting as a system administrator searching for how data might have been compromised and where access had been gained. She couldn't see any traces of her own activity and she also found that she could actually go back and eliminate all traces of her activity on her end before anyone might even become suspicious as to where a possible breach was coming from.

When they finally arrived in Manhattan, she would surely have to find another job that gave her access to computer networks so she could continue to pursue her new hobby. She was finding that it gave her the most professional satisfaction she had ever experienced. After all, programming and accounting could quickly become a little boring.

Alex was glad that Mac had scheduled a meeting for this morning, he had a long list of things they needed to put into motion in anticipation of their opening. He planned to go over these items in detail with Mac during their time together. They were fast approaching the first of the year and he wanted to be sure to get things off to a strong start. He was thinking about all his conversations with Mac and getting more and more eager to get to Manhattan. Living in the city again would be exciting and invigorating. It would also put an end to fighting traffic behind the wheel like this on a daily basis, and he could not wait.

Alex pulled into the lot at the front of Mac's office and parked his car. He gathered his things and headed in.

The receptionist greeted him. "May I help you, sir?"

"I'm Alex Coswell. I'm here for a meeting with Andrew McNeeley," replied Alex.

"One moment, please. Let me see if he's available."

"He should be expecting me. He set up our meeting today."

"Very good. I'll let him know you're here. Why don't you help yourself to some coffee and have a seat. I'm sure he'll be with you in a few minutes," she said. She turned away and picked up her phone to make a call.

Alex made himself a cup of coffee and sat in the waiting area. He pulled out his notebook and began reviewing his notes. He was organizing and prioritizing them as he sat there waiting. Before he knew it he had been waiting for nearly an hour.

"Mr. Coswell, you can go in now," said the receptionist. "Mr. McNeeley's office is the last door on the left."

Alex headed down the long hall and knocked on the open door to Mac's office. It was a large, sprawling space with photographs of hot rods and model cars along one wall. Alex assumed that these were all part of Mac's collection. He had heard a lot about Mac's collection and actually seen a couple of his cars over the past few months. On the other wall were bookcases filled with an assortment of what appeared to be products from Mac's various companies. There were photographs of Mac's boat and famous people that he had met over the years. Some of the photos were quite old with Mac looking very young. There were also several photos of political dignitaries posing for photographs with Mac. The furnishings were unassuming, basic office furniture with a small conference table and chairs. The focal point of the Mac's office was clearly the huge desk and chair.

As he entered, Mac's large leather chair was facing the window away from the door. He approached the desk, sat in one of the guest chairs and said, "Good morning, Mac."

The big leather chair slowly turned toward Alex. When he saw who was sitting in the chair, a look of confusion spread across his face and his heart may have nearly stopped. David Sohlmann was sitting there with a sinister grin on his face.

"Hello, Alex. Nice to see you again," said Sohlmann with obvious contempt in his tone. "I bet you didn't expect to see me, did you?"

"Mr. Sohlmann, w-what are you doing here?" asked Alex.

"That is a very good question, Alex," replied Sohlmann in a very calm tone. "I'm sure that over the next few minutes I will make that very clear to you."

Alex didn't hear Mac enter the office. He sat in a chair off to the side of his desk without saying a word. He didn't make eye contact with Alex, rather he focused on Sohlmann.

"I'm sure by now you're well acquainted with my friend Mac, here?" asked Sohlmann.

Alex looked at Mac, then back to Sohlmann trying to make sense of what was happening, but coming up with nothing.

To Mac, Alex said, "I'm sorry, am I missing something here? I'm not sure I understand—"

"Let me begin to explain things for you, Alex," Sohlmann interrupted. He was very calm and collected, showing no emotion what so ever. It was almost as if he were speaking to a small school child.

Again, Alex looked at Mac for some hint as to what was going on. Mac just shrugged his shoulders. David Sohlmann shot to his feet and slammed his large hand on Mac's desktop startling both Alex and Mac.

"Don't look at him for any help in understanding this! This is my meeting!" screamed Sohlmann.

His face was immediately red and any sign of calm emotions were instantly gone. Sohlmann had erupted.

"I told him to set up this little meeting, now sit there, keep your mouth shut and listen!"

Sohlmann sat back down in Mac's chair and tried to calm himself. He was still flushed and the veins in his neck and across his temples were looking like they would burst at any second. His breathing was shallow and he thought he might be close to having a heart attack right there. He gained control after a few seconds and stared intently at Alex. He had a look on his face like he might just want to explode again.

After a minute, he was able to calm himself and began to speak.

"You know," said Sohlmann calmly, "you think you're so smart, Coswell. You think that you know everything there is to know about everything, don't you? You think that you can do anything and do it better than anyone else, that you're one of the best financial minds out there. Well, I have some news for you; you're not as smart as you might think. In fact, I think you're pretty stupid. And as I expect, your reaction to our meeting today will be proof of exactly that. You are stupid. You see, no one is as smart as I am. No one."

Sohlmann was once again heading toward the boiling point. His emotions were all over the place. He was going from calm to beyond irate in seconds. Mac just sat there.

"Now, let's see, where shall I begin? How about the beginning? Will that be okay with you, Alex?"

Alex was at a total loss. He felt like he'd lost all sense of time and space as he sat there. His mind was racing but had no ability to make sense of what was taking place. He felt as if he were somehow glued to his chair with no escape from it, like gravity was suddenly much stronger than it was just moments ago. It was as if he were spinning in place, yet not moving.

"I actually had very high hopes for you back then. You came in to Sohlmann & Stein, you remember that firm, don't you, Alex? Of course you do! You're the one responsible for bankrupting it. Anyway, you proved that all my research on you was correct. There wasn't another young prospect out there that would be able to perform as you did. You were a natural, a genius when it came to the world of finance.

"Your ability to see what others couldn't see was remarkable. Your discipline, your drive, your motivation to excel was quickly the talk of Wall Street. Your innate gift to determine trends and steer away from unseen landmines was like nothing any of us had ever seen before. You could find paths to successful investing opportunities that even amazed me. I might have even been jealous of you. You reminded me of myself when I was the shooting star, only I have to admit you were better.

"But then what? You let it all go to your head or something! You lost sight of all reality. Your self-acclaimed moral and ethical compass failed you, Coswell. You thought you could steal from me! That proves stupidity! The fact that you thought you would somehow get away with it is even more proof of just how stupid you are! That's where you and I are so different. I don't have an ounce of stupidity in my entire being. You? That's a different story."

Sohlmann was close to losing control again. His emotions were running high and once again, he was feeling like a heart attack was on its way. He took a sip of water and continued.

"Do you have any idea how much money you cost me? Not just the losses to the firm when the market crashed and the loss of my personal investment portfolio, but the losses of future business on Wall Street? Of course you don't. How could you? But then, it never really mattered to you, did it? It never mattered to you if your actions caused someone to lose or win. All you cared about was you. As I think about it now, that's not necessarily a bad trait. In fact, it's probably a very good one. I don't really care either, never have. I guess we're actually very much alike in that way. But I digress, back to you and how much I have come to despise you. No, that's not a strong enough word. More like loathe. Is there a stronger word for hate? Anyway, your actions were inexcusable. They couldn't go unpunished.

"I don't care about the money, really. That firm and my portfolio at the firm were just a drop in the bucket to me, a pretty big drop, but still just a drop. I think it cost Stein everything; I'm sure he's not happy with you. In fact, as I think about it now, I should have invited him to this little party too. I bet he would be enjoying this. Anyway, the loss of my money is not what has been driving me for the past two years. All I care about is winning.

"So when your actions, your selfish and quite illegal, I might add, actions caused me to lose, well, then it became a very different story, it became personal. You see, Coswell, I always win. I always have and I always will. I make sure of it, no matter what it takes. And on the rare occasion that I lose, I take steps to avenge my loss—especially when it's the result of an intentional attack against me. And no matter how you try to spin what you did or what your intentions might have been, that is how I will forever look at it. You attacked me!"

Sohlmann rose from his chair and crossed the room to close the office door. He was at a point where he needed absolute privacy. When he returned to his seat, he stared at Alex for a few moments without blinking or saying a word. This was part of the plan. He wanted to give Alex some time to let all this settle and try to figure things out in his mind before he continued. As it turned out, that's what was happening. Alex was reeling. He desperately tried to sort this out. No luck.

"I never lost sight of you, Coswell. From the moment you left Wall Street I followed you. Your embarrassing position at that little bank was the perfect place for me to keep tabs on you. I could tell that you were floundering. I loved it! It was like taking a thoroughbred and forcing it to pull a plow.Then I came up with this brilliant idea. It would be the ultimate payback. I would lead you down a path that would guarantee the outcome I was looking for.

"Mac and I have been friends for years. Probably since you were in diapers attached to your mama's tit.We have been business partners on many deals over those years. I've helped him make and manage a fortune and he has helped me in the same ways.We've both seen the best and worst of each other and always helped one another through them. But, in the score column, he owed me a favor from way back and I never forget when someone owes me. Never.This plan of mine would be a perfect time to cash that chit in. So I placed a call. I knew in an instant how my vengeance against you would play out and Mac would need to be an integral player in this scheme. I explained what I needed him to do and he was all in, after all, what could he really say? And here we are!

"It was no coincidence that Mac walked into your office this past summer. I planned it.Your wife being hired by Kodak—real, but orchestrated by me and Mac. Did you know that he sits on their board? All that mystery and the 'too good to be true' opportunity that seemed to fall into your lap at a Podunk bank? Part of my plan. Oh, the investments were real.The money you generated for Mac—real.The commissions you earned—real. It was all part of my plan. But Coswell, I'm sorry to tell you that that's almost where reality ends for you.Almost.

"That lawyer of Mac's—Robert Mills? Fake. Part of my plan.The plans for you to run a boutique investment firm on Wall Street?—Fake. Part of my plan.The SEC filings for the firm? Real, but you'll never see the inside of that firm. Part of my plan.The office space you looked at on Wall Street, furnished and everything? Fake. Part of my plan. The resignation from the bank and the legal wording to make it impossible for you to ever hope to go back? Real. Part of my plan. The apartment that Mac showed you? Real, he owns it. But you'll never be using it. Part of my plan. The partnership agreement and compensation package? Fake. Part of my plan. The advance of your salary to be deposited into your account by December 1st? Fake. Part of my plan. That realtor that brokered the sale of your house? Real. Part of my plan. The couple that bought your house? Fake. Part of my plan. The actual sale of your house at an above market price? Real. I now own it, thank you. Part of my plan. The money you spent on a moving company? Real. Part of my plan—which I needed your help with, so thank you. The money you spent to rent a storage facility? Real. Part of my plan. Again, thanks for your help with that. The money you are spending to stay in a hotel, since you are now broke, unemployed and homeless? Real. Part of my plan.

"So, you see, Alex, I'm smarter than you. My plan worked flawlessly. It looks like I win after all. And that means you just lost—in a very big way. I love the feel of winning. I'm sure it's something you'll never understand. I hope you have a completely miserable life. Please give my worst to your wife. I have a plane to catch and a holiday to enjoy down in the Caribbean."

With that, Sohlmann stood, smiled at Alex and walked out of the office with Mac in tow.

Chapter Thirty-seven

Alex Coswell sat silently in his 9-year-old Jaguar with his head in his hands. His car was running but the heater fan was on the blink again. His breath was fogging the windows and the interior of the car was cold. He shivered.

It was the day before Thanksgiving and the snow was piling up fast. It was 11:30 in the morning and the forecast was calling for another 6-8 inches of snow before the evening rush hour. This amount of snow this early in the year was a bit unusual but not unheard of. Rochester got a lot of lake effect snow. The drive from the city out to his hotel in Scottsville was going to be a real challenge, even at this hour. Alex had no desire to drive there. Cold car or not, he feared a colder reception from his wife. There was no doubt that Janey loved him. She'd proven it time and again over the past few years, moving from job to job with him. Each move causing her to uproot her career and start over again. But there was only so much she could take.

He wondered how it had come to this. His entire world was crashing down around him—again. This time, though, it was complete destruction. Everything was in jeopardy. He had reached the end of the rope. Janey wouldn't understand this time. She never really did, but she went along. This time he feared it was going to be different.

He sat there for what seemed like forever, trying to warm himself, but the coldness that he was feeling came more from what he had just experienced than from the weather. He tried to come up with a way to explain the events of the morning to Janey, but couldn't find an acceptable answer. In his mind he was replaying the conversation over and over, trying to recall every detail. It wasn't really a conversation at all. It was more like a sentence passed down by an evil judge and jury that Alex had been forced to listen to.

He pounded his fist against the dashboard. It caused a crack in the old plastic because of the cold, but at least the heater fan started. He tried to warm his hands, then decided to make his way back to the hotel. He could at least try to clear his mind and make some sense of his situation in the hotel's exercise facility before Janey got home from work. What would he say? How would he explain this?

As he started to back out of his parking space, a Rochester Police car pulled up behind him, lights flashing, blocking him in.

He walked up to Alex's widow and tapped on the glass. Alex put the window down and asked, "Can I help you, Officer?"

"Sir," said the officer, "we received a phone call from the owner of this business complaining of a suspicious car in the parking lot. The description matches your car."

"Seriously?" Alex shook his head in disbelief. "Look, I basically just got fired, that's the only way I can explain what happened here today. I'm leaving right now."

"Well, I'll have to follow you out, just to be sure," said the officer.

"You do whatever you want to do. I can promise you I'll never return to this place. I'm heading home."

The officer followed Alex until he reached highway I-390 and headed south. The drive was slower than he expected due to the heavy snowfall. Traffic wasn't moving more than 35 miles per hour, which was suited Alex just fine, he was in no hurry to get anywhere. As he drove, he wondered how much further this plan of Sohlmann's would go.

Janey lay on the bed in their hotel room in a state of shock. She was staring at the ceiling not saying a word. She hadn't said a single word since Alex started talking. It was almost if she were in a catatonic state. He had just finished telling her all the details of the meeting. How McNeeley had set him up. How Sohlmann blindsided him. How McNeeley just sat there in total silence, which Alex was now convinced was "part of the plan." He told her about the deception and those things that were real. He told her about Sohlmann's fits of rage followed by complete calm. Everything; he didn't leave anything out. Including Sohlmann's look of satisfaction as he left Alex sitting alone in Mac's office. He also shared Sohlmann's comment about giving Janey his worst.

To top it off, Alex shared the whole police thing, the suspicious car story and then following him for at least 20 minutes after he left McNeeley's parking lot.

She was physically exhausted from the past few days and now the mental strain of what she just heard was causing her to shut down. She was as stunned as Alex was. She never saw any of this coming. As much as she tried to keep her emotions in check and with the few red flags that had surfaced through her research, this was completely unexpected. It was unbelievable, really. How could someone carry that much of a grudge for that long? Who would go to those lengths to get back at someone? How much money did Sohlmann have to spend to carry out this plan of his? How could someone harbor that much hatred? At first it seemed hard to imagine, but as she lay there and thought about it she began to understand. She, too, was starting to feel hatred grow within her. It was a feeling she had never experienced before, but it was very real and very strong.

Maybe it was that she felt that Alex had been personally attacked by Sohlmann and McNeeley. Maybe it was that she felt she had been attacked by Sohlmann and McNeeley. Whatever the reason, she was feeling an emotion that was new to her. Now was not the time to deal with her emotions; she would have to address that later. Now she just wanted to stare at nothing.

Understandably, neither Alex nor Janey had any desire to eat. They both lost their appetites during the long one-sided conversation about the current state of their lives. Janey's salary would help for a while, if she could un-resign in the morning and if she would even still have a job now that she learned that her employment at Kodak was part of the set up. But they were without a home. They didn't have the money to stay at the hotel past December 1st. And what about all their belongings?

They decided to try to get some sleep and work out their situation in the morning. With no energy left for anything other than sleep, Alex pulled the curtains shut and turned off the lights.

"Who does that?" asked Janey in the darkness of the room.

It was more of a rhetorical question and she wasn't looking for an answer. It was her way to release the tension of the situation.

"I mean really! What kind of person would go to those lengths to get back at someone? How much hate does he have to have inside to even be able to come up with something like this? What a miserable person he must be!

"And Mac! That really surprises me. He seemed like a genuinely good person. I can't believe he would do something like that. I can't believe he would allow himself to be used by Sohlmann like that.

"What are we going to do? Where are we going to live? What about Daisy? What are you going to do? What happens next?"

Janey was venting. Alex was listening but chose not to say anything. He really didn't have anything more to say. He was completely at a loss. He heard everything Janey had said and was actually thinking the very same things. There were no answers to her questions, so why try to come up with any? He was defeated. Literally defeated; physically, professionally and emotionally.

Janey began to cry as she lay in bed. She tried to keep her sobs quiet, to keep her emotions to herself, but found it to be nearly impossible. She buried her face in her pillow and let the tears flow.

Alex wanted to comfort her, but just didn't have it in him to offer any solace. He didn't have the energy to try to find some way to ease her pain. He knew she was hurting but he also knew that she was a strong woman. Sometimes she needed to work things out for herself. Maybe this was one of those times.

He wanted to scream, to let out some type of primal release in the hope that it might make him feel better but decided against it. That would probably just make things worse. He let her cry and longed for better days from their past. He wished there was just one thing he could do for her that would ease the pain she was feeling.

PART THREE

Chapter Thirty-eight

The Student had awakened in Alex and he bolted upright in bed. He was sweating and out of breath and his heart was racing. Looking at the clock on the bedside table he could see that it was 2:15 A.M. Something deep in his mind must have surfaced while he was sleeping. It could have been the mental trauma of the day, or stress. Maybe it was something else altogether. Whatever it was it had awakened a part of him from the past. It had uncovered a plan that was now his own, and it was crystal clear. He knew exactly what needed to be done and exactly how to do it. He needed some time to prepare, and all the preparations that would be necessary was clear as well. He decided that there was no need to delay acting on his plan so he slipped out of bed and silently began to pack only the essential items he would need. Everything else could be picked up later or improvised on the fly.

Memories were flooding back from times he'd spent with the Colonel in the desert many years ago. He was being bombarded with flashbacks of his days training at the cabin, with the things he learned as a young boy and with those he learned as a teenager. His feelings of defeat were being pushed aside by feelings of anger and resolve. It was time to act.

Alex jotted a quick note as he prepared to leave.

Dear Janey,

I'm sorry for what has happened. I know this hurts you and it's all my fault and I hate to see you this way. There is something that I have to take care of and I don't know how long I'll be gone. I'm taking most of the money from our equity to do what needs to be done. I promise to replace it one day....

I love you the most!

Alex

P.S.: Happy Thanksgiving!

Alex looked at his wife sleeping and placed the note on the pillow beside her head. He wanted to wake her and tell her everything he was planning, but knew that it was best if she didn't know anything about what he was about to do. He slipped out of the hotel room and quietly closed the door behind him. He wasn't sure when he would see her again. *Some Thanksgiving*, he thought.

He headed to the parking lot with his duffel bag and his plan. Alex Coswell was now a man on a mission. There was no turning back. The same drive that pushed him to succeed on Wall Street was now pushing him in another very different direction. The difference now was that there was another motivator in play—vengeance.

He made a few phone calls from the lobby before he headed out. The first call was to the airline, there were several flights daily leaving Rochester to Las Vegas, so Alex had flexibility. This gave him plenty of time to take care of some very important business. His second phone call was the most important and he hoped it would be received well. It was answered on the second ring.

"Hello?" said Marcus Dunsmore.

Marcus Dunsmore was a fraternity brother of Alex's. He wasn't the typical computer science major in their class; he was also double majoring in Graphic Design. Marcus was a rough-around-the-edges kind of guy from Upstate New York that seemed to know everybody. He wasn't much of a party boy himself, but he was pals with all the frat boys, the athletes and those guys with the reputations for running little businesses on the dark side. He was very likeable, a very bright student, but struggled when it came time to take tests. His friendship with Alex came in very handy there.

He and Alex considered rooming together after their sophomore year, but decided that some distance might be best if Alex was going to be helping him pass his tests and finals. So their friendship was solid, not that they would stay close after graduation beyond an occasional phone call, but solid nonetheless. It was one of those relationships that are forged in college and stands the test of time very well.

"Marcus, it's me."

"Me who?" asked Marcus cautiously.

"Me who got you through." It was all Alex needed to say.

"What are you calling at this hour for?" asked Marcus knowing exactly who he was talking to now and being very careful. His line of work demanded discretion. His tone changed immediately. "Are you in trouble?"

"I need your services and I need them right away. I'm willing to pay your going rate and I won't take no for an answer."

"You know I can't take any money from you, bro!"

"We can discuss the money later," said Alex. "Right now, I need to come by to see you."

Marcus gave him an address. It took him into the heart of the city to a nondescript workshop that was as high-tech as anything Alex had ever seen. Alex reconnected with Marcus when he returned to Rochester and stayed in touch with Marcus ever since. If there was any doubt whether he should give Marcus a call it was erased by the big bear hug Alex got when Marcus opened the door. This was the one friend that could help him.

Marcus didn't ask any questions when Alex sat at his table and told him what he needed. He was curious but that's as far as it went. He nodded, gave a few grunts and uh-huhs and listened. He agreed to help and promised secrecy to his dying day. He told Alex not to worry about a thing, especially calling at that late hour. As it turned out, most of his clients preferred to visit his shop during the late hours of the night, so he was still awake when Alex called. He explained that he would need about six or seven hours to get Alex what he needed and offered him a place to crash while he waited. Alex accepted his offer but there were some errands that he needed to take care of first. He would be gone for about 3 hours or so.

While the first part of his plan was being completed, Alex drove to one of the worst areas of the city. He trolled the seediest areas of town until he found what he was looking for. Rochester, like many cities, had a dirty secret that wasn't talked about much—heroin. Drug abuse was a serious problem and it was growing. Alex had seen the news reports of the growing number of overdose victims plaguing the city. As he pulled his car behind an old abandoned warehouse he found what he was looking for. There were two junkies rummaging through the pockets of one of their own. When Alex's headlights hit them, they scattered like roaches into the darkness of their world. Alex found the man to be dead, an obvious OD, with the needle still hanging from his arm. Looking around to make sure no one was left in the area, he picked up the man and stripped off his clothes. Fortunately, he was close to Alex's size. He quickly traded clothes with the dead man and hoisted him into the driver's seat of his car. Alex tossed his wallet onto the ground next to the car, picked up large rock and smashed the front passenger window. He poured some lighter fluid on the front and rear seats, then soaked the headliner as well. He lit a match, tossed it into the car and calmly shuffled away. He looked like one of the many homeless residents of the city and would draw no attention at this hour. He figured it would be at least 5 minutes before the entire car was engulfed in flames. He was right. In this location and at this hour it would burn completely before anyone even noticed there was a fire. He felt no remorse for what he was doing, but did feel bad for the pain it would cause Janey.

He made his way back to Marcus' shop under the cloak of darkness and the silence of the snowstorm. He saw not a single soul on the streets as he walked. He had to consciously force himself to walk slowly to maintain his cover should anyone see him.

The following afternoon, after a little sleep, a shower, some clean clothes and some quality time with Marcus that included an unsuccessful argument about paying Marcus for his services, he pocketed his new items from his friend and got ready to head to the airport. He handed Marcus an envelope and asked him to get it to Janey at the hotel any time after Tuesday of next week. Marcus promised and Alex was out the door.

Once at the airport, he purchased a ticket to Las Vegas, made rental car reservations and waited for the flight to leave. In his mind, he went over his plan again for what the next several days and weeks would look like. There was much to be accomplished and timing would be important. He hoped that Alex Coswell would soon be forgotten, that was his plan.

As Alex was waiting at the airport, David Sohlmann and his lady friend were aboard *The Endeavor* anchored off the southwestern shore of Tortola, British Virgin Islands. They were about a half-mile out from the resorts at the West End, just off Frenchman's Cay which offered some of the most beautiful turquoise waters, breathtaking scenery of nearby islands, warm trade winds and as much privacy as one desired. Local captains knew to give a vessel like *The Endeavor* plenty of space. It wasn't just anybody that could afford a ship like that, and when the owner arrived at the Beef Island airport in a private jet, word tended to spread very quickly to steer clear. Not too long ago, a charter boat captain let the curiosity of his passengers persuade him to check out a large private vessel a bit too closely. It didn't take more than six weeks for him to be out of business after the owner placed some very angry phone calls to the right contacts throughout the British Virgin Islands. There wasn't a single local captain in all of the BVI that was interested in experiencing the same fate. The business of securing charters was tough enough as it was, who needed enemies?

Since their arrival yesterday during the late afternoon, they had been enjoying the sun and warm temperatures. The fact that it was Thanksgiving Day meant that there weren't nearly as many tourists as might be found at any other time of the year. Sohlmann enjoyed diving, but his friend was content with snorkeling, she wasn't a strong swimmer. Sohlmann couldn't understand why anyone would settle for looking at the beauty of the ocean from the surface when you could dive and experience it up close and personal. There was so much more to encounter below the surface, and it opened an entirely new world to explore.

They spent the day snorkeling at both coral reefs and the shipwreck of RMS Rhone. The Rhone was a three-hundred-ten-foot mail ship. She was a British two-masted sail and steam-powered vessel with an iron hull and a bronze propeller. It was only the second bronze propeller ever built and was considered to be a very innovative advancement in the design technology of the day. She was on a route from London to the Caribbean, which was a very lucrative and prestigious route. On the fateful day of her wreck, the captain was concerned about the changing weather conditions and moved the ship to what was thought to be a safe area. As the hurricane developed and moved across the path of the Rhone, her captain made the decision to anchor off the coast of Salt Island, hoping to weather the storm on the leeward side, but as the hurricane passed, the winds shifted. The Rhone was doomed when she tried to escape the hurricane by heading for open seas by passing through a narrow pass between Salt Island and Black Rock point. When the eye of the hurricane passed directly over her, she was slammed directly into Black Rock Point, causing her to split in two.As seawater poured into the engine compartment, the cold water caused the hot boilers, which were running at full steam, to explode. She sank swiftly on October 19, 1867, off the southwestern shore of Salt Island, killing one hundred twenty-three crew members and passengers.There were twenty three crew members that survived the wreck. Her bow lies in 80 feet of water and the stern originally rested in only 30 feet of water.

Sohlmann was very interested in learning as much as possible about the areas he dived in.Whether it was a coral reef and the fish he was to encounter or a shipwreck, he would research and learn whatever he could about the location.There were two reasons for his obsessive study. First, he was truly interested in what he was studying, the species of fish that were indigenous to the area, the makeup of the coral reef, the history of the shipwreck, all of it interested him; it had since he was a child. Secondly, it gave him a feeling of superiority over his guests. If he knew more than his guests about where there were and what they were doing, and he always made sure he did, then, naturally, he felt superior.

There wasn't any schedule to follow for this trip other than the gourmet dinner planned for tonight. He and his most recent female companion would be dining aboard ship on the upper sundeck, complete with white linens, fine silver, crystal, and his personal wait staff that knew how to appear and disappear as needed.This would be a Thanksgiving dinner to remember and the promised after-dinner activities with his guest was something that Sohlmann was hoping he would be remembering for a long time as well.The forecast for the evening was for light breezes and warm temperatures. The water was calm and things were exactly as he had hoped for.

In the morning he planned to do some research to find out when the coming full moons would occur. Every month there was a Full Moon Festival at Trellis Bay. The festival included local island cuisine, live calypso music and steel drum music, Moko Jumbies, which are dancers on stilts, and spectacular fireball sculptures. They had missed the November festival by only a few days, and it was something that Sohlmann wanted to see. He would definitely make plans to return soon for those festivities. He wasn't sure if it would work out, but thought it would be nice to have the same female companionship when he returned. However, if she could make the trip he would have her meet him here so he could enjoy a couple of days of diving before she arrived.

Chapter Thirty-nine

Janey sat in the hotel room trying to make sense of what she was experiencing. She was holding the note Alex had left on her pillow and was trying to understand what the meaning of the note was. She considered throwing it away, but thought better of it. For some reason, something in the back of her mind was telling her to hang on to it. She had read the note several times and was battling mixed emotions. She was angry that Alex had left without saying goodbye or letting her know what he was thinking, and at the same time, she was worried for him because of the state of mind he was in last night.

She wasn't sure what he meant by saying there was something he had to do. What could he possibly need to do on Thanksgiving morning? Was there a message buried in the note? Was there something she was missing? The fact that he was taking their money was also unsettling for her. But in the end, she knew Alex. She knew him to be true to her. She knew that he loved her completely, and that gave her some small sense of comfort. Still, he was gone, and after the day they had yesterday she could use some company.

She called her boss at home, apologizing for disturbing his holiday, and asking if she might keep her job after all. He was happy to accept her change of heart. She was a valuable asset to his department. After learning that their plans for relocating to Manhattan had suddenly fallen through he offered a sincere apology for what he could only imagine was an unpleasant turn of events. He was a wise enough man to know not to ask too many questions when situations like this arose. For that, Janey was grateful. She told him that she would see him on Monday morning.

After learning what Alex had told her about the job offer being manipulated by Sohlmann through McNeeley's position on the Kodak board, she was very happy to hear her boss tell her she could keep her job. But now there was a measure of doubt in the back of her mind. She would never be able to shake the feeling that there was another surprise waiting for her regarding her job. Sohlmann had proven to be the most ruthless, controlling person she had ever known, so she put nothing past him.

How much did her boss know about this whole mess? Was he aware at all of the events that had taken place leading up to yesterday? Was he a part of this plan to ruin their lives? Jane decided that she would have to continue to perform as she had for the past two years, without tipping her hand to her boss of any of the details. At the same time, she would have to be very careful and very aware of what was going on around her at work. If she got even a hint that something was off, she would need to act.

She decided that she and Alex needed a plan of some sort to fall back on. They would need an income, that was certain. If her job was in jeopardy, she needed a plan. She had no idea what that plan might be or what it would entail, but she knew that it was necessary.

Alex, where have you gone? she said to herself. *I really need you right now!*

Chapter Forty

Alex slept the entire 6 ½ hours from Rochester to Las Vegas. The flight departed at 2:30 P.M. and he gained three hours as he traveled west. Being Thanksgiving Day, the flight was only about 1/3 full which gave him space along with peace and quiet, which he was quite thankful for. He arrived at just before 7:00 P.M. local time and picked up his rental pickup truck from an off-airport discount company that specialized in cargo vans, large passenger vans and pickup trucks. His first stop was at a local grocery store for some food and other provisions and supplies. He wasn't sure how long he would be staying so he was careful to stock up on canned food items and other things that wouldn't be subject to either going stale or rotting. He liked the idea of prepackaged protein bars and trail mix and grabbed some bags of nuts. He wanted to avoid having to return to town as much as possible during this phase of his plan.

He also picked up several boxes of matches, pencils, rolls of gauze, athletic tape, rubbing alcohol, cotton swabs, dish towels, laundry detergent, bleach, a roll of thread and a sewing kit and anything else he could think of that might come in handy.

Next, he canvassed the areas near the airport searching for a place to purchase some other necessary supplies that a grocery store didn't carry. Luckily, he came across a military surplus store that was open 7 days a week, 365 days a year. He entered the store and the lone employee was eating a plateful of turkey and all the trimmings at the counter. He was a young kid of about 20 years old.

He shrugged and apologized. "Sorry, dude, my mom just stopped by with some dinner since I got stuck working tonight," said the clerk. "We don't close until 9, then I have to lock up and straighten up the store before I can leave. I won't get home 'til after ten. My boss knew it would be slow tonight, so he said I could eat during my shift, but he wanted to remain open until our normal closing hour."

"Don't worry about it," said Alex. "Enjoy it while it's hot. It sure smells good! I'm going to pick up a few things."

"Anything I can direct you to?"

"I think I should be able to find what I need, thanks."

Alex spent the next 25 minutes gathering hiking boots, black tactical trousers, shirts, T-shirts, sweaters, skivvies, socks, a field jacket, gloves, knit caps, camouflage face paint, scissors, tape, batteries, flashlights, a large hunting knife along with a smaller folding knife. He found an old military compass and a small knapsack, three green wool blankets and 6 military gas cans.

Walking up to the counter and dumping his supplies in front of the clerk, he said, "I think this should about do it."

"Looks like you're going on a hunting trip! What are you going after?"

"Well, that depends on what I find."

"Man, I wish I was going on a hunting trip. My dad and I used to go all the time, but he and my mom got a divorce a few years back and things just haven't been the same since. It's like my mom doesn't want me to have a relationship with him anymore. And when I'm with my dad all he talks about is how bad my mom treated him. I guess it's easier to keep to myself. I've actually been thinking about joining the military, but I'm not convinced that would be the best path for me."

Alex immediately liked the clerk, he was a friendly and engaging kid that made easy conversation. He felt bad for his situation and could understand where his was coming from, but there was nothing to be done about it. Alex wasn't worried about the kid remembering him, none of his plan would have him conducting any of his business anywhere near the state of Nevada.

As the kid was ringing up Alex's purchases, he said, "You might need some of these." He reached down and picked up a large package of waterproof matches. "We just got these in last week. I tried them during a rainstorm we had a few days ago, they work great!"

"Well, you sold me! Throw them in."

"I also have some new military MREs if you want to give them a try. Several different types of meals come in each case."

"I'm good for food, but thanks for the offer," said Alex. Looking at the display behind the counter he added, "Why don't you throw in that pellet gun there and a tin of pellets. You never know when a pellet gun will come in handy." He handed his credit card to the clerk to pay for his purchases.

After adding the pellet gun to the purchase, the clerk said, "I'll need to see some ID."

Alex handed him his driver's license.

After running the credit card he handed the card and the California driver's license back to Alex and said,"Thank you very much, Mr. Baker. I hope you have a fun time and that your hunting trip is successful. My name is Curtis if you ever need any more supplies. Here's one of our business cards. We have an 800 number and we ship anywhere for free if the purchase is over $300.00."

"Call me Tom. It was a pleasure doing business with you Curtis. Happy Thanksgiving!"

Alex gathered his things and headed out to his truck. Twice in the past hour he had successfully used his new credit card and driver's license without a glitch. Not that he had expected anything less from Marcus, but it was still one of those things that had the potential of creating stress. He stopped at a gas station and filled the new gas cans and headed north.

As he drove, he thought about the other items he had purchased from Marcus. He had another credit card and a passport. He had a book of checks tied to a Los Angeles bank account in the name of Thomas Baker that somehow had $8,000.00 in it, plus or minus. His credit limit between the two credit cards was over $15,000.00. Alex didn't know how the money got into the accounts and didn't really want to know. All Marcus told him was that he was covered for about 6 months before anything would start raising red flags. If he needed more time, all he had to do was contact Marcus and he would work his magic again. When Alex was finished with whatever it was he was doing Marcus would simply erase any trace of Thomas Baker. Alex thought he would cross that bridge when he came to it. Right now all he was focused on was his plan and the steps he needed to take to make it happen.

The drive to the cabin took longer than Alex had remembered. The fact that it was nighttime made the trip seem even longer. Add to that the fact that adrenaline that was now building within him and he realized he was very keyed up. It had been several years since a young Alex made the last trip out to the desert, but he knew exactly where he was going. Every turn was as if he had made the trip last week. As he approached the cabin, he was surprised at how dark it was in the desert. There was no moon tonight and the sky was as black as ink. He made the decision to sleep in the truck and make the final 2-mile drive in daylight. He knew there were safety measures in place surrounding the cabin to protect it from any curious hikers that he had to be careful with. No sense in trying to deal with them when he was so tired and in the complete darkness that was the desert at night. He also knew that there would be no chance of him being disturbed by anyone.

The morning sun crested the mountains and Alex awoke with a start. It took him about 5 seconds to get his bearings and clear his head. He was stiff from sleeping in the truck and decided to take a short walk to stretch his legs and breathe some fresh air. Looking around, he saw no sign of any life other than local wildlife and that suited him just fine. He needed to be alone.

The inside of the cabin was exactly like he had left it all those years ago other than a layer of fine dust that covered every surface. His first task would be to run a thorough check of the security systems to be sure that everything was in working order. Next he went to the cabinet above the refrigerator and pulled out the notebook that contained an inventory of all the supplies that had been accumulated over the years when he and the Colonel had been regularly visiting the cabin. Finally, he would clean the cabin. There were vivid memories of inspections by the Colonel and part of Alex still did not want to disappoint him when It came to squaring things away. It was his way of honoring his father one last time.

Alex unpacked the truck and got the cabin ready for the specific use it had been designed for. He had fired up the generator and made sure all the lights worked and that the fridge was operating. He made up his bed, then went out to the old well with a bucket of water and primed the pump until it brought up water. Once everything was in its place, he settled in and began to review his notebooks from his days of training.

Chapter Forty-one

Janey was at her desk early on Monday morning. The office was deserted at this hour following a long weekend. Having spent the holiday alone with her thoughts running all over the place she was ready for a distraction. She looked at the schedule of tasks that needed to be accomplished for the day and dug right in. She was very skilled at taking her workload for the day and stretching it beyond the actual amount of time that was required for her to complete her list of responsibilities. This was how she justified, in her mind, spending company time on her *other* activities. By midday she was caught up on her work and entered into the underworld of computer programming. She always kept several programs open that she could quickly jump into should anyone enter her workspace unannounced. This gave her the peace of mind she needed to sink deep into her secret world.

About 1:30, Janey's desk phone rang. "Hello, this is Jane," she answered.

"Jane, it's Frank." Frank was Jane's boss. "I need to see you in the conference room right away."

"Okay, I'll be there in five minutes," replied Jane. She quickly closed out all her programs, careful to follow her own security protocols. She grabbed her purse and a notebook and headed to the conference room.

As she entered, her heart sank. Frank was there with the head of HR and two uniformed Rochester police officers and another man in a suit. Janey immediately feared that she had been caught and her heart began to pound. Her mind raced to come up with an explanation for what she had been doing on the company computers during company time. At the same time she was scrambling to figure out where she had failed to cover her tracks.

Frank said, "Jane, this is Detective Blankenberg, and these are officers Davis and Ventura."

"A pleasure," said Blankenberg as he shook Jane's hand. "Please take a seat."

Jane had a bewildered look on her face as she sat down at the conference table. Blankenberg and Frank also sat at the table with the HR director. The two officers stood without showing any emotion nor attempting to engage in any form of pleasantries.

"Jane," Frank said, "Detective Blankenberg needs to talk to you about something. He asked that I be present while he's here. He also suggested that HR be present as well."

"What's going on?" It was all Jane could get out as she looked around the room.

"Mrs. Coswell, I'm going to jump right in. There just isn't an easy way to do this," said Blankenberg.

"Okay." Janey was visibly shaken at this point.

"Can I get you some water?" asked Frank.

"Yeah!" Jane quickly blurted out. "I mean yes, please. That would be great."

"Mrs. Coswell, when was the last time you saw your husband?" asked the detective.

Immediately, Janey's mind shifted gears. She went from fear to panic. She had no idea where this might go.

"Alex and I were together on Wednesday night last week at our hotel. I haven't seen him since then."

"Your hotel?" asked Blankenberg. He was taking notes and looking quizzically at Jane.

"Yes, we're staying at a local hotel. We just sold our house and we're in the process of relocating to Manhattan, at least we were.... Can someone tell me what this is about, please?"

"It seems there was an accident over the weekend. A car with license plates registered to you and your husband was found late Thursday afternoon by these two officers. It was in the parking lot behind an abandoned warehouse. There is a lot of questionable activity that goes on in that area. Do you know why your husband might have been in that part of town?"

"What kind of accident? And why am I just now hearing about it?" Janey was starting to get agitated. "Where is my husband?"

"Ma'am, the address that the vehicle was registered to is vacant. The neighbors didn't have any information as to your whereabouts. We finally tracked down your husband's employer this morning and they informed us that he had recently resigned. One of the bank secretaries mentioned that you worked here and here we are." Blankenberg had a sheepish look on his face as if he were a bit embarrassed by the turn of events that had led him to Jane Coswell 3 days late.

"Please, someone tell me where my husband is!"

"Ma'am, the vehicle we found was burned beyond recognition. It appears that it was intentionally set on fire." Blankenberg paused. "Also, there was a charred body inside the vehicle that matches the approximate height and weight of your husband that appears on his driver's license. The officers found this next to the car buried in the snow."

Blankenberg gently placed Alex's wallet on the table. "I'm sorry."

Janey completely lost any composure she had and began sobbing uncontrollably. She took Alex's wallet in her hands and laid her head on the table. After a few moments, she lifted her head and said, "I have a note."

Blankenberg said, "Excuse me? A note?"

Janey reached into her purse and took out the note that Alex had left for her. She handed it to the detective.

He read the note and asked, "When did you receive this?"

"It was on my pillow when I woke up Thursday morning. He must have left during the night. I have no idea where he was headed or why, nor do I know what he meant by '…something to take care of….' I can't believe what I'm hearing." She started crying again, this time more quietly.

"Mrs. Coswell, if you will confirm that this is your husband's wallet, I think it will be enough for us. There's no need for you to come to the morgue to identify the body; it's beyond recognition due to the extensive burns."

Jane nodded and cried a bit harder.

Blankenberg placed his business card on the table and left the room with the officers in tow. To Frank he said, "If she thinks there is any other information that she can share with us, please have her give me a call."

Frank sat at the table with Jane and didn't say a word. The HR director let her know that she could take as much time as she needed, then left the room. Jane asked Frank to leave her alone in the conference room and could he please turn off the lights.

"Is there anyone I can call for you, Jane?" asked Frank.

"No," replied Jane.

He left quietly allowing Jane to sit in the silence of the room while she cried.

Chapter Forty-two

Andrew McNeeley was at the garage (actually it was a warehouse, but he liked to call it a garage) spending the day with his car collection. It was actually a large warehouse that had been outfitted specially for maintaining the perfect climate for restored automobiles. The temperature, humidity, lighting and flooring were all designed to provide the optimal environment for preserving fine automobiles. He had visited with museums, auto manufacturers in the U.S., Italy and Germany and with architects from several geographic regions to ensure that his garage would have the most state-of-the-art design features available. Being in Rochester, New York, he had to be mindful of changes in weather and how those changes might affect the collection.

The warehouse was separated into 4 distinct sections; the main garage was the largest space and where he stored his collection, there was a completely furnished auto body/mechanic's shop complete with a staff of two master mechanics that worked full time. There was a small area where the cars were washed and detailed—dust was an enemy that had to be continually kept at bay and an office area. The office was one of McNeeley's private spaces where he found solitude when he couldn't be out sailing his boat.

During the winter months he would spend every Wednesday at the garage. He enjoyed washing his cars, making sure the engines would fire and constantly moving the cars around to avoid tire rot.The space was massive with over 50 vehicles on display.There was enough room in the main garage to move the cars easily and it gave him the regular opportunity to sit behind the wheel of every one of his cars and actually drive them, even if for only a few hundred feet at a time. There were some cars that were drivers, like the Mustang and a GTO, but there were others that were only for display. Some were far too valuable to risk taking out on the road.

On this particular Wednesday, McNeeley was sitting at his desk listening to a local oldies radio station, surrounded by photographs of his cars at various auto shows, trophies, ribbons and as much automotive memorabilia as you would expect to find. He was reading the local newspaper when his eye caught a small article that took him by surprise. He read the 3-paragraph article twice, then picked up the phone and dialed the number by heart.

"Hello?" answered David Sohlmann.

"David, it's Mac. I thought I would get your answering machine. I'm surprised you answered," said McNeeley.

"It's actually raining here today," said Sohlmann. "Not the best weather for snorkeling. If we were diving, rain wouldn't be an issue, but don't get me started."

"I'm sorry you're having bad weather down there, would you like to trade?" said McNeeley. "The snow stopped a couple of days ago but we have well over a foot on the ground."

"No way! That is exactly why I have a jet and a yacht. I can avoid weather like that very easily. But I'm sure you didn't call me to talk about the weather."

"No, I didn't. You're not going to believe what I saw in today's paper. I'm sitting in my office at the garage killing some time and I came across an article buried on page 6 of Section One. It was the headline that caught my attention. Let me read it to you: *'Local Investment Banker Found Dead in Warehouse District.'* It seems that our friend Alex Coswell was doing something in the abandoned area of Rochester late last Wednesday night after our meeting and came upon his untimely demise. The article says that he was found in his car and both were burned beyond any recognition. The only way he was able to be identified was by the license plate number on the car and his wallet, which they found a few feet from the car. There was no money in the wallet so they think it was some type of robbery, there are lots of junkies in that area. The article also says that there will be an ongoing investigation, but you and I both know that these cases go away very quickly."

"Well, I certainly won't be losing any sleep over it," replied Sohlmann. "But it does tie up that loose end for us, doesn't it?"

"That it does, David. I mean, he was clearly devastated when we left the office last week. I guess desperate people do desperate things but I can't imagine what he would have been doing down there that got him killed."

"Not my problem," said Sohlmann. "Thanks for letting me know. I'll talk to you later." He hung up and left McNeeley with his thoughts.

As he sat in his office McNeeley actually breathed a sigh of relief knowing that Coswell was out of the picture. He didn't like the idea of

Sohlmann taking such a drastic measure of revenge out on Alex, but now that he was dead the book was closed. He tossed the paper into the trash and headed out into the garage to wash one of his Ferraris.

Alex was finishing up a full day of physical training at the cabin. He knew he would need to be in top physical condition for what was ahead of him. He was pleased that everything was exactly as he had hoped it would be.The area surrounding the cabin was just as deserted now as it had been back when he spent every weekend here with the Colonel. It caused him to consider how much thought had gone into the selection of this place or if it was simply pure luck. He was free to move around the area both day and night without being disturbed, and the various physical training courses were easily brought back to an operational state. The firing ranges were also easily rebuilt and ready for use. He and the Colonel had amassed plenty of supplies and ammunition back in those early days and with his memory now refreshed he was ready to start the next phase of his training, He had spent the last week reviewing his notebooks, making new notes, reacquainting himself with the various weapons that were stored in the armory of the cabin and carefully inspecting the explosives and detonator supplies. Everything was in perfect condition.

Alex kept a special notebook for his new plans. He was never specific with details but was very clear in how the schedule of events would play out and exactly what would take place.Anyone that might read this notebook would never understand what they were actually reading, but to Alex it was crystal clear.

Chapter Forty-three

February 1990

Jane sat at her desk again finding it difficult to concentrate. It had been 6 weeks since the small funeral for Alex and she saw no end in sight to her feeling like a ship adrift at sea. The pain she felt from the loneliness was more than she ever expected and there was nothing she could do to make it any better. She didn't have any real friends that she could call on for support and her exercise only went so far to distract her. To make matters worse, there was the unexplained package of money that had been delivered anonymously to her hotel the day after learning that Alex had been killed. It was close to the amount that Alex had taken, but she couldn't make any sense of it. How could Alex have gotten it back to her? Why would he take it just to return it? Who delivered it? She was lost, hurt and confused all at the same time.

After the first of the year she rented a small apartment and moved a few pieces of furniture out of storage into the cramped space. The landlord did not allow pets, so Daisy had found a new home with an old neighbor. Everything about her life was upside down and sitting there staring at her computer screen she came to the realization that there was only one person to blame: David Sohlmann.

Jane suddenly had clear focus. Admitting that Sohlmann was responsible for the issues she was left to deal with was like releasing all the pressure that was building up within her. She spent the remainder of the day getting caught up on all the projects at work that she had been neglecting. When she finally left the office it was well after midnight. She needed to start the day tomorrow with a clean slate; there would be a lot to do and she didn't want any work hanging over her head that might be a distraction for her.

Frank walked into Jane's office at 7:15 the next morning and it was obvious that she had been there for quite a while. "Good morning, Jane," said Frank with a look of surprise on his face. "How long have you been here?"

"I got in around 5:30 this morning. I couldn't sleep so I decided to come in early."

"I just saw the ticket log, you're all caught up on your work. How late did you stay last night?"

Jane replied, "I stayed until my work was done."

"Is everything okay? I mean are you okay? I know it's been a rough time for you. I don't want you to feel...."

"I'm fine, Frank," interrupted Jane. "What else am I going to do with my time?" She gave him a look that made it clear that this conversation was over.

Frank took the hint and headed out the door.

Jane turned back to her computer screen and the chatroom conversation she was having with someone named "The Dark Detective." She had connected with "The Dark Detective," known online as TDD, when searching for a tutorial on how to access personal computers. She wanted to learn specific skills that would allow her to apply her finely honed hacking abilities into corporate mainframe computers to the fast growing world of personal computers.

The Dark Detective promised he was full of information for Janey. He would be happy to share his knowledge with her in exchange for some of her knowledge about mainframes. After some initial bantering back and forth to develop a comfort level with each other, part of the underworld dance to ensure safety, they agreed to connect later in the day in a private chatroom that Jane had created. She would send TDD the password later in an encrypted message on the chatroom page they were currently communicating on.

The rest of the day was spent working on projects for Frank and researching everything she could about personal computers. Understanding how they connected to other computers was going to be an important part of what Jane was interested in trying. Computer networking wasn't new, it had been around since 1961, but most of the early networks were all internal. By 1969 computers were starting to connect remotely using telephone lines and modems. By the early 80s, BITNET connections were becoming the common connection between IBM mainframe systems. Jane was an expert in gaining access to mainframes via these connections, as were most hackers out there. Firewall technology was being developed as a security measure by the late 80s and were so rudimentary that someone with Jane's skillset could easily work around them without leaving a trace.

But Jane wanted to know how the connection from a personal computer with connectivity through a home telephone line and a dialup modem could be accessed. If she understood the mechanics of how the process worked, the technology would begin to make sense. Then she could figure out how to gain entry into the personal computer she was hacking and whatever computer it was connecting to via the phone line. Once she had this knowledge, she would begin educating herself on how to explore the exact interactions between the two. It would be a steep learning curve, but her motivation was high and her energy level had been renewed.

Jane connected with TDD after business hours. She referred to herself in the underworld of hacking as "Mainframe."The office was empty so there was no threat of distractions from any coworkers.The chatroom session lasted several hours and by 10:00 P.M. Jane had filled up a notebook of valuable information from her new chatroom friend.They agreed to connect again at the same time over the next several days. They would use the same chatroom with a rotating password that Jane created using a complex algorithm and some basic binary code that TDD would understand.

For the next week, Jane and TDD exchanged information that both thought was very helpful.TDD was learning about accessing mainframe computers in new ways and Jane was learning everything she needed to know about accessing personal computers via phone lines; that would be her key. She was able to locate TDD's physical location by using her skills and applying some of what she had been learning from him over the past few days. TDD was trying to do the same with Mainframe, but quickly learned that she was a master at concealing any trace of her identity and presence in the networks they were using. This gave him an uneasy feeling that was new to him. Until now, he thought he was the smartest hacker out there. His skills were unmatched and there were many "clients" out there that looked to him for advice and education. In fact, with the exception of Mainframe, they all had to pony up serious money to tap into his knowledge of hacking skills. He viewed himself as a sort of professor. Mainframe, however, paid with a different currency; one that would allow him to access money in very different ways which would make his life and business much easier. The skills she was teaching him would give him a new approach to earning a very comfortable living.

One of the skills that Jane never brought up with TDD, and he had never inquired about, was concealment. It was a critical skill of any hacker, for sure, but she had always taken it to the extreme. Her early days of exploring the hacking world were consumed by paranoia. It was the most important part of what she was learning. Now, with the foundation and confidence of invisibility built into her approach, she was free to come and go as she pleased in any mainframe computer she could identify. She was constantly running tests to try to expose her presence and was absolutely sure that no one could ever find a trace of her access. She had far too much to lose if she were ever found out. Now, with her new focus and what she would be trying to do, it was extremely important to maintain complete invisibility.

Her first test would be to access her own computer. She went to a local electronics store and purchased a high-end personal computer and dialup modem. She connected it to her home phone line and signed up for a local internet service provider that gave her access to both CompuServe and the new service named Prodigy. She found that she could access news reports, file sharing, chatrooms and other information sharing sites. She set up several different information service accounts that permitted access only with a login that had both user name and password requirements. She would search very specific but unusual topics that would be easily identified. Then, leaving the phone line connected, she would go to her office and try to access her computer to see what she could see. It was much more difficult than she expected, but after a few weeks of trying she finally gained access to her system. Before long, she was able to see her login profile, her user name and her password. This was a huge victory for her. Armed with the skills to access her computer, she began to bolster the complexity of her profile and passwords. Every time she accessed her home computer, it was like she was given a roadmap of exactly where she had been, what she had done and how she had done it. The only thing was that she had to access her computer while the telephone line was connected.

Solving this problem required her to gain access to the local telephone company mainframe. She was able to enter her phone number, then insert some code that would alert her any time the line was in use. Simple, really, she had been experimenting with this type of access for years. She set up the alerts to send an encrypted message to her work computer with a time stamp. Now, all she had to do was access the phone company computer through a trap door she created, enter a phone number and the telephone company computer would identify all the information tied to that number. Name, address, city, state, billing records, call history of incoming and outgoing calls. It was all there for her to see.

Jane started entering random phone numbers to see what she came up with. It turned out that she could enter several numbers at a time and retrieve all the information she needed. Most of it was useless information, but it proved that it was working for her. She also began entering consecutive numbers and learned that many home accounts had multiple phone lines coming into a single address. This was valuable information for her also.

Her next step was to randomly access in-use phone lines to see if she could get lucky and find a line connected to a modem. When she hit the first "live" line connected to a computer, she actually let out a squeal of excitement. Someone in Ithaca, NY, named Marvin Williams—user name marvwill, password 042131—was connected to their local newspaper reading obituaries. Jane assumed that his password was his birthday. He had logged on to a Veterans Administration site before navigating to the newspaper. This gave Jane a boost in confidence and launched her to the next level of her personal project.

Chapter Forty-four

Alex was ready. He had been training and preparing at the cabin for over three months. He was comfortable with the skills that he had redeveloped and his fitness level had never been better. As he was loading and packing his truck to leave he realized that he needed to exchange his pickup truck for something a bit more functional for his plans. A closed panel van with no windows would be best. It would give him privacy for the cargo he was carrying, a place to sleep while he was on the road and some room to work as his plan unfolded.

Over the past few months he had made two trips back to the military surplus store for heavy-duty storage bins that locked and a few other supplies, making sure that Curtis was not in the store when he made his purchases. He didn't want there to be any recognition by an on-the-ball clerk like Curtis that might create a lasting memory of him; especially since he was changing his appearance. All that would do would be to raise questions, and Alex didn't need that.

He stopped at the same truck rental facility near the Las Vegas airport and made the truck exchange without any problems. Once he was packed and ready to hit the road, he looked at himself in the rearview mirror. The face staring back at him was nearly unrecognizable compared to the clean cut Alex of the past. He hadn't shaved since arriving at the cabin and his hair was long and unkempt. He was wearing an old dirty ballcap and his tight black T-shirt would cause people to notice his ripped muscles rather than what the face beneath the beard looked like. All of this was part of his plan.

The drive ahead of him was over 2,900 miles. He would take the southern route through Texas and over to Charlotte to avoid any bad weather that he might run into. He was in no hurry and he wanted to take his time to be sure that he never reached the point of exhaustion. He would be stopping frequently for exercise and rest, and constantly reviewing his plans. He estimated that the drive would take over twelve days before he reached Rochester. That was about 5 or 6 hours of driving per day, if he tried to stay off the interstate system. He figured a slow and steady route would provide him the best opportunity to stay relaxed, and focus only on the upcoming weeks.

Alex reached Rochester by the third week of March. They were experiencing unseasonably warm weather, which suited Alex just fine. He would be spending several days in his van and on foot conducting a detailed stakeout for his first phase of his plan. He needed to be sure that he understood the movements and habits of his first target.

He made contact with Marcus for another set of identity papers and the accompanying bank accounts and credit cards. With his new look he needed to be able to move about without any problems or explanations. While he was waiting on Marcus to complete his work, Alex made the decision that he had been wrestling with since he first left town; he still wasn't sure if it was the best decision but he felt he had no choice.

"Marcus, I need you to do me one more favor," said Alex.

"Anything for you, my brother," replied Marcus. "You name it."

"I need you to get in touch with Janey for me. I need you to find a way for me to talk to her."

Marcus stared at Alex for a few moments before he said anything. When he spoke, it came from his heart. "Alex, you've always been a great friend to me. I could never repay you for what you've done. But are you sure this is the best idea? I mean, I don't know what you're into and it's probably best that I don't know so I'm not gonna ask. But I do know what's been in the news about you; you're a dead man—literally a dead man. I can't imagine how your wife would react to some big black guy tellin' her that her dead husband wants to talk to her."

"You think I haven't thought about this every day for the past 4 months? It's tearing me up inside knowing that she's out there and I'm here and she has no idea that I'm alive and well and…." Alex put his head in his hands and ran his fingers through his long black hair. He was still struggling with the idea of reaching out to Janey but he actually needed her for his plan to work. Alex said, "I just want to talk to her. No, I need to talk to her."

"Okay, you're the boss. Just tell me how you want me to make this happen and I'll arrange it," replied Marcus.

Alex laid out the plan with Marcus for connecting with Janey. Marcus would make contact with her and let her know that he was a friend and could be trusted. He would invite her to accompany him to a meeting with a mutual friend that was very important. If she was hesitant or if she resisted, Alex gave Marcus one fact to share with Janey that would make it obvious that it was Alex that was reaching out. If he didn't need to convince her to join him he was to bring her to the meeting not knowing who she would be meeting with.

Alex left Marcus' office with his new identity and any trace of Thomas Baker gone forever. He headed out to his first location and began the tedious task of learning the detailed movement habits of Andrew McNeeley.

Marcus watched Alex walk out the door. He was struggling with what Alex had asked him to do. He understood what Alex was asking, but he really didn't agree with him. It had the potential to really mess things up for everyone involved.

First, how would Jane react to hearing that her dead husband was alive? Second, would she go to the police? What about the insurance company? Finally, it would link Marcus to Alex, and that would be a bad thing on so many levels that Marcus decided right then to scrap the idea completely. He would explain it to Alex when the time was right, but there were just too many landmines in that part of Alex's plan.

Jane sat at her desk in her dark office staring at her computer screen. It was well after business hours but it was now her habit to work late. Her boss Frank had tried several times to get her to ease up, but there was no stopping her. She was taking on more and more projects to give her something to do with her time and Frank was happy with all the extra work that was getting accomplished. He gave her a raise because he felt obligated to reward her for all the additional time she was spending at the office. In reality, her time in the office after dark was being spent tracking down the financial empire that was David Sohlmann.

Over the past few days, she was able to see him contact three separate offshore bank accounts from his Manhattan office computer. One was in Grand Cayman, another in Basel, Switzerland, and the third was located in Curacao. It had taken her about two months before she was able to imbed a Trojan Horse program on his computer that would provide her with his passwords. After another couple of weeks, she had gained access to his accounts and was now able to login without Sohlmann being online at the same time.

At first, she wanted to see how deeply she could explore his accounts without raising any suspicions. For the first several ventures into to financial world of David Sohlmann, she would limit her access to the few minutes immediately after David Sohlmann had logged out of his account. That way, she reasoned, if there were any hint of unusual activity, it would most likely be dismissed as user error by Sohlmann since all the times would match up with his activity in the accounts. The amount of money Sohlmann had in his offshore accounts was mindboggling—it was well over a billion dollars. He was accessing these accounts at least three times a week, transferring money from one of his offshore accounts to another, finally to a bank in Athens, GA, and then to his Manhattan bank account.

After several of these exploratory test runs she was confident that her plan would work. She was able to log into his numbered account at Scotiabank Global Private Bank located on the island nation of Curacao in the south Caribbean Sea. Having passed the initial entry barriers, she found herself with access to eleven different sub-accounts, each with their own password. She had a very detailed notebook that contained bank names, account numbers, user names and passwords that she was referencing. Her first test was to transfer balances from one sub-account to another, then monitor Sohlmann's personal email tied to that account to see if there was any hint of detection. She moved twenty million dollars, thinking that it was a large enough sum to attract some attention. After a week, there was no hint of detection so she moved it back to its original account. She had logged in to the other two banks and did the same thing and finding similar success.

Tonight would be the first step in her plans to strike out at David Sohlmann. It meant that she would need to monitor the dummy email accounts very regularly and keep a close eye on the offshore banking activity of Sohlmann's accounts. She would need to be prepared to react quickly if anything looked like it was unravelling, but she was certainly up for that challenge.

As she logged in to his Switzerland account, she searched for the sub-account with the lowest balance. There was one account that had only twenty-five million dollars in it. It showed limited but regular monthly activity so this would be a good place to start. She navigated to the settings page and changed the password to the account. She also changed the email address to the account, directing any communication from the bank to the dummy account she had set up for herself.

Her heart was pounding as her finger hovered over the "accept and save changes" button. There would be no going back now. She closed her eyes and clicked. She immediately felt a rush of adrenaline. She felt power and control like she had never felt before. She pushed back from her desk and said out loud, "I'm just getting started, you SOB!"

But there was more work to be done. She knew that she would have to return in twenty-four hours and change the password again or Sohlmann would be able to use the original password to make the change back. This meant that Jane needed to access the account on her own time without Sohlmann showing any activity. This might pose a problem, but things were in motion now so she had no choice.

Depending on how this turned out, there were more plans in store for Sohlmann that Jane was considering. She would take it slowly, making sure that she kept her activity limited to what she knew would be untraceable, with the exception of Sohlmann not being able to access certain accounts any longer. She hoped that he would very quickly learn that something was wrong with his money.

As Jane sat there she wondered where all this would go. She wanted to get back at Sohlmann, but how far did she need to take it? She had become completely disconnected from any emotion tied to what she was doing beyond her hate for him. She said to herself, *I'll take it as far as I can until I see that he is hurting*.

She closed out the computer programs she was working on, tidied up her desk and headed for home. She needed to get some sleep and think about everything that she would need to do on a daily basis going forward. As she walked to her car, she allowed herself to smile. For the first time since last fall, she seemed almost happy.

Chapter Forty-five

Alex had been watching the warehouse for over two weeks. He was getting tired of the monotony of the long hours sitting in the van logging activity but knew this was a necessary step in his plan to make McNeeley pay for his role in Sohlmann's game. When the two employees left the warehouse on Wednesday afternoon at 5:15, as they did every day, Alex waited. It would be another thirty minutes or so, then McNeeley would raise a garage door and drive out in one of his cars and head for home. Alex was aware of McNeeley's Wednesday routine at the warehouse from his previous dealings with him while he was working at the bank. Now that he had confirmed the schedules of the two mechanics, he was ready to get things started.

The days were getting longer and his work couldn't start until after darkness had fully set in. This gave him time to grab a bite to eat and connect with Marcus. He used a pay phone at a gas station to make the call.

"Hello?"

"Marcus, it's me," said Alex. "I thought I would have heard from you by now."

"Listen, man, I'm sorry. Are you sure about this? I mean, you gotta do whatever it is you gotta do. I think I understand that... no, I really don't. But you coming back from the dead might be hard to take for your wife. It's been months! Have you thought this through from every angle?

"In my business, I have to look at things from every possible angle. I have to take extreme care to understand every possibility so things don't come crashing down on me or my clients. I'm just wired that way. I've been rolling this over in my mind ever since our last conversation and I can't see where it helps. I guess I'll do whatever you tell me to do, but there might be a better path is all I'm sayin'."

Alex was silent for a while. He knew Marcus was making a very good point, but he wanted to see Janey in the worst way, and he needed her help. At least that was what he thought.

"Marcus, it's time for you and I to have a confidential conversation. I need to talk through some things with someone that can be trusted. What are you doing right now? Can you grab some dinner?"

"You mean right now?" asked Marcus.

"Yes, I mean in 10 minutes. Can you meet me?"

"Yeah, I'll pick up some takeout. Meet me at my place. It sounds like we might need some privacy."

Alex talked for over an hour giving Marcus the details of what had happened over the past several years. Starting with his being hired by Sohlmann & Stein, the crash, the move to Rochester, the Sohlmann scams, everything. He also shared his intentions going forward, but only in vague detail. He purposefully left out his history with the Colonel and his time spent in the desert as a kid and the specifics of what he was doing the past several months in training.

"Wow! I had no idea about any of this. When you turned up in Rochester and reached out to me, I just thought you and Jane were trying to escape the rat race in the Big Apple. This story is unbelievable!"

"You can't make this up. I mean, who does that?" replied Alex.

"So this guy Sohlmann has the ability to control all these events? What kind of money must he have spent on this?"

"You know, at this point, all I can think about is...." Alex stopped himself. He had already shared more than he was comfortable with, but he knew that if anyone could keep a secret, it was Marcus.

Alex gathered his things and cleared the table of the takeout trash. It was time to get started at the McNeeley warehouse. It was now well after dark, so he should be able to get his work done without any interruptions. Marcus had convinced him that he should wait on contacting Janey. He didn't really like it, but decided that it was the best path for now.

As he headed for the door, Marcus was pulling on a black stocking cap and jacket.

"What are you doing?" asked Alex.

"I'm coming with you, that's what I'm doing. I don't know the details of what you're heading out to do, but I know this, I'm with you. Even if I'm just your gopher for whatever you're doing, I'm in. Two are better than one, so let's go!"

They got into the van and headed over to the warehouse.

"You're going to see things that you're going to have to forget immediately," said Alex.

"Bro, in my business, my memory lasts about ten seconds. Not something you have to worry about."

Alex shook his head and looked at Marcus, then smiled.

It took the two of them until after 4:30 A.M. to complete the work at the warehouse. Alex figured the help from Marcus cut at least four hours out of the time needed to do what had to be done. With all the trips back and forth from the van to the warehouse, Alex was glad that Marcus had offered his help. The work on the exterior of the warehouse was the easy part which they completed first. Getting inside the building was another story. After an hour of struggling, they were able to get in through a rear access door.

"Can I ask you a question?" asked Marcus.

"Sure you can. Doesn't mean I'll answer it," said Alex.

"Who owns this place? I mean there has to be millions of dollars' worth of cars and equipment and supplies in here. This place is incredible!"

"Well, let's just say it's not Sohlmann. But who knows for sure? At this point, I don't know what to think anymore."

"So what happens now?" asked Marcus.

"We have one more stop to make. I need to go to the marina for about 15 minutes. I can handle this job by myself, so you get to wait in the van." Marcus looked at him with a look of disappointment on his face.

"Man, are you serious? I hate to wait in the car! My momma used to make me do that when I was a kid. I hated it then and I hate it now!"

"Well, sorry. But you need to sit tight. I'll be right back." They drove to the marina, then Alex grabbed a duffle bag and jumped out of the van before Marcus could say anything else. He headed to the fence and kneeled down and got to work.

After Alex was done with his work at the marina and the two were headed back to Marcus' place, Marcus again asked, "So what happens next?"

"You get to go home and get some sleep. That's what happens next," replied Alex. "I'm going back to the warehouse until the two mechanics arrive for work in a few hours. I need to be sure that they don't suspect anything once they get into the building."

"When does all this go down?"

"Marcus, it's best that you hear about it on the news like everyone else, trust me," said Alex. "You don't want to be connected to anything that happens next."

"I'm already connected, in case you don't realize that!"

"Just go and get some sleep. If you're that interested in helping me, there might be another opportunity in a week or so. I'll be in touch. Now, go home."

Alex stopped about three blocks from his destination. Marcus got out of the van and headed in the direction of his office. Alex drove back to the warehouse and got comfortable in the back of the van and waited. He set an alarm on his watch to wake him up before the mechanics arrived between 7:15 and 7:20. At least they were consistent. He closed his eyes to try to get some sleep, but it was useless. If he wasn't thinking about his plan he was thinking about Janey. Now that the first phase of his plan had started, adrenaline was kicking in, and dealing with adrenaline wasn't something that could be trained for. It came only with experience.

So he waited....

The slamming of the car door startled Alex awake. One of the mechanics had arrived early today for some reason. It was 6:50 A.M.; not once since Alex had been watching the warehouse had either of the mechanics come in earlier than 7:15. Alex's heart began to race as the mechanic walked around the perimeter of the building looking at the foundation, getting on his knees and searching for something. Alex was starting to panic. Had they left something out in the open? Was there a security camera that he was unaware of?

He breathed a sigh of relief when the man reached down to pick up a stray cat and it was followed by several kittens. He pulled out a container of what looked like milk and food and fed the family. After they were done eating, he petted the mama cat on the head and set her on the ground. The cat scampered off around the corner, followed by her kittens. He heard the mechanic say, "See you next week, little lady!"

Chapter Forty-six

The next few days went by very fast for Alex. Everything was in place at the warehouse and there was nothing left to do to prepare for his confrontation with McNeeley. Alex spent time with Marcus, working out and pulling together the details of the next phase of his plan. He made travel arrangements and did some important research on Marcus' computers, which was a huge help. He wasn't sure exactly where the next phase would begin, but he had to have his bases covered.

Tuesday night was restless for Alex. He forced himself to get some needed rest and rehearsed the day in his mind over and over. In a perfect world he would have constructed a replica of the warehouse area and walked through the plan several times before actually conducting the "operation." The Colonel made it very clear on several occasions during his training sessions that the seven Ps were critical: Proper Prior Planning Prevents Piss-Poor Performance. There was no substitute for preparation, and preparation and success went hand in hand.

Alex looked at his watch, it was 5:00 on the dot on Wednesday afternoon.The mechanics would be leaving soon and Alex had one last task to accomplish once they were gone. He was dressed in black tactical fatigues and boots, he had a black stocking cap on his head and his face was covered in black camo. He was wearing tactical gloves and had a protein bar between his teeth. He glanced at the pellet gun sitting on the seat next to him. He had two trigger-switch detonators and a third timer detonator attached to the harness he was wearing. His two silenced 9mm pistols were strategically placed, one on his right hip and the other in a holster in the small of his back. He had no need for extra magazines of ammo.There shouldn't be any gunfire tonight, but he was prepared for anything.

There was a long strip of nails in the back of the van right behind the driver's seat.As soon as the second mechanic pulled out of the parking lot and was out of sight, Alex slipped out of the van, grabbed the strip of nails and eased over to the garage door. He placed the strip of nails across the driveway where McNeeley would be exiting. Attached to the strip of nails on each side were one-gallon plastic milk jugs with pebbles in them. Once the nails were in place Alex took his gear and sat down next to a dumpster across the parking lot from the warehouse. He needed to be a safe distance from the building to not be seen, yet close enough to do what needed to be done. It was a quiet night and it seemed that the area was more deserted that usual on this Wednesday evening. The weather was cloudy but there was no forecast of rain, which helped.

McNeeley was later than usual departing the warehouse. It was almost 6:30 before Alex heard the garage door opening.Alex started to feel the rush of adrenaline kick in. He slowly reached for the pellet gun and waited. McNeeley eased out of the warehouse in a perfectly restored 1967 Pontiac GTO. Before he could get the garage door closed, he rolled over the hidden strip of nails, puncturing the tires and the milk jugs created a very unusual sound as they were dragged by the car. McNeeley immediately stopped the car to inspect the noise. This is exactly what Alex had been expecting him to do. As soon as McNeeley was out of the car, Alex fired a single shot from the pellet gun. The sound of the shot was masked by the rumble of the GTO's engine. The sodium vapor light that illuminated the driveway shattered and sprinkled broken glass to the ground, casting the driveway in darkness. This startled McNeeley and he quickly spun around to look up at the light fixture.

He stood there scratching his head and looking at the shattered light, then back to the car and the milk jug. As he bent down in the darkness to look at the nails in his front tire, Alex pressed the first trigger detonator. The sounds of the small explosions coming from the warehouse were more like firecrackers than anything else. They echoed throughout the warehouse, but McNeeley couldn't tell what they were.

"What was that?" McNeeley said out loud to no one.

He started to walk back into the warehouse just as Alex pressed the second trigger detonator. This time the sounds were much louder and produced very visible results. McNeeley was thrown backward into the rear of the GTO. He fell to the ground and scrambled away from the building. It seemed that the entire interior of the building was now glowing. Fires were breaking out all over the warehouse, in the ceiling, along the walls, under the cars and there seemed to be some type of accelerant creating an inferno.

"What is going on?" screamed McNeeley. "Why isn't my fire alarm going off? My collection!

Alex held the timer detonator and pressed the button to activate it. The detonator started beeping and red LED numbers lit up and started counting down from three minutes. Alex tossed the timer and it landed at McNeeley's feet. He was still hidden from McNeeley, but he could see him. The look on his face was total confusion now. He frantically started pressing buttons on the detonator trying to get it to stop the countdown. No luck.

"I think you better back away from the building!" said Alex in a loud voice.

"Who's there?" cried McNeeley, searching for the voice. "Do you have any idea what you're doing? Those cars are priceless! Many of them are irreplaceable! Make it stop!" He was still pressing the buttons on the detonator and finally hurled it into the open door of the warehouse which was now burning out of control.

"Just shut up and watch," shouted Alex.

McNeeley fell to his knees just as the large explosions started to shake the ground. There were small fireballs that burst into the evening sky. In about thirty seconds, the entire building was collapsing in on itself and the fire was starting to burn his face.

Shielding his face from the heat, McNeeley asked, "Why are you doing this to me?"

The final explosion came just as McNeeley slumped to the ground. The fireball was huge. It was a combination of C4 explosives and the fuel tank stored in the warehouse for the cars. The early evening sky turned black with smoke as the entire building was quickly reduced to a pile of burning rubble. There wasn't a single car, piece of equipment or furniture that was salvageable.

McNeeley was stunned but he gathered his composure. He looked toward where Alex had been hiding and growled, "Do you have any idea what you've just done? Do you know how much history you've just destroyed? Do you know who you're dealing with? You're never going to get away with this! Whoever you are!"

Alex had already walked away and didn't hear McNeeley's comments.

Once it was clear that no fire department was coming, not that it would have done any good, McNeeley headed for home. He had to find a taxi since all his transportation has just gone up in flames. As he walked in the front door of his house, his wife said, "Why are you coming in the front door?" After getting a look at him she said, "What on earth has happened to you? Mac, are you alright?"

"I'm fine, get me a drink, please."

"What happened? You look like you've been in a fight!"

As he started to answer, he was interrupted by the telephone ringing. "Hello?" said his wife. "Yes, he's right here. One moment, please." She handed Mac the phone.

"Hello?" said McNeeley in an angry voice. It was clear that he was not in the mood for a phone call right now. "What? ...When? ... How?" He was silent and then just hung up the phone. He walked over to the living room and slumped into one of the chairs with a bewildered look on his face.

"Mac, who was that on the line?" asked his wife. "Will you please tell me what is going on?"

"That was George Carpenter, the marina Harbor Master. My sailboat just exploded and is sitting at the bottom of Lake Ontario." McNeeley said this with no emotion or any expression on his face. "I look the way I do because I just came from the garage, which also exploded, ...burned to the ground. Nothing left...."

"How can that be?" asked his wife. "This isn't making any sense. What do you mean, the garage exploded and burned to the ground? Buildings don't just explode, Mac. And don't you have the best fire suppression equipment available to prevent even the worst of fires in there?"

"Someone was there. Someone did it," said McNeeley.

"Someone who?"

"I have no idea who, but someone was there. He spoke to me while he was doing it. I couldn't see him, but I heard him. Like it was a ghost or something."

Chapter Forty-seven

It had been two weeks since Jane had changed the passwords on Sohlmann's accounts. She was monitoring his email activity and nothing had surfaced that showed any hint of a problem. This made her mad and she hated Sohlmann even more for it. After all, what good was it to access his accounts, move money around, change passwords or anything else if he was completely unaware of it?

As she sat alone in her small apartment, she became more and more angry. Not only had he taken her husband and ruined her life, but now it seemed that he was completely unaffected by her plan. Well, she would see about that.

Late in the evening the next day, after all other employees had left the building, Jane went to work. She not only accessed and changed the passwords of several accounts at all three offshore banks, but tonight she moved fifty million dollars of Sohlmann's money to a numbered account that she opened in her name at a bank in the Cayman Islands. She immediately opened four more numbered accounts in other locations and began moving the money from location to location. She had learned that this was the best way to hide her tracks. One fifty-million-dollar transaction might raise some eyebrows, but she was betting that Sohlmann has moved that kind of money before so it might not look unusual. She now had to start making time each day to create many transactions of less than one million dollars. She was hoping that small transactions over several days to several accounts in several banks in several different countries wouldn't interest anyone that might be looking.

The next day, early in the morning, she went in and changed the passwords again to prevent Sohlmann from changing them back. Her hope was that this would generate some serious heartache for him. She also started the routine of moving money.A little here, a little there. She opened six more accounts and was now juggling fifty million dollars in eleven different numbered accounts in eight different offshore banks. It would be a challenge to keep track of everything, but she was certainly up to the task.

One Week Later...

David Sohlmann was sitting at his desk in his Manhattan office taking care of his many interests across the country. Things had calmed down significantly over the past several months now that he was no longer consumed with ruining the life of Alex Coswell. He had settled back into the life he enjoyed, which was a mix of both building his wealth and living a life of luxury.

He was looking at his itinerary for another trip to the British Virgin Islands. He would be enjoying some diving and timed this trip to allow him to participate in the Trellis Bay Full Moon Party on Tortola. His companion for this trip was a recently divorced woman nearly half his age and an accomplished diver, something that Sohlmann researched well before making his move to endear himself to her with an offer she wouldn't refuse.

They would be flying in his private jet to Lettsome International Airport located on Beef Island, then meeting *The Endeavor* for 10 days of fun in the sun. His plan was to spend the entire trip exploring the islands of the British Virgin Islands, then spend 5 days taking his yacht up to Miami for some scheduled maintenance. Normally, he would have his staff deliver the yacht to the Miami marina, but he had given them much needed vacation time. His lady friend would be flying back to New York from Tortola on his jet after the week of diving was complete.

The thought of this trip had Sohlmann in an unusually good mood as he made final preparations for his departure. Everything was in place. The flight crew was in place and the flight plan had been filed with the FAA, the staff of *The Endeavor* was preparing the yacht for the two weeks of use, provisions were being ordered and everything was looking good. He had a report from NOMAA (National Oceanic and Atmospheric Administration) showing favorable weather conditions for the entire trip. Sohlmann was happy about this for obvious reasons. It wouldn't be the first time that Sohlmann captained his own vessel, he was an expert seaman, but he preferred the staff to be there. Maybe more for the cooking than anything else; however, he knew that he would be able to impress his guest on his own. Not only with his cooking skills but also with his seamanship abilities.

At 4:30 P.M. his phone rang. "Hello?"

"Mr. Sohlmann, there seems to be a problem." It was his personal accountant on the line.

"You know what I say about problems! You get paid to solve problems before they ever make it to my desk!" Sohlmann's pleasant mood was immediately starting to evaporate.

"Well, this problem is proving difficult to solve and definitely needs your attention," said the accountant.

"What is it?" barked Sohlmann.

"I can't access several of the overseas accounts and there are automated payments that have not gone through over the past two weeks. I'm getting phone calls."

"What do you mean you can't access several accounts? That makes no sense!" Sohlmann was getting very angry and the accountant knew it. He had experienced Sohlmann's anger in the past and felt lucky to still have his job.

"My access is being denied in over twenty-five accounts at banks in Switzerland, Curacao and Cayman. It's telling me that the passwords are incorrect. I've been trying all day to gain access with no success."

"That's ridiculous! Let me see what's happening!" He slammed the phone down without another word. He spun around in his chair to face his computer and logged in to the bank in Switzerland. It was a long process, but he finally got connected. He was able to access the first account he tried to open, but when he entered the password for the second account he was denied. He tried another, same result. The third account was also locked out.

Now, he was furious. Long gone were the thoughts of enjoying the sun. He could feel his anger rising as he logged into the settings for each account and tried to change the passwords. No luck. Without the previous and current password, he was unable to make any changes. It was as if anyone that happened to stumble into the account were trying gain access, they would be denied—security protocols were in place to safeguard every numbered account. He slammed his fist on the keyboard and it broke into pieces. With a quick swipe of his arm, he flung it off his credenza.

He picked up his phone and placed a call to his banker in Switzerland. Because of the six-hour time difference between New York and Basel, Switzerland, there was no one at the bank at this hour at night. That didn't stop Sohlmann. He had been given a private phone number that rang directly to a key accounts manager. The manager maintained a list of numbered customers and the corresponding numbered accounts attached to the customer number but no names. This was to protect the identity of the accountholder.

Sohlmann called the banker.

"Gueten Oobe." This was the standard evening greeting in Basel's native Swiss/German language.

"English!" screamed Sohlmann.

"Hello? Who is this?" replied the startled banker.

"This is customer 476749930567," said Sohlmann. "And I cannot access several of my accounts! What are you going to do to fix it?!"

"I'm sorry, but it is late at night. There is nothing I can do until I get to the bank in the morning. For obvious security reasons, I do not keep sensitive account information at my home, nor do I have the ability to access our computer system. I will be happy to take care of your questions once the bank opens at 9:00 local time tomorrow morning," replied the banker in a very calm and polite voice.

Sohlmann was ready to explode. He did the calculations in his head and realized that the bank wouldn't open until 3:00 A.M. Eastern time. "I can't wait that long! I need answers to my questions and I need them right now!"

"I'm very sorry, sir. But please understand that it is very late here. There is nothing to be done until tomorrow. Goodnight." The banker hung up the phone and the line went dead.

Sohlmann was coming unglued. He wanted to log into his accounts at the bank in Curacao and Cayman, but his keyboard was destroyed. He picked up the phone and called his bank in Curacao. They were in the same time zone as New York. Unfortunately, island culture being what it is meant that banks were pretty much deserted by 3:00 each afternoon. He had the same experience trying to call Grand Cayman.

Sohlmann sat at his desk and fumed. Looking around his Manhattan office, he realized he was powerless to do anything about this. He was not accustomed to being powerless. Someone would pay.

Chapter Forty-eight

Marcus Dunsmore was a very unique character. Alex was learning this as he spent more time with him. He proved to be much more valuable than simply being able to create new identities for Alex and provide him with passports, credit cards, bank accounts and histories. His current identity was that of a Canadian trust fund playboy named Patrice McDavid. While it was unnecessary for what Alex needed to do, it made things easy for him to move around. His Canadian passport would soon be put to the test, but Alex wasn't worried. Marcus had proven to be very reliable with the work he had done for Alex last time.

Alex explained to Marcus what he needed next in the way of information. Marcus had so many contacts with so many favors to cash in that the next phase of Alex's plan seemed to come together quite easily. It was actually quite surprising to Alex just how well connected Marcus was to very influential people.

When Marcus put Alex in touch with a contact at the FAA he learned about the flight plan that Sohlmann's flight crew had filed for the trip to the Caribbean. This put very specific details about location and timing around Alex's next steps. The challenge now would be getting his supplies down to the British Virgin Islands.

"Marcus, how am I going to get my cases out of the U.S. and into another country?" asked Alex. It was more of a rhetorical question than anything else.

"Sounds to me like you are going to need to sidestep both commercial airlines and customs."

"Exactly, that's my biggest hurdle right now, and the clock is ticking. I'm trying to figure out the best way to deal with this."

"Why don't you make your travel plans as the Canadian playboy heading down to the Caribbean for some fun? You can drive up to Ottawa and fly from there. It's only a 4- or 5-hour drive. Then you'll be able to rent a vehicle and actually stay in a hotel while you're in the islands.

"Let me worry about getting your supplies down there. You just let me know where you'll be staying and I'll make it happen. I got you covered, buddy!" Marcus winked at Alex. "Wasn't that *your* line back in our college days?"

"What would I do without your help?" Alex smiled.

"Take a look around. None of this would be possible without the help you gave me way back then."

"Man, I really want to see Janey," said Alex. He looked away and was immediately lost in his thoughts.

After a moment, Marcus said, "Take it one step at a time, my man. If it's meant to happen it will happen, but only at the right time. Don't rush things, rushing will get you in trouble every time."

Alex turned and left Marcus' place. As he was heading out the door he turned back and said, "There's some shopping I need to do. I'll be back later. Marcus, thank you!" Alex closed the door and was gone.

Marcus made the necessary phone calls to his connections and arranged for the cargo to be delivered to the Caribbean. Customs would not be an issue and no questions would ever be asked about what the cases contained. He also suggested that there might need to be a return of the cargo to Rochester, but those details were yet to be finalized.

Alex went shopping for some specific gear that would be needed for his trip to Tortola. Not only did he need some warm weather clothing, but there were some other items that would be necessary for what he was planning that the training at the cabin could never provide.

The trip to the Caribbean was uneventful. He made a stop in Quebec City with a 2-hour layover that allowed him to eat, then flew directly to the British Virgin Island of Tortola. He was immediately hit with the humidity and the warm temperature. He carried only a duffle bag with a few necessary toiletry items and some shorts and T-shirts. After making his way through Customs and picking up his rental car, he headed over to his motel. It was only about 5 minutes from the airport and came at a cheap price since it didn't have beach access nor a view.

He got settled in, showered and shaved his beard off. He found a pay phone and called Marcus. After relaying the information about his hotel accommodations to Marcus and exchanging some small talk, Alex headed out to start getting familiar with the Island. He found a small general store and was able to buy some sunscreen, some snack food and a large straw hat that would provide protection from the sun, but also some measure of concealment, should there be anyone that might spot him. This was a very remote possibility, he knew, but one that the Colonel never allowed him to overlook. It was drilled into Alex's brain from early on that your best chance of getting spotted was when you were sure there was no one looking.

There were a few things that Alex knew about this phase of his plan, but still a few things that he would need to learn to ensure his plan would come together. He knew that Sohlmann was due to arrive in three days, this gave him some time to plan and familiarize himself with the area. He also knew that Sohlmann owned a yacht, but nothing beyond that. Alex was assuming that he would be staying on the boat, but not how to identify which one would belong to him. He also knew that Sohlmann was an avid SCUBA diver, so there should be some tank rentals in his near future. What he didn't know was how he would be making contact with Sohlmann and how he would orchestrate the things he was planning for him.

Alex spent the entire next day in and around Trellis Bay. He learned that there was a party being planned for a week from today—they called it a Full Moon Party. Locals came from every walk of life to celebrate the full moon each month. It was believed that the full moon caused abnormal behavior in humans and animals. People came from everywhere to sell souvenirs, T-shirts, all manner of local island food and drink, provide festive live local Calypso music, huge decorative fireballs, Moko Jumbies, which are native stilt-walkers, and burning statues located just off the beach. Everyone that Alex talked to strongly urged him to participate. It was one of the hottest parties of the month and every tourist in the area would be there. If he was looking for a good time, this would be the place to find it.

Early the next morning, Alex was awakened by his motel room telephone ringing.

"Hello?"

"Hey, buddy, you enjoying some sun and sand down there?" said Marcus.

"Not really, but you certainly can't complain about the weather here."

"I hear you. I'm gonna have to get myself down there one day. Listen, I got some good intel for you. You should be getting a knock on your door sometime between 2:00 and 3:00 this afternoon. All your cases, including the two new ones will be delivered by a guy I know. It won't be hard to recognize him, he's a relative of mine, if you know what I'm sayin'.

"Also, I did you a solid with some research during my spare time. Here's what I learned from a friend. Sohlmann owns a big boat, actually, it probably qualifies as a ship. It's called *The Endeavor* and it's well over a hundred and fifty feet long. It's due to arrive in BVI this afternoon and there are several scheduled deliveries that will be made out of Trellis Bay tomorrow by local companies that specialize in outfitting sailboats and yachts. Also, I heard that there is some diving equipment that's being delivered as well. I was able to get a diagram of it for you. It will be in one of the cases."

"Wow! That's incredible! How did you get that information?" said a shocked Alex.

"Wait, there's more. The FAA is going to spring a surprise inspection on Sohlmann's Gulfstream that will delay any departure from BVI for over a week."

Alex said, "Marcus, where are you getting all this information and how are you able to make these things happen?"

"Now it's your turn to not ask questions. Let's just say it's best if you forget where you learned any of this."

"I owe you, Marcus. This time, I really owe you. You have no idea how helpful this is to me," said Alex.

"Just shut up and get to work. I'll talk to you soon. I got someplace I need to be." Marcus hung up and the phone went dead.

Alex headed out to spend the day on the beach. He had to play the part of a fun-in-the-sun tourist to blend in to the local surroundings and not raise any suspicions. It would also give him the ability to keep an eye on the bay for any large vessels that might show up. He struck up a light conversation with a group of young women from Nashville that were celebrating a long bachelorette party weekend. They were clearly more interested in consuming local alcoholic drinks than anything else. The local Painkiller drink was a favorite, but the drink was named improperly. There would plenty of pain in the morning. He maintained easy on-and-off conversation for most of the morning, not getting too deep into anything that would require much thought about being Canadian. When they left the beach for lunch, he headed off toward the small pier.

As he was approaching the pier, his afternoon plans changed when a large ship came around the end of the island. He wasn't able to identify the vessel because it dropped anchor with its stern turned away from the beach. A large starboard hull door opened and a small shore craft emerged and headed his way. As the four crew members came ashore Alex was able to read *The Endeavo*r on their crew shirts.

Marcus was right, this was no ordinary yacht. It was massive! *The Endeavor* was a super-yacht by anyone's stretch. It was obvious that Sohlmann spared no expense when it came to the time he spent on the water. This made Alex smile to himself. He would take great pleasure in seeing his plan unfold.

The crew of *The Endeavor* were very familiar with the single deckhand working the pier. They greeted him by name and he let them know that their taxi was waiting at the end of the dock. As they headed off, Alex looked at his watch and headed over to one of the local beach bars for a quick burger. Once he finished eating his lunch he headed into town to talk to one of the local dive shops. He made some arrangements with the shop owner then headed back to his hotel to wait for his delivery.

Chapter Forty-nine

Alex was startled by the heavy pounding on his motel room door. As he opened the door he was facing the back of a large black delivery man who was bent over looking at one of the several cases being delivered. He was sweating profusely and his shirt was soaked through. When he stood and turned around, Alex stepped back, stunned.

There stood Marcus!

"What are you...."

"Yeah, let's just get these cases inside your room," interrupted Marcus. "We can talk about why I'm here in a minute. You know how hot this sun is on black skin?"

Alex again just shook his head. They hauled the cases into his motel room and shut the door. Marcus stood in front of the weak air-conditioning unit, completely blocking any airflow from the rest of the room.

"Are there any more surprises you want to tell me about?" asked Alex.

"Nope. I'm all yours for the next two days. I figure you got a lot going on, so here I am to help. I'll do whatever you need me to do. Just please don't ask me to stand out in the sun for very long!"

Alex and Marcus spent the rest of the day preparing the equipment that Alex would need for his encounter with Sohlmann. As they worked, he shared all the details with Marcus about what would be coming and how Marcus could help. Alex would need several explosive devices, some small, some very large. Marcus was able to help with all of it. Alex kept the detonators separate from the explosives to keep things safe, but Marcus proved to be a very quick study and took directions well.

Once the explosives work was complete and the detonators were ready, the two developed a plan to watch the crew of *The Endeavor* coordinate the deliveries of supplies to the ship. Alex headed back to the beach and Marcus found a comfortable stool at one of the local beach bars in the shade. They spent the evening and the entire next day observing the crew. Once the four crew members said their goodbyes to the worker on the pier and headed toward the airport, they figured the preparations and prearrival work on *The Endeavor* had come to an end. It was now time to get things started.

Chapter Fifty

David Sohlmann was beside himself with rage. Never in his life had he been so completely stonewalled. There were no acceptable answers from anyone in Switzerland, Curacao nor Grand Cayman. Each bank was telling him the same story—numbered accounts were numbered for a very specific reason and that was to protect the identity of the accountholder. To each of these banks, he was nothing more than a twelve-digit number calling on the phone. No bank would simply override account passwords and give access to someone who claimed to be the owner of the account just by providing a valid customer and account numbers. He would have to visit each bank personally and handle the matter face to face. It would be a long and tedious process and require that Sohlmann schedule appointments with each bank's identity security officers.

This was not something that Sohlmann was looking forward to. It meant unscheduled international travel, not that that was an unusual thing, just that it was a hassle and very time consuming. It also meant that he would have to go through all the secrecy required to even have a conversation about his accounts. The worst thing was that he would have to do it three times. Each bank was the same, yet different at the same time. They each had their unique way of doing business and Sohlmann was the one that would have to adjust to their way of doing it.

His accountant was calling every day now with more and more payments that were not being made. Sohlmann was juggling making payments to various creditors from accounts that were not designed to be liquid. Especially when the activity in these accounts were ones that were tied directly to Sohlmann by name. These payments had been set up in offshore accounts under shell company names for a very specific reason. Now his anonymity was in jeopardy. All this extra activity had the potential to raise the eyebrows of the IRS and Sohlmann did not want that.

But today he had other things to worry about. He was scheduled to fly to Tortola with his lady friend this afternoon which meant that he would not be able to deal with the offshore banks until he returned. Right now he wanted to focus on everything that this trip would provide. He forced himself to leave his office and head up to his living quarters to pack. His driver would be downstairs at 1:30 and he and his companion would be in the air an hour later. There was a lot to do before he departed. As he was heading upstairs, his office phone rang. He decided to ignore it. As he entered his living quarters, the house phone rang. There were very few people that had this number, so he decided to answer.

"Hello?"

"David, it's Mac," said a lifeless voice on the other end of the phone.

"Mac, I have a lot going on this afternoon. I'm trying to get ready to fly down to the Caribbean in about two hours. What do you need?"

"What I need is someone to talk to. It's personal," said Mac.

This was very unusual. Sohlmann knew that when Mac needed to talk, he always talked to his wife. She was his only confidante when it came to anything personal.

"Well, I don't think I'm your man for that," replied Sohlmann. "You should know me better than that. Isn't this your wife's department? Besides, I'm not really interested in being your shrink or giving out any hugs. No offense."

"I lost my boat and my cars," said Mac. "I feel like part of me has died!"

"What do you mean you lost your boat and your cars?" said Sohlmann in a confused tone. "Look, I don't have time to talk about this right now. I'll call you when I get back to the States in two weeks. We can sort this out then. In the meantime, go talk to your wife."

Sohlmann hung up and shook his head as he walked to his master suite. He said to himself, *McNeeley must be getting old or something! Why on earth would he think that I would care about his personal problems? Or that I would be interested at all in talking about it with him! Friggin' sissy!*

Sohlmann started packing and gathering his personal items. Something in the back of his mind started nagging at him but he didn't know what it was. He pushed it out of his mind and focused on the trip.

The flight to Lettsome International Airport in Tortola was exactly as Sohlmann expected it to be. A luxurious Gulfstream airplane with impeccable service and every creature comfort one could imagine. The flight took just over 3 hours and Sohlmann and his guest were delivered to *The Endeavor* by dusk. The weather was clear and the setting sun provided just the right mood for a late evening meal on the rear deck. Sohlmann noticed that his liquor cabinet was fully stocked, which meant that the kitchen would also be ready for his use. He headed down to the lower deck to inspect the hold and saw several dive tanks ready and waiting for the coming week.

After he finished preparing the meal they both headed to the rear deck and spent the remainder of the evening enjoying the food and the location. The breeze was blowing gently and the stars were starting to twinkle above. Sohlmann wondered to himself when it might be time to retire and stop dealing with the frustrations of his daily business dealings. After just a few seconds he banished those thoughts from his head. He would never be ready to quit the game. It defined him. It drove him every day, and if he was honest with himself, even with the current frustrations he was going through with his offshore banks, he loved it. He couldn't imagine life without it.

Alex knew he had a limited window of opportunity to get the work done that needed to be done. He waited until dark to begin his initial reconnaissance of *The Endeavor*. He opened one of the new cases that he purchased back in Rochester and pulled out his SCUBA gear. He had everything he would need with the exception of tanks. Those had been rented on the island under the name of Patrice McDavid and he would pick them up tomorrow morning.

Alex told Marcus he was heading out to watch the activity on Sohlmann's boat for the night to see if there were any pieces of helpful information he might learn. Marcus opted to head back to the beach bars to see if he might pick up on any loose talk about the activities surrounding the big shot that owned the big yacht. It had already attracted the attention of the local vendors; that boat had been here before many times. When it arrived, money would flow from it. Everything from fishing guides to sailboat captains to tourist excursion purveyors—they all knew that The Endeavor came with lots of money to spend in the local economy. It didn't take long for the current batch of tourists to pin the nickname "Big Shot on the Big Yacht" on Sohlmann. His presence in the BVI generated special treatment from just about everyone. The visiting tourists quickly learned that they took a back seat to whatever it was that Sohlmann wanted.

Marcus had given Alex a diagram of *The Endeavor* that allowed him to become somewhat familiar with how the ship was laid out. It didn't really matter, he would never set foot aboard it. He only wanted to know what might be going on based on where interior lights were visible after dark. The main living cabin space, the galley, and the master stateroom were the main areas that were showing activity tonight. There was a constant blueish glow from what Alex assumed was a television pulsating in the living cabin on the second deck. The lights in the galley area flashed on and off over the few hours that Alex was watching the ship. At just after midnight, the lights in the living cabin went out and the galley lit up for a few minutes. The master stateroom lights went on, then seemed to dim for remainder of the time that Alex watched from his perch on the rocks just off the airport property.

He waited for another hour, then turned his attention to the airport. Sohlmann's Gulfstream sat in the dim light off by itself. The airport basically shut down after the last flight departed at 9:30 P.M. local time. The various employees straggled out of the airport over the next several hours. Alex didn't know what they were doing in there, but by 2:00 A.M., even the security guard was fast asleep in his little jeep. Alex would watch the airport again tomorrow night to be sure that the guard kept the same schedule.

He headed back to the motel and found Marcus watching TV.

"Well, you were out late," said Marcus. "Learn anything interesting?"

"I don't know if it's interesting, but helpful—yes," replied Alex. "It seems that about midnight is when things shut down on *The Endeavor*. Once the lights go out in the main living space, they are out for the night."

Marcus sat up and said, "That doesn't mean that someone isn't walking around in the dark, Alex."

"I know, but the night vision goggles didn't reveal anything. I need to watch again tomorrow night to see if the schedule is close to the same. I also need to watch the airport tomorrow night to be sure that the night security guard keeps a regular routine.

"What were you able to learn tonight over on the beach? Anything worth noting?"

"Well," said Marcus, "Sohlmann has obviously been here before because all the locals know the boat and that the boat means money! He gets some pretty preferential treatment from just about anyone that is fortunate enough to get his business. Anything from food and drinks, to souvenirs, to whatever he wants to spend his money on.

"Also, it seems that boat is equipped with a small motorboat that he uses for his dive excursions. The local dive captains feel left out since he never spends money with them."

"Yeah, I saw the small motorboat when the crew came ashore. By small, I mean it's a twenty-plus-foot boat that looks very comfortable in its own right," replied Alex.

"Well, then it should be pretty easy to tell when Sohlmann comes and goes from the boat," said Marcus. "What's your plan now?"

"Tomorrow is another recon day, just to be sure that I have my information correct. Both on the ship and at the airport. What time is your flight out?"

"I leave at 1:45. Is there anything else you need me to help with before I bug out?"

"No, you've done way more than I could have asked already, my friend."

Alex sat on his bed and fell back against his pillow. He stared up at the ceiling in silence, his arms crossed behind his head.

"You really miss her, don't you?" asked Marcus.

"More than you'll ever understand."

"You know, I've had my share of ladies in my life. Some good, some not so good. But I ain't never had whatever it is that the two of you had goin' on."

Alex rolled over, turned off the light and tried to get some sleep.

Marcus sat in the dark and looked at his friend. He said to himself, *This is one hurting white boy!* He wished there were more that he could do for his friend. He just didn't know what it would be. He really wanted to stay with Alex to help see this thing through, but he had to return to Rochester tomorrow to meet with some important long-time customers. They were the type of client that didn't take kindly to any deviation from a prearranged schedule and Marcus knew it was in his best interest to go home.

As Alex slept, Marcus pulled out the large envelope he had brought with him and scribbled a note on it for Alex. It read:

My man, you're gonna have to get outta here when you done. This is another set of identity papers that should be good for at least 6 months. Be sure to burn the old ones along with this note. See you soon! - M

He placed the envelope in Alex's duffle bag and turned off the TV and settled in for some much needed sleep.

Chapter Fifty-one

Alex and Janey learned to love the Caribbean when they took their first trip down there during that fateful weekend back in '87. There aren't many locations on the planet where the water is as beautifully clear as it is in the Caribbean. While this was one of the most attractive features of that part of the world, it presented challenges when it came to underwater stealth. Alex had come to realize that he would have to complete his underwater operation under the cover of darkness.

Even with the approaching full moon in the next day or so, night was black in the Caribbean. In fact, souvenir shops sold postcards that were completely black, and said "BVI at Night!" The deep darkness would give Alex the cover he needed to accomplish his work beneath *The Endeavor*.

He loaded up his rental car with the necessary supplies and dive equipment he would need, then prepared to head off to a remote beach to the north and west of the airport. While this would require a much longer swim, it gave him the privacy he needed. He had three two-tank rigs for the dive, but hoped he wouldn't need all of them. He checked and double checked his gear, then locked up the car and found a small local restaurant for some light dinner and waited for the approaching darkness. After he ate, Alex found a place to keep an eye on Sohlmann's boat for a while. He was pleasantly surprised to see the motorboat moving away from *The Endeavor* just before dusk.

As luck would have it, Sohlmann and his guest decided to leave *The Endeavor* and enjoy dinner on the island tonight. Alex smiled, then headed back to his car to get into place for tonight's dive. He had strategically placed the extra tanks along the shore for use as needed. There was a bit of cloud cover, so Alex would enjoy even darker than normal skies tonight. The light from the moon would be hidden which gave him the ability to complete his work in total darkness.

Alex knew that the best location to place a large catastrophic underwater explosive on a ship like *The Endeavor* would be on or near the drive shaft. Flooding the engine compartment would be very important for the ship to go down as fast as possible. He was also planning to place explosives across the stern. However, since Trellis Bay was only about fifteen to twenty feet deep, there would need to be several smaller explosives just below the water line around the perimeter of the vessel. These charges would be wrapped in small containers of gasoline. Alex had never seen how gasoline and explosives reacted when detonated underwater, but hoped for the best.

He slipped silently into the water about two hours after darkness had fully set in. At first, night diving was very disorienting and Alex felt the need to surface frequently to be sure he was heading in the right direction. After about thirty minutes, he gained some confidence that his internal compass was accurate. The swim to *The Endeavor* took just under an hour and 10 minutes. The two tanks were enough to get him to his destination, but not enough to allow him to complete his work. He was glad he had changed out rigs earlier. Alex was in no hurry, but didn't want to waste any time. His work beneath the ship went without a hitch. He was able to attach all sixteen charges to the hull of *The Endeavor* in less than forty-five minutes.

While swimming back to where his car was located, he exchanged his tank rig one last time. He would retrieve the spent tanks later. He still had plenty of work to be done later tonight at the airport. When he returned to his motel, he showered quickly and took a nap. At 1:30 A.M. he got dressed in his black tactical gear, complete with black camo face paint and a single pistol, just in case. He grabbed his second bag of supplies for the night and headed over to the airport.

The night watchman at the airport was fast asleep, just as he was last night at this hour. Alex made a few quick cuts in the perimeter fence and slipped onto the airport grounds. He was able to make his way over to Sohlmann's Gulfstream with no apparent detection by the sleeping guard. It was an extremely humid night, so Alex was hoping that the guard would be sapped of any energy he had. He was also hoping that the uneventful, sleepy routine of guarding the Beef Island airport kept the night security guard on a very low level of alertness.

Alex was finished working on the plane in fifteen minutes, and slipped back through the slit in the fence he had created without making a sound. He made his way back to his car and was in his motel room before 4:00 A.M.

The easy work was complete. Now came the challenging part of Alex's plan. It would require him keeping a very close watch on Sohlmann and finding a way to engage him when he was least expecting it. Alex wasn't sure how that would unfold, but he was patient and he was prepared.

Alex had been mingling near the pier for the past two and a half days hoping for his chance, but so far there was no sign of Sohlmann. He was sure to always have his backpack of supplies with him in the event that an opportunity presented itself. Tonight his patience was rewarded.

The Full Moon Party was a bigger bash than Alex had anticipated. There were people everywhere eating, drinking, dancing and just having a good time. Locals were set up with food tables selling local dishes that ranged from jerk chicken, barbequed goat, ribs, seafood and just about any other type of local calypso cuisine imaginable. There were tables set up all along the beach for people to sit and eat. There were souvenir stands scattered throughout the beach area selling all kinds of local souvenirs and plenty of extra chairs surrounding all the beach bars.

There were young families, singles looking for a party—maybe more, there were middle-aged tourists and elderly alike all enjoying the island atmosphere. The Moko Jumbies were making their way through the crowds and thrilling them with their agile dancing and moving to the music. Some were spitting fire. There were fire dancers with burning batons that they were spinning. The fires were blazing in the large ornate iron balls, the music was blasting, both from speakers and from the live Calypso Band located at the far end of the Trellis Bay beach. People were packed into the beach area as tightly as could be waiting on the moon.

Just as Alex was losing hope for tonight, he saw the motorboat pull away from *The Endeavor*. It slowly made its way to the pier and

Alex watched from the shadows as Sohlmann and his guest climbed on to the pier.They made their way to the first beach bar and ordered something to drink.They stood at the bar for a few minutes and quickly downed their drinks. They ordered another round, then headed out into the crowds.Alex thought for a few moments, then followed them from a distance.

He would have to do this right for everything to work as he planned. His heart was once again racing just like with McNeeley. He forced himself to calm down. Sohlmann and his lady friend made their way up and down the beach taking in all the sights and sounds of the party. They were genuinely having a fun time on the beach. They grabbed some food and looked for a place to sit.There were so many people and so much noise that Alex didn't worry about being careful. As long as he stayed in the shadows, he would be fine.

Suddenly, a voice was calling out,"Patrice! Patrice!"

It took a minute for Alex to recognize that it was his false name that was being called. He turned to see one of the young ladies from the bachelorette party waving and heading his way. She seemed to be alone, but was definitely coming over to see him.

"Patrice! Hi, it's Jamie. From Nashville, remember me?" she said.

"Yes, Jamie. Hi, nice to run into you tonight."

Alex got up on his toes to look above the crowd to be sure he didn't lose sight of Sohlmann.

"Are you by yourself tonight? You shouldn't be alone at a party like this! Let's go get a drink or something. Let's have some island fun. Come on!"

She grabbed him by the arm and started to pull him toward the crowds and spilling her drink. Alex was now struggling to keep an eye on Sohlmann, but all the people were getting in the way.

Alex stopped and turned Jamie around to face him. "Actually, Jamie, I'm waiting on a friend that is just arriving here tonight," relied Alex, surprised at how easily this excuse came to him. "I can't spend any time with you tonight."

"Oh, okay. I'm sorry. Well, I hope you have fun tonight!" Jamie said.

"I'm sure I will," replied Alex.

Jamie bounded off into the crowd and disappeared.

Alex breathed a sigh of relief and slipped back into the shadows to keep an eye on Sohlmann. He found him a few minutes later and kept close. Tonight would have to be the night for him to finalize this. He felt like things were getting too dicey and he didn't want to lose his nerve. Plus, an environment like the Full Moon Party was the perfect setting for what he wanted to do. He watched Sohlmann for another hour as he and his lady friend drank, danced, ate some more local food and joined in the fun. Finally, Sohlmann got up from his table, alone, and headed to one of the beach bars for refills on their drinks.

Chapter Fifty-two

Alex reached into his backpack and pulled out his large straw hat and one other item he would need. He pulled his hat down low on his head and started to move through the thick crowd. As the evening got later, the crowds grew larger. Everyone was waiting for the moon to rise; that was when the art sculptures just offshore would be set aflame and the real party would start. Alex couldn't imagine it getting any more raucous that it already was, but then again, for most of the partiers, this would be a night they would remember for a long time.

Sohlmann was slowly making his way through the crowds to one of the beach bars, bobbing to the beat of the festive music when he felt a strong grip on his right arm and a sharp pain in his left kidney. He tried to spin around but the grip was too tight.

"Keep walking," said Alex in a calm tone. "You and I are going to take a little walk. If you try anything stupid, you'll be very sorry. Do you understand me?"

The crowd was oblivious to anything that wasn't related to the party, food or drink. It was so loud that Alex could have been screaming at Sohlmann and no one would have noticed.

Alex led Sohlmann between two of the small beach bar buildings away from the beach and the crowds. It was very dark once they moved away from all the activity of the Full Moon Party.

"Who are you!" Sohlmann said with pure contempt in his voice.

"My name is Patrice McDavid," said Alex. "But that doesn't matter. You're the rich guy that owns the big boat, right? I think they call you the Big Shot from the Big Yacht."

"What? What are you talking about?" Sohlmann's ego wouldn't let him deny that he owned the yacht. "Yes, that's my yacht. Why does that matter to you? Where are you taking me?"

"Be patient, my friend. Be patient."

Sohlmann tried hard to escape from Alex's grip by twisting and dropping to a knee. Alex jerked him up and gave him a quick punch to the kidney with his free hand that dropped Sohlmann almost to his knees.

"I told you you'd be sorry if you tried to break free," said Alex. "Keep walking and you better think twice about trying that again."

He led him further away from the Full Moon Party to an area between the beach and the airport. He kept a very tight grip on Sohlmann's arm and was careful to not let up. He needed to maintain complete control of Sohlmann until they reached their destination, but after the kidney shot he was sure that Sohlmann wouldn't be trying to break free again. Alex led him for another five minutes or so to the spot he had selected on the rocks two nights ago. It provided them with a view of both the airport and *The Endeavor* floating peacefully in the bay.

Alex pushed Sohlmann down on the rocks and pointed his silenced pistol directly at his face.

"If you make any attempt to get up, run, move quickly in any way, or if you start to yell for help.... Not that it would do any good with all the noise coming from the beach, I'll shoot you right here. I'll dump you in the water and the crabs will devour you before daylight."

"What do you want from me?" Sohlmann was visibly shaken but still very angry. "If you're looking for money, we can probably come to some type of peaceful agreement. Let's just talk for a minute. What did you say your name was? Pat?" Sohlmann was grasping at straws for any advantage that might be there.

"Yeah, we're going to talk. We are sure going to talk tonight," replied Alex. "And the name is Patrice. I'm curious, with all the money it takes to operate a boat like that, you must have built quite an empire for yourself. What line of business are you in? What kind of boss are you?"

"What the hell kind of questions are those? Why does any of that matter to you? Have we ever met?" Sohlmann had a quizzical look on his face.

"Well, Mr. Big Shot from the Big Yacht, those are important questions to me. I want to hear how you answer them. After all, that's why I brought you here tonight."

"None of that is any of your damn business!" Sohlmann was now getting angry.

Alex could sense that his time was running out.

"You don't want to answer any of my questions? Okay. Your choice." Alex reached into his backpack and pulled out a small box. He showed it to Sohlmann. "Do you know what this is?"

"No. Should I?" asked Sohlmann, a bit sarcastically.

"Well, Mr. Big, this is a very painful thing for you." Alex pressed the button on the detonator.

Suddenly, there were several pops that sounded from behind them. With the sounds from the beach, it was almost impossible to hear them. Alex turned to look toward the airport.

"You might want to stand up and take a look at this," said Alex.

Sohlmann stood and looked toward the airport. There was no mistaking his Gulfstream sitting alone on the tarmac. Only now there were small fires starting to engulf the entire plane.

"What was that?!" cried Sohlmann. "That is my airplane! What just happened?"

He was looking from the Gulfstream to Alex and back to the Gulfstream. "Do you have any idea how much that cost me?"

"Don't know, don't care," said Alex in a calm voice. "Keep watching."

After about thirty seconds, there was a huge explosion that split the fuselage in two. It fell to the ground, snapped at the center. The fireball was incredible. Sohlmann stared in silence as his plane was enveloped in such intense flames that it seemed to melt before his eyes.

Sohlmann screamed, "What do you think you're doing? Do you know who I am?! Your life is over!" Sohlmann was pointing a finger into Alex's chest.

Alex quickly pushed him back to the ground as he pulled the second detonator out of his backpack. He showed it to Sohlmann and extended his arm to him. "Would you like to do the honors this time?"

Sohlmann looked at him with a blank expression on his face.

After a few seconds Alex shrugged and said, "No? Okay. I will. It will actually be fun for me!"

He pressed the button just as the art sculptures were being set aflame on the beach over at the party. The perimeter of *The Endeavor* started to light up with an eerie glow and muffled sounds of the explosions. As the gasoline charges reached the surface they created huge fireballs that lit up the night sky and pounded the entire area with deafening sound. The partiers on the beach started to cheer as if it were part of the Full Moon celebration. Then the large explosions rocked the night. It was as if *The Endeavor* had been lifted out of the water for a few seconds. The entire stern was blown off the ship and the explosion from well below the surface seemed to break the ship into pieces.

Now the sounds of voices coming from the beach were of shock and awe. This was certainly not part of the celebration. The night sky was nearly as bright as daylight as the explosions lit up the entire area. The explosions were so overpowering that the entire beach party seemed to come to an immediate halt. Some people were even knocked off their feet.

Sohlmann was in shock. He turned to look at Patrice McDavid. "Do you have any idea what you've just done? Do you have any idea who you're dealing with? You're never going to get away with this! I will destroy you! I will make it my life's mission to make you wish you were dead! You have no idea what's coming your way, *Patrice*!"

Alex just stared at him. He removed his hat and pulled his hair away from his face. It took Sohlmann about fifteen seconds to recognize him. Sohlmann started to say something....

Alex cocked his head and put up a finger to silence him as if Sohlmann were an insolent schoolboy and said, "I know *exactly* what I've just done! I know *exactly* what I've destroyed! And believe me, I know *exactly* who I'm dealing with, Sohlmann! And yes, I will get away with all of this.

"I'm dealing with the man that ruined my life! I'm dealing with the man that lied to me countless times and proceeded to turn my life upside down and inside out. I'm dealing with the man that set up a complex psychotic scheme that involved my wife, who had zero involvement in any part of what happed at the firm, and crushed her dreams. I'm dealing with the man that treated me like a worthless pawn to be used in a really twisted game, the man that, as far as my wife is concerned, is responsible for my death. I'm dealing with the man that was so much of a coward that he had to solicit the help of a friend to see his crazy scheme through. That's who I'm dealing with!"

Sohlmann sat staring at Alex. He pointed a shaking finger at Alex and said, "McNeeley's boat and cars. You!"

"That's right, me," replied Alex with a grin on his face.

There was nothing Sohlmann could say to Alex now. He turned to look at his boat, but it was nearly unrecognizable as it sank to the bottom of Trellis Bay in small burning pieces. In less than ten minutes, it would be as if *The Endeavor* had never existed.

Alex turned and started to walk away, then turned back to face Sohlmann. "Oh, and one more thing, I'm dealing with a dead man!" He pulled the pistol from the small of his back and placed a well-aimed silenced shot right between Sohlmann's eyes.

Chapter Fifty-three

June 1990

His name was Albert Constantine. He was single and looking to stay that way. He had no desire to complicate his life any more than it already was by bringing a woman into the picture. There were plenty of local women that would love to spend time with Albert. He was relatively new in town and, according to the ladies, very easy on the eyes. However, the time wasn't right for companionship—not yet. He wanted to live a quiet, simple life away from everything and everyone. He needed to be alone. He lived in a small apartment about a block from the beach and was able to bus a few tables and take care of the daily trash at a local restaurant in exchange for two meals a day. Life was good and he had very little to worry about. He would prefer it to remain that way for as long as possible.

He made some friends here and there; it was a very friendly area. But Albert tried his best to keep them at a safe distance. He was friendly enough, but didn't want to get too deep into any relationships because it would just be too difficult. He was content to remain the loner, regardless of what people in town might say or think about him.

He was sitting under a royal blue umbrella in a beach chair on an empty beach along the coast of Mykonos, Greece, same as every other day lately. He was wearing a pair of khaki shorts and a blue T-shirt and had a red ballcap on. There was a brown leather satchel with three books and two newspapers in it sitting next to his chair; he was reading a third. He had a large container of water and some fruit tucked in there, as well. His goal each day was to stay up to date with the news events of the world from multiple news outlets from across Europe. There was a local merchant named Niko that stocked newspapers from all over the world, but Albert trusted only a few of them. He had learned that many were either controlled by corrupt governments or were not interested in the truth. Either way, he would stick to his trusted favorites. The merchant also carried a large catalog of used books that tourists would leave for him or exchange for something they hadn't read yet. Every day, Albert would maintain his daily routine of picking up his newspapers, fruit, maybe a new book and heading to the beach to read and learn the local language.

The weather on Mykonos was perfect and promised to only get better as the coming months approached. He was already showing the obvious signs of living along the coast. His skin was tanned bronze from the sun and his short hair was starting to lighten from the salty seawater and sunshine. Everything in his life was easy and stress free, except for one thing—the gaping hole in his heart.

It had been two months since he left Tortola, never to return. The fact was that he now had nowhere to return to. In the United States,

Alex Coswell was dead. He'd been dead since last November. There was no longer anyone on the planet named Thomas Baker nor Patrice McDavid. Those men might as well have been ghosts. Marcus has seen to that. The local authorities in BVI were searching frantically for a murderer, their only hopeful suspect was the Canadian playboy seen on their beaches. On top of that, they were trying to figure out how an airplane *and* a luxury yacht happed to blow up at the same time.

Albert Constantine had purposefully severed all contact with anyone from his past. He knew that any attempt to make contact with anyone now would only open doors that could lead to disaster for him and others, like Marcus and Janey. He had finally resigned himself to his new life and would forever purge Alex Coswell from his consciousness. It wouldn't be an easy task, in fact it was very painful, but one that he would have to face—every day.

The loneliness was bad, but it was the monotony that bothered him the most. Yesterday looked exactly like today for Albert. Tomorrow would look exactly like the next day. The only change would be the dates on the newspapers and the stories that were told. There had been three stories in the international papers about Sohlmann, but they stopped completely after ten days with no progress on solving his murder. Albert finally gave up on seeing anything related to his past in the news which allowed him to relax a bit. Still, there were times when he longed for his past life. High finance, the thrill of Wall Street and everything it involved, and Janey. He missed it all. Especially Janey.

Marcus had quite a bit of work to do upon his return to Rochester. In his line of work, you never knew who might make contact for some work to be done. He had grown accustomed to receiving everything from mundane information requests, to creating identity papers, to some of the most complicated corporate espionage jobs one could imagine. There wasn't anything that Marcus couldn't handle, although he drew a very distinct line at National Security—for any country. That was one area that he didn't want to get into. Ever.

His friend Alex, now Albert Constantine, had gone somewhere after leaving Tortola and Marcus needed to know where so he could keep track of him. It was easy to find him, really. When you knew exactly what to look for, it didn't take long. Marcus knew the name of who he was looking for and location of where to start his search. Also, he was able to sidestep all the normal information channels and bureaucracy that bogged one down when searching for someone and work directly from his office without worrying about where he was getting his information. In less than a week, Marcus had Alex comfortably in his sights. He could monitor him from afar with a few clicks of his computer keyboard.

Jane Coswell was another story. Marcus wasn't sure of the best way to approach her. After all, she was a recent widow and he knew nothing about her nor how she was handling her new normal. So, he went to work. He learned where she worked, where she lived and how she spent her money. That was easy. What was proving to be difficult was what it was she was doing at work all those long hours, then longer hours in her apartment. He knew that she was online, but she was very good at covering her tracks. He had tried many ways to break into her activities, but he was stonewalled every time.

One night while working late, he had a thought. It was a gamble, but worth a try. He logged into one of the chatrooms he used and tried to make contact with a former student/teacher. Nothing. He tried again the following evening. Still nothing. On the third night he got a hit. He took a longshot to see if he might be on the right path. He sent a message that read: *Mainframe, I know what you've done. The Dark Detective.*

It took over an hour for the response.

Please follow the attached link to move to a secure chatroom. The message included an encrypted link for Marcus to follow. He logged on immediately.

What do you want from me, TDD? Marcus knew his instinct was correct. He had Jane Coswell properly identified. Now the question was how to handle her with such care so he wouldn't lose her. Her skills were top notch and if she didn't want to be found, she could disappear forever.

The Dark Detective replied, *I am a friend. You can trust me.*

Are you stupid enough to think I would believe that? Jane stared at her screen with a combined feeling of panic and shock.

What can I do to make you believe me?

Let me think on it for a day. Meet me in the attached chatroom tomorrow night at 9:30 P.M. sharp.

Deal.

Marcus had some serious work to do between now and tomorrow night. Now that he had identified Jane's computer he could start some very detailed research into what she had been up to. He worked through the night and by 11:15 the following morning had learned quite a bit about Jane Coswell and her after hours activities. He was actually very impressed. If the circumstances were different, he would be making her a job offer that would pay her much better than her day job. However, there was no way he could compete with what she did after hours. He was surprised by what he was able to learn over the past ten hours or so.

Marcus logged in to the chatroom five minutes early. He was put into a holding cell until Jane arrived.

Good evening TDD. - Mainframe. It was a friendly, but interesting greeting.

Good evening to you, Jane. Marcus had taken a huge gamble by using her name. He was hoping for the best.

Jane was horrified! The fact that whoever the Dark Detective was knew her name was one of the most unsettling things she had ever encountered since she started dabbling into hacking.

I'm going to ask again, what do you want from me?

I actually want to help you. I know about Switzerland. I know about Curacao. I know about Grand Cayman.

…?…

You have nothing to fear from me. I truly am a friend. Because I know things, lots of things, I want to help you get out from under the burden you must be feeling. I want to help you protect what you have AND keep what you've taken. I don't care about that. I want to help get you to where you can start a new life. Let's say we have a joint vested interest in seeing this through for you.

Tomorrow, same time, follow this link. Jane clicked off. She sat at her computer shaking. She tried every trick she knew to find out who was contacting her. No luck. The Dark Detective was good. He had upped his game since last time.

The next night, she sent a pointed message: *I am very well connected, if you are not being completely honest with me, there will be some heavy trouble for you.* Jane had no idea how she would follow up on her threat if it was necessary, but she had to say something that gave at least a small feeling of control.

Please trust me. You will be receiving a package at your door in the next ten minutes. Don't be afraid, just look through the peephole of your door once ten minutes has passed. There will be a large yellow envelope in the center of the hall, you'll see it. At this hour it should be safe for you to retrieve it. Once you get the package, send me a message for further instructions.

Now Jane was really spooked. She pushed back from her computer and ran her fingers through her hair. For the first time in a long time she felt completely exhausted. She stared at her screen. Her mind was racing.

When ten minutes had gone by she slowly moved to the door of her apartment. She hesitated to look through the peephole, but when she did, she saw the yellow envelope right where it was supposed to be. Quickly, she unlocked her door and grabbed the package. She slammed the door a bit too hard and immediately locked it. Her heart was pounding. Her name was written on the front—Jane Franklin Coswell.

Again, she was perplexed by seeing her full name. She opened the envelope and studied the contents. She was stunned by what she saw. After about twenty minutes she began to type: *Please explain what you've just sent to me and why you would do this.*

As I mentioned earlier, we have a mutually vested interest in your wellbeing. Please be quick to follow the instructions, and be sure to follow them to the letter. There are people that are very close to uncovering the Sohlmann theft, but I'm misdirecting them. (I don't think they will return to the right path any time soon.) Not that it matters anymore. But you need to move quickly. I'll be tracking your progress to ensure that no one is on your trail. When you arrive at your destination, there will be another package for you with further instructions.

Jane had a decision to make, right now! She considered everything that had transpired over the past few nights and decided that it really was time to make a move. Whoever this was was right about a lot of things. One of them was the burden she had been carrying. If there really were people on her trail, then she had to do something. Until now, she didn't have an idea what that something would be. Now, however, it seemed that a guardian angel was laying out a path for her—a very clear path that she would follow tonight.

When she arrived at her destination two days later, she was beginning to trust the Dark Detective's plan and his claim to be a friend. The package that was delivered to her apartment gave her a new identity complete with a driver's license from England, a British passport, a detailed background of who she was now, some cash and stern instructions to leave anything with her former name on it behind. She felt like she was entering Witness Protection. Everything seemed to be working smoothly.

The package that was waiting for her when she stepped off the plane contained a new laptop computer and a cryptic, but clear message, if that made sense. She was to introduce herself to anyone she met as Jackie Frye, her new name. There were to be no exceptions.

Next, she was to settle in to a local hotel where a reservation was waiting for her. No need to worry about payment, it was already taken care of. Early the next day she was to eat a healthy breakfast and follow the enclosed map.

It was an unusually windy afternoon, Albert was dozing beneath his umbrella, his newspaper draped across his chest. The wind was blowing and the pages of his newspaper were flapping in the wind. There were several families enjoying the sun on this particular day and suddenly, he was awakened when a stray beachball rolled to his feet. As he looked up to see who it might belong to, his heart skipped a beat. As he looked down the beach, he thought to himself, *How on earth? Can this really be happening?*

He remained in his chair to be sure as the lone beachwalker approached. He recognized her immediately. His mind raced for what to do. He was searching for words, for some way to at least say something, but nothing came to him. His mouth was as dry as the sand he was sitting on. He simply dropped his head to shield it from the wind and waited.

Jackie didn't notice him at first but as she got closer, she stopped. Tears immediately started streaming down her face. She looked around. She couldn't believe her eyes at first. How could it be?

Albert stood and faced her. "Ma'am, are you alright?" he asked. He also had tears in his eyes.

"What…? Alex, it's you!"

She threw her arms around his neck and squeezed with all her might. Neither of them said anything for what seem an eternity.

He pulled himself away and looked deeply into her blue eyes. "My name is Albert," said Alex. "Albert Constantine."

Janey tried to compose herself and said, "It's nice to meet you, Albert. I'm Jackie Frye."

"Well, Jackie, we have a lot to talk about, don't we?"